I0822483

Measured Agony

Judy Smith

Celeste Plumadore

ISBN: 9798991852548

Author's Note

This story serves as a companion book to the novel *Veils of Verdant*, detailing the events between the novel's conclusion and the epilogue ten years later.

Prologue

Jack West sat in his parked car, engine off, watching the lights of the police station flicker through the steady early morning rain. His fingers were stiff against the steering wheel, gripping it as if it might anchor him to this moment—the last moment before everything changed. Outside, officers moved between squad cars, normal people living normal lives. He was about to walk in there and end his own.

His hands were numb, but he felt a pain in his chest, a feeling he recognized well. Guilt. Not for what he'd done to Brad—that was necessary—but for what he was doing to his family. Their faces flashed through his mind in painful succession: Tabby's eyes, filled with worry she couldn't quite conceal, as she'd connected the dots, asking questions that he couldn't fully answer. Ruby's face, her usual cheerful exuberance replaced with a quiet sadness. She knew. He was certain she did. Jason's tightly controlled anger when he'd confronted Jack in the driveway, demanding the truth.

He'd tried to shield them all, to bear the weight of his actions alone. But the trouble with loving people—truly loving them—was that they refused to let you carry your burdens in isolation. Despite his best efforts to insulate them, they had remained stubbornly involved, their concern for him a mirror that reflected his own love for them.

Jack closed his eyes, feeling the weight of the future pressing down on him. His son would grow up without a father. His wife would sleep in an empty bed. His sister would visit him in a place surrounded by concrete and steel. All because of a choice he'd made that now left only destruction in its wake.

He opened the car door, the sound of rain growing louder as it drummed against the asphalt. Each step toward the station felt both impossibly heavy and strangely liberating. Perhaps in unburdening himself, he could finally allow his family to move forward, even if he couldn't move with them.

The station door opened with a pneumatic hiss. Jack entered, catching a whiff of coffee on the burner too long. A police officer looked up from the front desk, expression neutral, unaware that in moments she would become the recipient of a confession that would change multiple lives forever.

"Can I help you?" the officer asked.

Jack stood straighter, his decision solidified in the moment of its execution. "I killed a man," he said.

1
Confessions

The officer behind the desk stopped typing, her fingers hovering above the keyboard as if the air had suddenly solidified. She studied his face, searching for signs of intoxication or mental disturbance, finding only the clear-eyed certainty of a man who had made a decision he could not unmake.

"Sir?" Her voice carried the practiced neutrality of someone accustomed to filtering emergencies from pranks. "Could you please repeat that?"

"I killed someone," Jack said, water dripping from his coat sleeve onto the worn tile floor. Each drop struck with a soft, persistent rhythm, marking seconds in a life now divided into before and after. "I need to report it."

The station, which moments ago had seemed an unremarkable government building, now revealed itself in hyperreal detail. The scuffed floor tiles beneath his boots. The outdated wanted posters yellowing on a corkboard. The metallic taste of recirculated air. The officer—mid-thirties, dark hair pulled back in a practical bun, wedding band on her left hand—reached beneath the counter and produced a notepad. Her expression shifted from skepticism to focused attention, professional training taking over.

"I'm Officer James," she said, pulling a pen from her breast pocket. "Why don't we start with your name?"

"Jack West."

"And when did this... incident occur, Mr. West?"

Jack noticed how carefully she avoided repeating his confession. Not yet a fact, just an allegation until verified.

"Two months ago."

Her eyebrows lifted slightly. "I see. And you're coming forward now because...?"

"Because it's the right thing to do." The answer sounded insufficient even to his own ears, though it was true.

Officer James nodded, pen poised over her notepad. "Can you tell me the name of the deceased?"

"Bradley Torres." The name felt strange in Jack's mouth, like speaking a foreign language.

She wrote the name down, her handwriting neat and compact. "And what was your relationship to Mr. Torres?"

"He was an acquaintance of my sister. He spent five years in prison for sexually assaulting her."

The officer's expression didn't change, but something shifted in her posture—a slight straightening of the spine, a new alertness in her eyes. "I understand. And what happened between you and Mr. Torres?"

"I didn't mean to kill him," Jack said, the words emerging before he could arrange them properly. "Brad was going to hurt my family, and I just wanted to stop him."

"Did Mr. Torres physically threaten you during this confrontation?"

Jack considered the question, weighing truth against consequence. "Not me. My family."

The officer's pen scratched across the paper, transcribing his own words into the narrative of his prosecution.

"I'd like to talk to a lawyer before saying anything else," Jack said, the words coming out more abruptly than he intended.

Officer James looked up from her notepad, pen still poised. "Of course. That's your right. But it would help us verify your statement if you could provide a few more details about where we might find Mr. Torres."

"Are you going to take me into custody?"

The question hung between them, transforming the atmosphere. Until now, he'd been a civilian reporting a crime. With these words, he acknowledged his new identity: suspect, perpetrator, prisoner.

Officer James glanced toward a door behind her, then back to Jack. "We'll need to verify your statement before proceeding with formal charges. In the meantime—"

The sound of approaching footsteps interrupted her. Jack turned to see a man in a dress shirt and tie walking toward them. He carried a folder tucked under one arm.

"Officer James," the man said, nodding to her before turning his attention to Jack. "I'm Detective Lyons."

"This gentleman was just—" James began.

"I heard," Lyons interrupted. He led Jack into a narrow room with walls the color of dead skin and handed him water in a paper cup.

Then came the advice. Quiet. Steady. Touched with something else—doubt, maybe, or curiosity.

"Stop talking. Get yourself a lawyer first." He slid a business card across the scarred metal table —as if it were a life raft thrown to a drowning man. "Call this guy. He's good with cases like this."

The look he gave Jack wasn't accusatory. It was speculative. As if he suspected that Jack's eager confession might be an attempt to protect someone else.

Jack stared at the card, the raised lettering of the attorney's name rough against his fingertips. "You're letting me go?"

"For now." Lyons said.

The weight of his confession—and what came next—settled over Jack like a heavy blanket. He'd expected to be led away in handcuffs, to begin paying his debt immediately. Instead, he was being sent back into the world, back to Tabby and their unborn child, with the knowledge that this reprieve was temporary.

Jack pocketed the card and walked toward the exit, each step feeling undeserved. The pneumatic door hissed open, and the rain-freshened air hit his face. He stood for a moment under the station's overhang, watching water sheet off the asphalt parking lot, and wondered how he'd explain to Tabby that he confessed to murder and was sent home with a business card.

The future stretched before him, uncertain as the rain-blurred horizon, but one thing was clear: the next time he walked through those doors, he wouldn't be walking back out.

Later that morning, Jack found himself standing before a tall brick building in downtown Leveret, business card crumpled in his fist. Jack stared at the card—Michael Campbell, Attorney at Law. He checked his watch: 8:57 AM. Punctuality, even for his own undoing, was a habit he couldn't break.

When the elevator doors parted on the fourth floor, Jack stepped into a reception area that felt deliberately impersonal. The walls were bare except for framed law degrees, the furniture all sleek lines and sharp angles. A receptionist looked up from behind a desk of polished cherry wood, her expression as neutral as the space around her.

"I have an appointment with Michael Campbell," Jack said. His voice sounded distant, as if it belonged to someone else.

"Mr. West?" When he nodded, she gestured down a hallway. "Third door on the right. Mr. Campbell is expecting you."

The corridor stretched before him, each step taking him closer to a confession he couldn't take back. Jack's shoulders tightened beneath his jacket, the muscles bunching like fists. When he reached the third door, he paused, his hand hovering over the handle. Inside this room, he would transform from a man with a secret to a confessed killer. The thought made his jaw clench so hard his teeth ached.

Michael Campbell stood as Jack entered, extending a hand across the desk. He was in his mid-fifties, salt-and-pepper hair closely cropped, his face bearing the deep lines of someone who had seen every variety of human trouble.

"Mr. West," Campbell said, his handshake firm and brief. "Have a seat." He gestured to a chair across from his desk where a mug of coffee waited, steam curling into the air.

Jack lowered himself into the chair, his hands coming to rest on the armrests. His fingers tapped an irregular rhythm against the leather, betraying the stillness he was trying to project.

"I understand you visited the Leveret Police Department earlier," Campbell began, pulling a legal pad toward him and uncapping a pen. His tone was neither accusatory nor sympathetic—just factual.

"Yes. I tried to confess to killing a man, but they told me to get a lawyer first."

Campbell's face remained professionally impassive, though his pen paused briefly above the paper. "That was good advice. You'd be surprised how many people walk in thinking confession is the answer, only to realize they've complicated their situation beyond repair."

Jack's gaze drifted past Michael's shoulder, where a row of law books stood like sentinels. Their spines were worn at the edges, testament to actual use rather than mere decoration. He wondered how many others like him had sat in this chair before, waiting for someone to translate their actions into the sterile language of the law.

"I killed him," Jack said, the words falling flat in the quiet office. "That's not complicated."

Michael's expression didn't change, but his pen made its first mark on the paper. A single note, perhaps just Jack's name. "Actually, Mr. West, it's almost always complicated. Especially when someone like you—a young man with stable employment, family, and no prior record—decides to take a life."

The lawyer's gaze was steady, clinical in its assessment. "So here we are." He tapped his pen twice against the pad. "I need you to tell me exactly what happened."

Jack's eyes fixed on empty space, focusing on nothing. "Five years ago, a man named Bradley Torres raped my sister, Ruby." His voice was flat, stripped of emotion. "He served time for it. Got out recently."

"And this Bradley Torres is the person you're saying you killed?" Campbell clarified, making a note.

Jack nodded.

Michael wrote without looking at the page, his eyes never leaving Jack's face. "And that's why you killed him? Revenge for your sister?"

"No." Jack shifted in the chair, the wood creaking beneath him. "I didn't go there to kill him."

"Then why did you go?"

Jack looked down at his hands. They were steady now, the trembling from the car gone. "To convince him to leave town. To stay away from Ruby. From all of us."

Michael nodded, making another note. His face remained impassive, but something in his eyes suggested he'd heard similar stories before. "Tell me about that day, Mr. West. Start from the beginning."

Jack drew a deep breath. The air in the office felt too thin, filtered through too many years of confessions and legal strategies. "I went to his apartment."

"Did you bring a weapon?" Michael asked.

"Yes. My gun." Jack met the lawyer's gaze directly. "I brought it for protection. I didn't know what kind of man he'd become in prison."

"You didn't intend to use it?"

"No." The word came quickly, firmly.

Michael leaned back slightly in his chair, creating space for Jack's story to unfold. "What happened when you got there?"

Jack closed his eyes briefly, the memory reassembling itself behind his eyelids with unwelcome clarity. "He let me in. We talked. He told me he was planning to vanish—not just leave town but disappear entirely. But not before settling the score. Then he described the violence he was planning against my family for putting him in prison."

Campbell nodded, his pen moving steadily across the page. "And what did you do after he made these threats?"

"I shot him," Jack stated flatly. The words hung in the air between them.

The room felt suddenly airless, the silence pressing in from all sides. Outside the window, Leveret continued its day, oblivious to the confession taking place above its streets.

Campbell made another note, his pen scratching against the paper. "Was anyone else present?"

"No," Jack said. "Just us."

"And the body?" Campbell asked, his voice matter-of-fact, as if inquiring about a misplaced file.

Jack hesitated, his chest rising and falling with a deep breath. "I took care of it."

Campbell looked up, his expression sharpening. "Mr. West, I need to be very clear about something. I'm your attorney, which means I'm bound by attorney-client privilege. But that privilege doesn't extend to future crimes. I can't help you cover up evidence or dispose of a body."

"I already did it," Jack said. "Months ago."

Campbell's posture shifted slightly as he processed this information, leaning back in his chair. He tapped his pen against the legal pad, his eyes never leaving Jack's face. "Alright, Mr. West. I'm going to need more details about what happened after the shooting. But first, let me ask you something practical. Are there any witnesses who might connect you to Torres around the time of his disappearance? Anyone who saw you enter or leave his apartment? Any evidence like phone records or text messages?"

Jack shook his head. "No."

"And the gun?"

"With the body."

"Mr. West, I need to understand exactly what happened after the shooting. How did you dispose of the body?"

Jack felt a peculiar calm settle over him as he described the aftermath. It was like watching himself from a distance, narrating a film he'd seen long ago.

Campbell wrote silently, his pen making soft scratching sounds against the legal pad. Jack noticed how the lawyer's handwriting slanted to the right, each letter precise and contained, much like the man himself.

"I drove to my parents' farm in Pennsylvania. I took him to the back acreage. There's an old section where we don't plant anymore; the soil's too acidic."

"And the location—would someone be able to find this grave if they were looking for it?"

Jack shook his head. "No obvious markers. It's near a copse of oak trees, away from the property line."

Campbell set down his pen and leaned back in his chair. His fingers formed a steeple beneath his chin as he studied Jack. "Did anyone help you? Anyone who might have knowledge of what happened?"

"No. I did it alone." Jack's pulse, visibly throbbing at his temple, the only outward sign of his distress.

The office fell into silence, broken only by the distant hum of a copier from somewhere down the hall and the mechanical ticking of a wall clock. Campbell reached for his coffee mug, now grown cold, and took a thoughtful sip.

"Mr. West," he said finally, setting the mug down. "I need to be very clear about the gravity of what you're facing."

"I know it's serious," Jack replied, his voice low.

"More than serious." Campbell leaned forward, his elbows on the desk. "Based on what you've told me, we're looking at voluntary manslaughter at the least, possibly second-degree murder. Voluntary manslaughter typically carries a minimum sentence of five years in New Jersey. Second-degree murder is a minimum of fifteen years, potentially up to thirty." Campbell's tone remained professional, but not unkind. "The evidence tampering and body disposal would add additional time."

"I understand," Jack said.

"The thing is," Campbell continued, "without physical evidence, the police might not pursue this case aggressively. You have no witnesses, no obvious connection to Torres at the time of his disappearance and no one has reported him missing."

Jack's brow furrowed. "What are you saying?"

"I'm saying that if you hadn't walked into that police station, you might never have been caught." Campbell held up a hand when Jack started to speak. "I'm not suggesting you should have kept quiet. I'm just outlining the reality of your situation. Given what you've told me, I believe our best approach is to negotiate a plea deal. If the prosecutor agrees to voluntary manslaughter instead of murder, we might be able to get you a sentence on the lower end of the range. However, there is another matter we need to discuss."

Jack waited, tension visible in the rigid line of his shoulders.

"The body," Campbell said. "If you want any chance at a favorable plea deal, you'll likely need to reveal its location. The prosecutor will want physical evidence."

Jack inhaled sharply, the implications clear. "My parents' farm. It would implicate them."

"Not necessarily. You've already stated they had no knowledge. But yes, it would bring unwanted attention to their property." Campbell's expression softened slightly. "This is the reality of your situation, Mr. West. There are no easy options here."

Jack rubbed his forehead, suddenly looking exhausted. "What happens next?"

"I'll contact the detectives at Leveret PD, see what their interest level is in pursuing this case. I'll feel out the potential for a plea deal without mentioning specifics about the body's location." Campbell made a final note on his legal pad. "One more thing," Campbell added, his tone cautionary. "From this point forward, don't discuss this case with anyone except me. Attorney-client privilege only extends to our conversations."

Jack nodded, understanding the implication. The conversations he needed to have with his family—the explanations, the apologies—would happen without the protection of privilege. Every word could potentially be used against him.

"When will you contact the police?" Jack asked, rising from his chair.

"Today," Campbell replied, standing to meet him. "I'll call you once I have a better sense of where we stand."

They shook hands across the desk, a brief, formal gesture that belied the gravity of what had passed between them. As Jack turned to leave, Campbell spoke again.

"Mr. West." His voice stopped Jack at the door. "For what it's worth, coming forward was the right thing to do. Not many would have had the courage."

Jack looked back, his expression unreadable. "It wasn't courage," he said quietly. "I just couldn't live with it anymore."

The door closed behind him with a soft click, leaving Campbell alone with his notes and the burden of a confession that would alter many lives. Outside, the sun continued its arc across the sky, indifferent to the human drama unfolding beneath it. Jack West had taken his first step toward atonement, but the path ahead promised no easy redemption.

2

Law Enforcement Discussions

Detective Marcus Lyons stared at the written confession he picked up from the front desk log. Jack West. Bradley Torres. Murder. He sank into a chair, weary and alert all at once. Detective Carter arrived with coffee, eyes bright with anticipation, as Lyons read from the statement: "I killed a man." Carter leaned in expectantly, while Lyons remained unmoved, tapping his pen like a clock counting down.

"Is this for real?" Carter asked, a current of energy under his steady tone. "We got a murder confession just like that?"

"Looks like it," Lyons said, eyes fixed on the paper.

"This is big," Carter continued, his voice building momentum. "We should jump on it."

Lyons raised an eyebrow, considering the paper as if it might reveal a deeper truth. "Jump on it, or jump the gun?"

Carter set his coffee down with a sharp thud, the sound of his resolve. "You don't think it's legit?"

Lyons let the question hang in the air. "I think," he said slowly, "this guy might be feeling guilty about something else. He tapped the paper, pointing to Jack's name. "He says, 'I killed him,' and now he wants to pay for it?" Lyons shook his head, the gesture precise and skeptical. "I don't buy it."

Carter ran a hand through his hair. "We need to dig deeper."

"Alright," Lyons said, meeting Carter's intensity with measured calm. "Let's think this through. You want to talk about murder?" We've got a long way to go before it looks like murder." He counted off on his fingers, as if teaching a reluctant student. "No victim, no crime scene, no weapon."

He paused, letting each word land with weight. "And no resources until we get some of those things. That's department policy."

Carter shook his head, unable to fathom Lyons' restraint. "You really think he's making it up? Lying about killing someone?"

Lyons opened the file again, reading over the words with care. "He could be lying about a lot of things." His voice held the faintest hint of something like intrigue. "Or he could be telling the truth about the killing and lying about the rest."

Carter leaned in further, his curiosity piqued. "Meaning?"

Lyons pushed the file across the table. "The sister. The threat to his family. That part of the story, I don't buy. Maybe Torres was never a threat."

"What are you saying?" Carter asked, a touch of skepticism coloring his words.

"I'm saying we don't know enough to say anything," Lyons replied. His voice was steady, but there was a current of interest that betrayed his calm exterior. He picked up his pen again, making a note on the edge of the file. "You really want to pursue this?"

Carter nodded, a quick, firm gesture.

Lyons leaned back, as if weighing the balance between caution and risk. "Let's see what we've got first," he said, opening the laptop. The glow of the screen cast a pale light over the room. Lyons' fingers moved over the keys with methodical precision as he ran a search for Torres's name. "If he's missing, we should know," Lyons said, his voice thoughtful but reserved. He adjusted his tie, a habit that seemed to comfort him when evidence was in short supply.

Carter crossed his arms, his posture a map of impatience and persistence. "He says the guy's dead. Missing is putting it mildly."

"Yeah, well," Lyons replied, the Boston in his voice like a line drawn through each word. "I'll believe that when I see it."

The search results blinked back at them, stark and unyielding. Lyons turned, meeting Carter's eyes with the certainty of procedure. "Not exactly the smoking gun you were hoping for."

Lyons glanced at the computer screen again, as if looking for something he'd missed. "No report of any altercation or threat. No missing person report. Torres doesn't seem scared." Lyons' voice was matter-of-fact. "Doesn't seem dead either."

Lyon's closed the laptop. "You really want to open the case? We start small. "Canvas his last known address," Lyons said, offering a compromise between duty and department policy. He began writing in his notebook, each letter clear and deliberate. "Assign some patrol officers to follow up. But I'm not throwing more resources at this until we know there's more than a confession."

Carter watched him, the frustration mingling with reluctant agreement. "What about Jack West? We let him walk until then too?"

Lyons gave a short, decisive nod. "We'll keep an eye on him. But without a victim, there's no way to hold him."

Carter paused, the tension hanging heavy in the air. Then, with a final look at the confession, he exited the room, leaving Lyons alone with the silence.

Lyons sat alone, the solitude breathing like a steady companion as he examined the confession. The phone rang—a precise, demanding trill—and he answered, voice calm. "Detective Lyons," he said. Michael Campbell's tone crackled down the line, cool and probing. "I'm calling about Jack West's confession," the lawyer announced, setting the stage for a verbal duel.

"What do you need?" Lyons asked, knowing the conversation would dance around evidence and expectation.

Michael's voice carried the smooth authority of a seasoned negotiator. "An understanding of where the department stands. Are you pursuing charges?"

"Not without more," Lyons replied, measured in his words. "A confession's just words until we find a body or physical proof."

Michael pressed on, undeterred by Lyons' restraint. "Anything on a missing person's report? Forensic evidence? Anything to back up my client's statement?"

Lyons leaned back, the silence a canvas for his thoughts. "Not yet," he admitted, the Boston edge in his voice growing sharper. "Without proof, it's unsubstantiated. Department policy's clear."

Michael absorbed the response, recalibrating his approach. "I see. You're holding off until you have something tangible. But the confession, that has to count for something."

"Counts for nothing without evidence," Lyons countered, tapping his pen in steady rhythm. "You know that."

Michael paused, letting the tension hang like a dropped note. "If something surfaces, what's your next move?"

Lyons felt the undercurrent of strategy in Michael's inquiry. "That depends. You're expecting charges. We're expecting proof."

"Then you're not ruling out the possibility," Michael said, seizing on the opening.

Lyons offered a sound halfway between agreement and reserve. "Not ruling it in, either. Where do you stand on that?"

Michael's response was crisp and calculated. "Where I stand depends on what you find."

The room was filled with Lyons' patience, a thick, palpable thing. "Can't find what isn't there," he said, the words both factual and challenging.

"We'll see about that," Michael returned, his voice tightening like a noose around the uncertainty.

Lyons allowed a moment of silence to stretch, testing the limits of the call. "And if it turns out like I think it will?" he asked, drawing Michael out.

"We prepare for all possibilities," Michael replied, his tone never wavering.

The conversation circled its unyielding center, both men entrenched in their positions. Lyons' calm precision met Michael's sharp inquiry with equal force, each push countered by a pull.

Michael redirected, sensing Lyons' commitment to procedure. "Assuming the evidence appears, are you considering plea negotiations?"

"We consider everything," Lyons said, the caution in his voice unbroken.

Michael pressed further, trying to pierce the detective's pragmatic shell. "Say you find a body. That changes the scenario significantly."

"Say we don't," Lyons replied, his tone a reflection of doubt as much as possibility.

"But if you do," Michael insisted, "are we looking at voluntary manslaughter or second-degree murder? You know as well as I do, that makes a substantial difference in sentencing."

Lyons let the implications settle. "Depends on what we find," he repeated, his patience enduring.

Michael paused, recalibrating his approach once more. "You're not committing to anything," he observed, the edge in his voice clear.

Lyons gave a brief, dry chuckle, more like an exhalation of amusement than real laughter. "Commitment without evidence isn't my style," he said.

Michael remained unflappable, his lawyer's instinct pushing him to gather every nuance. "You must have some sense of where this might lead," he prodded.

"We follow where the evidence takes us," Lyons said, echoing the steady beat of his earlier words.

"And if it doesn't take you anywhere?" Michael challenged, pressing the weak spot.

"Then we go nowhere," Lyons said, letting the bluntness land with deliberate weight.

The phone line thrummed with unresolved tension, both men aware of the high stakes and low promises.

"You can't tell me you haven't thought this through," Michael said, the persistence of his inquiry a testament to his experience.

"I think things through when there's something to think about," Lyons said, the ambiguity intentional.

Michael pushed one last time, hoping to unearth a clue to Lyons' strategy. "Give me a hypothetical. Where's this going with physical evidence?"

"It's going to court," Lyons replied, the first hint of finality in his voice.

"And without it?" Michael asked, knowing the answer but demanding it be spoken.

"Nowhere," Lyons said again, the repetition as much an end as a beginning.

Michael absorbed the responses, recalibrating for the negotiations ahead. "We'll see what surfaces," he said, more a declaration than a farewell.

"Yes, we will," Lyons said, hanging up, the silence reclaiming the room.

He sat back, contemplating the confession. His pen tapped a thoughtful rhythm, his gaze unwavering as he prepared to watch and wait.

3

Family Reactions

The kitchen door creaked open, admitting Jack along with the morning chill. He stood in the entryway; his shoulders slumped beneath the weight of what he'd done. The house was quiet except for the soft ticking of the kitchen clock and the distant hum of the refrigerator—ordinary sounds that now seemed to mock the extraordinary chaos he'd unleashed on their lives.

Jack removed his shoes methodically, placing them on the rack that Tabby had insisted on buying—"the shoe spot," as they'd jokingly called it. His jacket followed, hung on the peg where it always went. These mundane rituals felt surreal now, as if he were an actor playing the role of a normal man coming home after a normal day. But nothing was normal anymore. Nothing would ever be normal again.

Tabby appeared, relief across her face as she took him in her arms. Jack returned her embrace, gazing over her shoulder at the kitchen table.

There, illuminated by the pendant light hanging overhead, a single sheet of paper, the creases softened from repeated handling. His letter to his unborn son—the one he'd left propped on the kitchen table before driving himself to the police station. The one that contained his feeble attempt at an apology for all he'd miss: his birth, his childhood, his life.

Tabby followed his line of sight. In the harsh kitchen light, Jack noticed what he'd missed at first glance—her eyes were swollen, the whites threaded with red, lashes still damp. She'd been crying. Recently.

"Tabby—"

"Why now?" She turned to face him, one hand still resting on her belly as if to shield their child from the conversation. "Why did you confess? After all this time"

Jack's gaze fell to the floor, his fingers clenched and unclenched at his sides, seeking purchase on a reality that kept slipping away.

Jack forced himself to meet her gaze. "I need to do this, so you're not burdened by my secret. So, our son isn't raised in a house built on lies."

"And you think this is better?" Tabby leaned against the counter, her knuckles white against the edge. "You think our son would rather visit his father in prison than live with not knowing?"

"This is my responsibility—no one else's," Jack insisted.

"What happens now?" Tabby asked, finally reaching out to take his hand. Her touch was warm, grounding him in the moment.

Jack held onto her fingers like a lifeline. "I don't know," he said honestly. "I don't know what comes next."

The calendar on the wall caught his eye, all those carefully marked dates stretching forward into a future that was now uncertain. But Tabby's hand in his was real, her presence a testament to the bond they shared, a reminder that whatever came next, they would face it together.

The doorbell's chime fractured the heavy silence. Tabby's eyes met Jack's before she moved to answer it. Ruby burst through the door first, her blonde hair escaping its practical ponytail, her face a careful mask that slipped the moment she saw her brother. Behind her, Jason entered with the cautious steps of someone crossing uncertain terrain, his shoulders rigid beneath his jacket, eyes scanning the room as if searching for threats.

"Jack," Ruby whispered, the single syllable carrying the weight of questions she couldn't yet form. She crossed the entryway in three quick strides and wrapped her arms around her brother, her frame slight against his solid build.

Jason remained by the door, one hand still on the knob as if preserving the option of escape. His perpetually messy blond hair caught the light from the pendant lamp, casting fragmented shadows across his face. He nodded once at Tabby, a gesture somewhere between greeting and condolence.

"Let's sit down," Tabby suggested as she led them toward the living room. "I made coffee. Or there's tea, if anyone wants."

No one responded to her offer. Instead, they arranged themselves in the living room like pieces on a chess board, each position revealing something of their strategy. Jack settled on the edge of the couch, elbows braced against his knees, hands clasped between them. Tabby lowered herself into the armchair opposite, her movements careful, measured. Ruby chose a spot beside her brother, close enough that their shoulders touched, while Jason took up a position near the window, his back to the gathering dusk outside.

They formed a circle of worried faces, connected by the secret they'd carried—a secret Jack had now decided to relinquish.

"I told them nothing about our discussions before," Jack said finally, breaking the silence. "As far as anyone knows, I'm the only one with knowledge of what happened to Brad."

Ruby's throat worked visibly as she swallowed. "You confessed to killing him?"

"I told them the truth," Jack replied, his gaze fixed on the family photos on the mantel. "That I went to his apartment to talk to him. That things escalated. That I acted alone."

"Why didn't they arrest you?" Ruby asked, her fingers twisting the sleeve of her sweater.

Jack contemplated this. "Likely they're waiting for evidence, which I haven't given them yet." Jack replied.

Tabby's hands trembled slightly in her lap. She pressed them flat against her thighs, inhaling deeply through her nose in a controlled breathing exercise that did little to calm the storm behind her eyes. "Yet?" she asked. The implication clear.

"I talked to a lawyer. There's no evidence and no proof only my confession. The prosecution might agree to a lesser sentence, but I'll have to give them the proof they need to prosecute." Jack explained.

Outside, twilight thickened into evening. The room grew darker by increments, shadows pooling in corners and stretching across the floor like spilled ink. No one moved to turn on a lamp. The gathering darkness seemed appropriate somehow, a physical manifestation of the future closing in around them.

Jason shifted his weight, the floorboard creaking beneath him. His jaw clenched and unclenched, a muscle twitching along its edge. Unable to remain still he began pacing restlessly.

"Your attorney—what are they saying?" Ruby asked, clinging to a sliver of hope.

Jack turned to her. "Campbell's looking into things. We'll know more tomorrow morning where things stand."

"Where things stand?" Jason echoed, incredulous. "You confessed to murder. Where exactly does he think things stand?"

"Manslaughter," Jack corrected quietly. "Campbell thinks we can make a case for voluntary manslaughter. With the threats Brad made, my clean record before this..."

"Jesus Christ," Jason muttered, turning away. His shoulders bunched beneath his shirt, tension radiating from every line of his body.

Tabby spoke up. "We need to focus on what we can control," she said. Her eyes were red-rimmed but dry now, her practical nature asserting itself through the shock. "Jason, this isn't helping."

"What would help, Tabby?" Jason spun back around, frustration giving his words a bitter edge. "Tell me what would help right now, because I'm at a loss."

Ruby's hand tightened imperceptibly on Jack's arm. He noticed how she positioned herself slightly between him and Jason, not confrontational but protective.

"Campbell thinks they'll need physical evidence before they can proceed with charges," Jack said. He looked down at where Ruby's fingers pressed against his sleeve, drawing strength from the contact. "They need to find Brad's body."

"And will they?" Ruby asked, worry etched in every syllable.

Jack met her gaze. "Eventually, yes. I told Campbell where to look."

Jason made a choked sound, halfway between a laugh and something more desperate. "So, you're just—what? Handing them everything they need to lock you up? After months of keeping this secret, you're suddenly throwing your life away?"

"It's not throwing my life away," Jack said, his voice rising for the first time. "It's taking responsibility."

Tabby leaned forward, pushing one of the untouched mugs toward Jack. "Whatever happens next, we face it together," she said. Her voice trembled slightly but held firm. "All of us. That's what we need to focus on now."

"There might not be much to face," Jack admitted. "Campbell said they're treating my confession as unsubstantiated until they find proof. No body, no crime."

"But you gave them a roadmap to the body," Jason said, slumping against the wall. "So, it's just a matter of time."

Ruby released Jack's arm and moved to the window, parting the blinds with two fingers to look out at the yard where, not long ago, they'd all laughed over Jason's attempt to teach their new puppy to fetch. "How much time?" she asked, desperate for certainty.

"I don't know," Jack said. "Days, maybe weeks. Depends on how quickly they move, how seriously they take the confession."

"And what do we do in the meantime?" Jason asked, the fight draining from his voice.

Tabby's eyes moved between them all. "We prepare," she said simply. "For whatever comes next."

Ruby attempted an optimistic smile. "We've been through worse," she said, looking directly at Jack. It wasn't entirely true—they hadn't faced prison before—but the sentiment behind her words rang clear: they would not abandon him.

Jason stepped toward them, running his hands through his hair one more time before letting them fall. "Fine," he said, the word an acceptance more than an agreement. "What do you need from us?"

The question hung in the air, an offering Jack hadn't expected. He looked up, taking in the three people who had become his anchor—Tabby, with her quiet strength; Ruby, with her unwavering loyalty; and Jason, with his reluctant but fierce protectiveness. Despite the fear that had driven him to confession, despite the uncertainty that lay ahead, Jack felt a surge of something like hope.

"Just this," he said finally. "Just you. All of you. Here."

The silence that followed was different from before—still heavy with the weight of what was to come but no longer suffocating. They were in this together, for better or worse. The family they had built would face whatever came next as one.

4
Corroborating Evidence

They met in a café thick with the scent of espresso, the air more caffeine than oxygen. Students crowded the tables, baristas juggling cups with effortless precision, the dull roar of conversation pressing against Jason like deep water. Every sound wave broke against him, the pressure mounting until he wanted to scream.

He stirred his coffee absently, his fingers tightening around the handle until the imprint burned into his palm. His phone rested on the table, untouched but never ignored. Rebecca, seated across from him, radiated a quiet patience that made his skin itch.

"You look terrible." The observation was clinical, not cruel—an assessment rather than an insult. Her gaze flicked over him, taking in the shadows under his eyes, the rumpled clothes that betrayed his unraveling state.

"Thanks for noticing," Jason muttered, dragging a hand down his face. His fingers came away damp with sweat.

He shouldn't have come. Shouldn't have agreed to meet at all. But the toll of keeping Jack's secret had reached its breaking point. He needed to get out of the house—away from the tension that permeated every interaction. Not that it mattered. He'd taken that tension with him.

His phone buzzed on the table, making him flinch. It was a reflex now, his body anticipating bad news with every vibration. He checked the screen—no new messages—and shoved it back in his pocket, trying to ignore the sinking feeling in his stomach.

Rebecca studied him, her expression softening—curious, patient. "Is this about Jack?" she asked. "At the pub last week, I could tell something was happening between you two. Something you didn't want to talk about."

Memories surged—sharp, unrelenting. The confrontation at the pub. Jack's anger when Jason had been too drunk to get Ruby home. By then, Jason had already pieced it together, even though Jack hadn't admitted it yet. Looking back, he could see his own behavior for what it was—an attempt to drown the truth in alcohol, whether intentional or not. Either way, it hadn't worked.

"It's not about that," he said too quickly. Even he wasn't sure if he was deflecting or outright lying. "This is... something else."

Rebecca held his gaze, steady and unwavering. "Then what is it about?"

Loyalty warred with fear, pulling him in opposite directions. He shouldn't say anything. He knew that. But the sleepless nights, the gnawing anxiety—it was breaking him down. His defenses, worn thin, finally collapsed.

"He turned himself in the other day."

Rebecca's brows drew together. "Turned himself in for what?"

"For something that happened months ago."

She leaned back slightly, crossing her arms. The shift was subtle, unreadable—searching. Jason felt like a live wire about to snap, the tension thrumming beneath his skin.

"He's... going through something." His voice wavered. He glanced at the baristas behind the counter, their movements effortless, their lives uncomplicated. The normalcy of it all only sharpened his resentment.

Jason shook his head, searching for a way to convey the weight of his turmoil without revealing too much. "Brad Torres." The name surfaced in his mind unbidden, a constant thread of chaos woven through his life from the moment he'd first heard it.

Only when Rebecca repeated it did he realize he had spoken aloud.

"Brad Torres?" she echoed, something shifting in her tone—curiosity laced with something deeper.

Jason swallowed hard. He needed to backpedal. Fast.

Rebecca's gaze sharpened, absorbing the weight of his confession. "Jason," she pressed, more insistent now. "Does this have to do with—?"

"Seriously." Desperation seeped into his voice. "I shouldn't have said that. Just... forget it."

Her eyes narrowed slightly, concern mingling with professional curiosity. "Is Jack in trouble?"

"I can't..." His voice cracked. "I really can't talk about it. I've gotta go," Jason blurted. The urge to escape hit hard and fast. He stood abruptly, his chair tipping over with a loud clatter. A few heads turned, but he was already moving.

"Jason, wait," Rebecca called.

But he was at the door, the café's dull roar swallowing her voice.

Outside, the cold air hit him, sharp and sobering, each step carrying him further from the mess he had just created.

Inside, Rebecca remained seated, her fingers curled around Jason's abandoned coffee mug, its warmth fading against her skin. Her thoughts raced, replaying the events of last week—the night she and Matthew had invited Jason out for drinks. That was when she'd met Jason's girlfriend Ruby. Ruby, who had spent the evening glued to her phone, texting her brother, much to Jason's irritation. Then Jack had arrived to take them home, and the tension between him and Jason had been unmistakable.

But now, what lingered most was her conversation with Ruby while the guys played pool. At the time, she'd assumed they were simply chatting about her work. But Ruby's words now echoed with new weight:

"Are you saying you work with murderers? What about someone who did something terrible but didn't want to? Someone who had no choice. How do you help a person like that?"

Rebecca had answered like a clinician then—detached, matter-of-fact, laying out outcomes with professional certainty. She'd noticed Ruby's subtle unease, the way her interest seemed personal. But she hadn't pressed.

Now, seeing Jason's concern for Jack, she understood what Ruby had been asking. Those questions weren't idle curiosity. She was worried about Jack. For what he'd done.

The yellow tennis ball bounced across the lawn, a bright spot against the fading afternoon light. Jason watched as Tristan, the puppy, glanced at it with mild interest before returning to his methodical investigation of a dandelion patch. The dog's indifference to the game of fetch had become a running joke between him and Ruby, but today Jason barely noticed, his mind circling back to the conversation with Rebecca like a tongue probing a sore tooth. The guilt of what he'd revealed sat heavy in his stomach, a constant weight he couldn't shake no matter how he tried to distract himself.

"Come on, buddy. The ball. Get the ball." Jason's voice lacked its usual enthusiasm. He sighed, retrieving the ball himself for the fifth time. "You're supposed to be the one doing the fetching, not me."

Tristan looked up at him with liquid brown eyes that seemed almost apologetic before returning to his exploration of the yard's perimeter. The animal's carefree wandering made Jason envious. How simple life must be when your greatest concern was which patch of grass smelled most interesting.

His phone vibrated in his pocket, the sudden buzz making him flinch. Jason pulled it out, squinting at the unknown number on the screen. For a moment, he considered letting it go to voicemail—nothing good ever came from numbers without names—but something made him answer. A premonition, perhaps, or just the lingering anxiety that had haunted him since his conversation with Rebecca. "Hello?" he said, tossing the ball again despite knowing Tristan would ignore it.

"Is this Jason Michael?" The voice was male, direct, with a hint of Boston in the vowels.

Jason's spine stiffened. "Who's asking?"

"This is Detective Marcus Lyons from the Leveret Police Department." The words sent ripples of panic through Jason's body. "I'd like to ask you a few questions about a conversation you had with Rebecca Simmons."

The tennis ball lay forgotten on the grass. Jason's mouth went dry, his free hand instinctively moving to the back of his neck, gripping the tense muscles there. "I, uh... what's this about?"

Lyons' tone was measured, professional, but Jason could hear the undercurrent of interest. "She mentioned that you disclosed some details about Jack West and Brad Torres."

His heart hammered against his ribs like it was trying to escape. "I don't know what you're talking about," he said, the lie sounding hollow even to his own ears.

"According to Ms. Simmons, you implied that Jack West was responsible for Brad Torres' death." Lyons continued, unperturbed by Jason's denial. "I'd like to clarify what exactly you told her."

"Look, I think she misunderstood me. We were just talking, you know? Just… conversation."

"What exactly did you say that she might have misunderstood?" Lyons pressed, his tone shifting slightly, becoming more focused.

"I don't remember exactly." Jason ran a hand through his hair, leaving it standing in agitated tufts. "It wasn't anything specific. Just… talking about Jack having a rough time lately."

"Ms. Simmons was quite specific," Lyons countered. "She noted that you mentioned Brad Torres by name and connected him directly to Jack West's recent behavior."

Jason's breathing quickened, shallow and irregular. "Yeah, I mean, maybe I mentioned Brad. But it wasn't like… I didn't say anything about…" He trailed off, unsure how to finish without incriminating himself further.

"Ms. Simmons stated that you confirmed Jack West's confession about killing Brad Torres." Lyons' voice hardened slightly. "Did Jack West tell you he killed Brad Torres?"

"No!" Jason blurted, too quickly, too forcefully. He moderated his tone, trying to sound calmer than he felt. "I mean, Jack never actually told me he did anything to Brad. That's not—I wouldn't have said that."

"You sound pretty certain for someone who doesn't remember exactly what was said," Lyons observed, the skepticism in his voice unmistakable.

"I just know I wouldn't have said that. Because it's not true. Jack never told me anything like that."

"She seemed quite convinced that you were confirming what happened."

"I don't know. Maybe she… maybe she was reading into things. People do that, right? They hear what they want to hear." Jason's words tumbled out too fast, tripping over each other in their haste.

"People do that," Lyons agreed, his tone neutral. "But Ms. Simmons seemed very clear about what you implied."

Jason's stomach twisted, acid rising in his throat. He swallowed hard, trying to steady himself. "Well, she's wrong. I didn't imply anything about Jack killing anyone."

"Then let me ask you directly: do you have any knowledge about what happened to Brad Torres?"

"No," Jason said, the lie bitter on his tongue. "I don't know anything about that."

There was a pause on the line, the silence more unnerving than Lyons' questions had been. When the detective spoke again, his voice had an edge that hadn't been there before. "Ms. Simmons mentioned that you were distressed when discussing Jack's recent changes in behavior. She specifically noted that you mentioned being concerned about Jack when he turned himself in."

Jason froze, the words hitting him like a brick. Had he really said that? Had he actually mentioned Jack turning himself in? His mind raced, trying to reconstruct the conversation with Rebecca, but everything was a blur of panic and half-formed thoughts.

"I... I don't think I said that," he stammered.

"You don't think you said that Jack turned himself in?" Lyons repeated, emphasizing the words. "Because that's a very specific detail, Mr. Michael. Not something Ms. Simmons would likely invent."

"I might have... I was upset. I don't remember exactly what I said."

"So, you might have mentioned that Jack West turned himself in?" Lyons pressed. "For what exactly?"

"I didn't say for what," Jason insisted, his voice cracking slightly. "If I said anything about him turning himself in, it was... it was just repeating what I'd heard, you know? Around town. People talk."

"People talk," Lyons echoed, his tone flat. "About Jack West turning himself in for killing Brad Torres."

"I didn't say that!" Jason's voice rose, panic breaking through his attempted composure. "You're putting words in my mouth. I never said Jack killed anyone."

"But you did mention him turning himself in," Lyons noted, calm in the face of Jason's growing agitation. "Which is interesting, since Jack West did indeed turn himself in to the Leveret Police Department recently."

Jason's legs felt suddenly weak. This was worse than he'd imagined. He'd thought—hoped—that Rebecca might not actually report him, that she'd recognize his slip as an accident, not something worth pursuing. But now Detective Lyons was on the phone, connecting dots that Jason had inadvertently laid out.

"Look, I don't know anything for sure," Jason said, trying a new approach. "If I said something about Jack turning himself in, it was just... speculation. Or something I overheard. I don't have any firsthand knowledge."

"Firsthand knowledge," Lyons repeated, as if testing the phrase. "That's an interesting choice of words, Mr. Michael. It suggests there's something to have knowledge of."

Jason closed his eyes, willing the conversation to end. Every word he spoke seemed to dig him deeper,

to make things worse not just for himself but for Jack, for all of them.

"I think we should continue this conversation in person," Lyons said after a moment. "We'll need you to come down to the station to make a formal statement."

Jason's eyes snapped open. "A formal statement? About what? I told you, I don't know anything."

"About your conversation with Ms. Simmons," Lyons clarified. "And anything else you might know about Brad Torres or Jack West. Given the seriousness of the situation, we need to document everything properly."

"Am I... am I being charged with something?" Jason asked, his voice small.

"No, Mr. Michael. We're just gathering information at this point." Lyons' tone softened slightly, almost sympathetic. "But I strongly recommend you come in voluntarily. It would be better for everyone involved."

The implication was clear: come in voluntarily or we'll find a way to make you come in. Jason swallowed hard, trying to think through the fog of panic clouding his mind. "Yeah. Okay. I'll... I'll be there."

"Good. Ask for me at the front desk." Lyons concluded.

The call ended, leaving Jason staring at his phone, the screen reflecting his stricken expression back at him. The quiet pressed in around him, broken only by the distant sound of Tristan barking in the yard, having finally found something more interesting than the tennis ball.

"Damn it," Jason muttered. "Damn it, damn it, damn it."

He stood on unsteady legs, moving to the guesthouse where Ruby would be, probably reading or working on her laptop, unaware that everything was about to fall apart. Again. Because of him. Because he couldn't keep his mouth shut.

Jason headed for the door. He had to tell her what had happened, what was coming. She deserved to know before the police showed up at their door, before the fragile peace they'd all been trying to maintain shattered completely.

The few steps to the guesthouse felt like miles, each one carrying him closer to a conversation he dreaded more than the one he'd just had with Lyons. How could he tell her that he'd betrayed them all? That he'd confirmed what Jack had been trying to keep contained, that he'd validated the confession and given the police the ammunition they needed?

Jason slipped inside the back door, his heart pounding against his ribs so hard he was sure Ruby would hear it before she heard him call her name.

"Ruby?" he called, his voice breaking on her name. "Ruby, we need to talk."

Ruby sat cross-legged on the bed, her laptop balanced on her knees, the blue light from the screen casting shadows across her face. She looked up at the sound of Jason's voice, her expression shifting from concentration to concern in the space of a heartbeat. Something in his tone—a tremor he couldn't quite hide—had alerted her to trouble before he'd even stepped fully into the room.

"What's wrong?" she asked, closing her laptop with a soft click that seemed to echo in the sudden stillness. Her eyes, sharp and assessing, tracked his movements as he paced from the doorway to the center of the room and back again, his body a coiled spring of nervous energy.

Jason couldn't meet her gaze. His hands opened and closed at his sides, fingers flexing as if searching for something to hold onto, something solid in a world that was rapidly dissolving beneath his feet. The phone call with Lyons replayed in his mind, each word a hammer blow against his conscience.

"Jason," Ruby said, firmer now. She set her laptop aside and swung her legs over the edge of the bed, feet planted on the floor in a stance that suggested she was bracing for impact. "What happened?"

He stopped pacing, forcing himself to look at her. The words stuck in his throat, thick and choking. How did you tell someone you'd betrayed their trust? That you might have just sentenced their brother to years in prison?

"I fucked up," he said finally, the admission tearing from him like something physical. "Ruby, I really fucked up."

She didn't move, didn't blink, just waited. But he could see the tension in her shoulders, the slight narrowing of her eyes that betrayed her growing alarm.

"It's about Jack," he continued, each word heavier than the last. "I was talking to Rebecca the other day, at that café downtown."

"Rebecca?" Ruby repeated, the name like a foreign object she was turning over in her mind. "Your friend from the pub that night?"

Jason nodded, running a hand through his already disheveled hair. "Yeah. He swallowed hard, preparing himself for Ruby's reaction. "I was upset, stressed about everything with Jack, and I just... I wanted someone to talk to who wasn't already involved."

Ruby's expression hardened slightly, a flicker of something—hurt? disappointment?—crossing her features before she masked it. "What did you tell her?"

Jason began pacing again, unable to contain the restless energy coursing through him. "I didn't mean to tell her anything specific. I swear, Ruby. But she kept asking questions, and I was so worn down from all of this..." He gestured vaguely, encompassing all the shared secrets and silent worry. "I mentioned Brad's name."

Ruby went very still, her posture rigid as a statue. "You what?"

"I didn't say Jack killed him," Jason rushed to clarify, though the distinction felt meaningless now. "But I mentioned Brad in connection with Jack's recent behavior, and she... she figured it out."

"She figured it out," Ruby repeated, her voice flat. She stood up slowly, her movements deliberate, as if she were moving underwater. "What exactly did she figure out, Jason?"

He closed his eyes briefly, shame washing over him in a hot wave. "That Jack's confession was real. That he actually killed Brad."

The silence that followed was absolute, a vacuum that seemed to suck all the air from the room. When Jason opened his eyes, Ruby was staring at him, her face a careful blank that frightened him more than any outburst would have.

She turned away from him, toward the window, her back a straight line of tension. "And did she report it?"

Jason's stomach twisted with dread. This was the worst part, the part he'd been dreading since the moment Lyons had called. "Yes. Detective Lyons just called me. That's why I came to find you."

Ruby spun back to face him, her composure cracking for the first time. "Detective Lyons? The police have already contacted you?"

Jason nodded miserably. "He wants me to come in and make a formal statement about my conversation with Rebecca."

"Jesus Christ, Jason." Ruby's voice cracked, her control slipping. She pressed her fingertips to her temples, as if trying to physically hold herself together. "Do you have any idea what you've done?"

He flinched at the question, though he knew he deserved it. "I didn't mean to, Ruby. I swear I didn't. It just... happened."

"Things like this don't just happen," she said, anger edging her words now. "You made a choice to talk to someone outside our circle. You chose to bring up Brad's name."

"I know," Jason admitted, his voice small. "I know I did. And I've been beating myself up about it since the moment it happened. But I can't take it back now. I can only try to fix it."

Ruby laughed, a harsh, brittle sound that held no humor. "Fix it? How exactly do you plan to fix this, Jason? The police already know. They've connected the dots."

"Maybe not completely," Jason said, clinging to a desperate hope. "Lyons said they're just gathering information at this point. Maybe I can downplay what I said to Rebecca, make it seem like she misunderstood me."

"You mean lie to the police?" Ruby asked, her eyebrow arching in skepticism. "That's your solution? Dig the hole deeper?"

Jason's hands were numb. "I don't know what else to do. I can't just confirm what she told them. That would be..."

"The final nail in Jack's coffin," Ruby finished for him, her voice suddenly tired. She sank back down onto the edge of the bed, the fight seeming to drain out of her. "God, Jason. Why couldn't you have just kept your mouth shut?"

The question hung in the air between them, unanswerable and damning. Jason stood there, feeling every inch the betrayer, every second of silence another indictment of his carelessness.

"I need to tell Jack and Tabby," Ruby said finally. "They need to know what's happening before the police show up at their door."

"No," Jason said quickly, stepping forward. "Let me. Please. I'm the one who screwed up. I should be the one to tell them."

"You think that will make it easier for them to hear? That their friend stabbed them in the back?"

Jason winced at the harsh assessment, but he couldn't deny its truth. "No. But it's the right thing to do. I need to own this, Ruby. Face them directly."

She studied him for a long moment, her gaze unreadable. Then, with a slight nod, she set her phone aside. "Alright. But I'm coming with you."

Jason felt a small measure of relief, though he knew the worst was still to come. "Thank you," he said softly. "And I really am sorry, Ruby. More than I can say."

"I know you are," she replied, her voice gentler now, though still edged with worry. "But being sorry doesn't change what's coming."

"What do you think will happen?" Jason asked, voicing the fear that had been growing since Lyons' call. "Will this... will this make things worse for Jack?"

Ruby ran a hand through her blonde hair. "I don't know. Campbell said they needed physical evidence before they could move forward with charges. Maybe this won't change that."

"But it confirms his confession," Jason pointed out, the guilt surging again. "It gives them corroboration from an outside source."

"Which is exactly what they've been looking for," Ruby agreed, the worry clear in her voice now. "But it's still just words, Jason. Not physical evidence."

"But it might be enough to make them look harder for that evidence," Jason said, the realization hitting him with fresh force.

Ruby closed her eyes briefly, as if warding off a sudden pain. "Yes. It might."

The weight of that possibility settled over them both, heavy and suffocating. Jason sank onto the edge of the desk chair, his legs suddenly too weak to support him. "What have I done?" he whispered, more to himself than to Ruby.

"You made a mistake," she said, surprising him with the lack of accusation in her tone. "A serious one, but still just a mistake. Now we have to deal with the consequences."

Jason looked up at her, grateful for the slim mercy of her understanding, undeserved as it was. "How? How do we deal with this?"

Ruby stood, straightening her shoulders in a visible gathering of strength. "First, we tell Jack and Tabby. Then, you go to the police station and give your statement. You tell them the truth—that you overheard Jack talking about turning himself in, that you don't have firsthand knowledge of what happened with Brad. You keep it as vague as possible without outright lying."

"And if they push?" Jason asked, dreading the prospect of facing Lyons' direct questions again.

"Then you say you can't recall exactly what was said. That you were stressed and emotional and might have misspoken or been misunderstood." Ruby's mind already working through contingencies. "The important thing is not to add any new information they don't already have."

Jason nodded, clinging to her guidance like a lifeline. "Okay. I can do that."

"And Jason," Ruby added, her voice dropping to a quieter register, "don't talk to Rebecca again. Not about this, not about anything. She's made it clear where her loyalties lie."

The reminder stung, even though he knew she was right. Rebecca had chosen honesty over their friendship, doing what she thought was best—but all she'd done was make things worse.

It was just another betrayal in a day full of them.

"I won't," he promised. "No more talking to anyone outside our circle. I've learned my lesson. Thank you," he said quietly. "For not hating me for this."

Ruby's smile was small but genuine.

She opened the door, letting in a wash of afternoon light that seemed at odds with the gravity of their situation. Together, they stepped out into the yard, walking side by side toward the main house where they would have to shatter Jack and Tabby's fragile peace with the news of what was coming. The sun beat down on them, indifferent to their troubles, the world continuing its steady rotation despite the chaos unfolding in their small corner of it.

Jason glanced at Ruby; at the careful composure she had reconstructed around herself like armor. Despite everything, he felt a surge of gratitude for her presence, for the strength she lent him even now.

Jason's mouth had gone dry by the time they reached Jack and Tabby's door. His rehearsed explanations crumbled into dust as Ruby rang the doorbell, her finger pressing with deliberate finality. The afternoon sun slanted through the trees, casting bars of light across the porch that seemed to point accusingly at him, illuminating his betrayal for all to see. He shifted his weight from one foot to the other, a restless pendulum of anxiety, while Ruby stood beside him, straight-backed and composed despite the storm he'd unleashed.

The door swung open, revealing Jack's questioning face. His eyes moved from Ruby to Jason, picking up the tension that hung between them like a visible thread.

"What's going on?" Jack asked, stepping back to let them enter.

Jason opened his mouth, but the words stuck in his throat. Ruby moved past him into the house, her shoulder brushing against his in what might have been reassurance or a warning.

"We need to talk," she said simply. "All of us."

Jack's expression shifted, a subtle tightening around his eyes that spoke volumes. He nodded once and led them through to the living room where Tabby sat on the couch, a book open on her lap. She looked up, her smile fading as she registered their expressions.

"Ruby? Jason?" Her hand moved instinctively to her swollen belly, protective and wary.

Jack settled beside her. The lamp beside them cast a soft glow that couldn't quite dispel the growing shadows in the room. Jason remained standing, his feet rooted to the spot just inside the doorway. He couldn't bring himself to sit, couldn't imagine the normality of perching on their furniture as if he hadn't just blown apart their fragile peace.

Ruby positioned herself near the kitchen entrance, arms folded tightly across her chest.

The silence stretched, elastic and dangerous. Jason felt it pressing against him, demanding words he didn't know how to form. The ticking of the clock on the mantle measured out the seconds of his hesitation.

"Somebody want to tell us what's happening?" Jack finally asked, his voice even but alert.

Jason cleared his throat, not meeting Jack's gaze. "I, uh... There's something I need to tell you guys." He swallowed hard, his Adam's apple bobbing visibly. "Something happened."

"Is everyone okay?" Tabby asked, her gaze sharp with concern.

"Yeah, everyone's fine," Jason rushed to assure her. "It's not that kind of... I mean, no one's hurt or anything."

Ruby made a small noise that might have been disagreement, and Jason flinched.

"It's about Rebecca," he said, forcing the words out. "My friend from the pub that night. Remember her?"

Jack nodded slowly, his expression unreadable. "What about her?"

Jason ran a hand through his already disheveled hair, leaving it standing in agitated spikes. "She, uh... she works as a psychologist. Works with criminals sometimes." He let out a strained laugh that sounded hollow even to his own ears. "Which is kind of ironic, given what's happened."

"Jason," Ruby cut in, her voice clipped. "Just tell them."

He nodded, drawing in a shaky breath. "Right. So, I was talking to Rebecca the other day. At this café downtown. I was... stressed, you know? About everything that's been going on. And I just wanted someone to talk to who wasn't already involved."

Jack's posture shifted subtly, a slight stiffening of his shoulders. Beside him, Tabby's body tensed visibly, her fingers finding Jack's hand and gripping it tightly.

"What did you tell her?" Jack asked, the question eerily echoing Ruby's earlier words.

Jason's gaze dropped to the floor. "I didn't mean to tell her anything specific. But she kept asking questions, and I was just so worn down from all of this..." He gestured vaguely around the room, encompassing all of them and the secret they shared. "I mentioned Brad's name."

The silence that followed was absolute. Jack exhaled slowly, the sound unnaturally loud in the quiet room. Tabby's eyes widened, her free hand pressing more firmly against her belly as if to shield their unborn child from what was coming.

"You mentioned Brad Torres to Rebecca? "Jack's voice was carefully controlled, but Jason could hear the undercurrent of disbelief.

"I didn't say you killed him," Jason rushed to clarify. "At least, I don't think I did. But I mentioned him in connection with... with everything that's been happening lately."

"He specifically mentioned Brad in the context of your confession," Ruby said, her voice even but edged with steel. "And Rebecca put the rest together."

Tabby held her gaze. "Put together what, exactly?" Her voice was steadier than Jason had expected.

Jason swallowed hard. "That Jack's confession was real. That he actually killed Brad." His words hung in the air, and his eyes dropped to the floor, which seemed to stare back, accusatory and unyielding.

Jack exhaled sharply, closing his eyes as if absorbing the blow. When he opened them again, his gaze locked onto Jason—sharp, unflinching, a force that made Jason want to shrink back.

Tabby inhaled sharply. "Jason."

Jason immediately sobered slightly. "Alright, alright. Bottom line—they know. But you already went to the cops, Jack. So, this isn't new information, right?"

Jack's expression tightened with concern. He had told his lawyer that no one knew what he had done. Now, this changed everything. It would complicate the case, pulling them into an investigation he had fought so hard to shield them from.

Ruby sighed, pinching the bridge of her nose. "We're handling this. We're keeping things as controlled as possible. And Jason—" she shot him another glare "—needs to stop talking now."

Jason nodded silently.

Jack exhaled, rubbing his forehead. "Alright. Fine. We move forward."

Tabby, despite her frustration, squeezed his hand gently. "We figure it out. Together."

5
Planning for Tabby's Future

Jack's fingers moved across the calculator with practiced precision, the quiet clicks of the buttons punctuating the kitchen's silence. The morning light filtered through the kitchen window, casting shadows across the notebooks and papers that covered the oak table—a battlefield of numbers where he fought against an invisible enemy: the financial uncertainty that loomed over his family's future. He paused, rubbing his eyes that burned from hours of concentration, then glanced at the clock on the wall—Ruby would arrive soon, and he needed to have these figures organized before explaining why, despite all his planning, he feared it wouldn't be enough.

The kitchen had always been the heart of their home, but lately it had transformed into his war room. Spreadsheets and bank statements replaced the family meals that once dominated the space. Jack reached for his coffee, now cold and bitter, and took a mechanical sip. His gaze drifted to the refrigerator where Tabby had pinned the ultrasound image with a tree-shaped magnet. His son's first portrait.

The sound of the kitchen door opened with a familiar creak pulling him from his thoughts.

Jack looked up, shuffling papers into neater piles as Ruby appeared in the doorway, her frame leaning against the jamb as she surveyed the scene. Her blond hair was pulled back in a tight ponytail, her face bare of makeup.

"How long have you been at this?" she asked, dropping her bag onto a chair and moving to the coffee pot.

"A few hours," Jack said, though they both knew it had been longer. "Coffee's fresh enough."

Ruby poured herself a cup, adding nothing to it before taking a sip. She grimaced. "Fresh enough is generous."

"Time management hasn't been my priority." Jack tapped his pen against a column of figures. "We need to talk about the numbers."

Ruby pulled out a chair across from him, its legs scraping against the floor. "So, talk."

His sister's directness was both familiar and comforting. No preamble, no emotional cushioning—just the facts. Jack pushed a notebook toward her; columns of numbers meticulously aligned in his neat handwriting.

"This is what Tabby brings in monthly from the library. After taxes, health insurance—which they're keeping her on, thankfully—and retirement contributions." He pointed to the figure circled at the bottom. "This is what we're working with without my income."

Ruby studied the number, her expression neutral. "It's not terrible."

"It's not enough," Jack countered, sliding another sheet forward. "Mortgage is here. Utilities average out to this. Car payment, insurance, groceries." His finger moved down the column. "And then there's everything for the baby." The baby. The word hung between them, weighted with all its implications. Jack's son would be born while he was inside.

Ruby took another sip of coffee. "Babies are expensive, but people manage."

"People who aren't single mothers with husbands in prison," Jack said, his voice lowered despite the empty house. "And that's not accounting for unexpected expenses. What happens when the water heater goes, or the car needs repairs?"

"That's where emergency funds come in."

Jack laughed, a short, humorless sound. "Emergency funds. Right." He flipped to another page. "Here's our savings. After legal fees, it's down to this." He tapped a circled number that seemed to diminish every time he looked at it.

Ruby's eyes widened slightly, the only indication of her surprise. "That's not much of a cushion."

"Exactly. Three, maybe four months of expenses if they're careful." Jack ran a hand through his dark hair. "And that's assuming nothing goes wrong."

The oak tree outside the window cast shifting shadows across the table as a breeze stirred its branches. Jack had climbed that tree to remove a dead limb that threatened the roof. He remembered how solid it had felt beneath him, how certain he'd been of each movement, each cut. Now nothing felt certain.

"So, what about my contribution?" Ruby asked, pulling him back to the present. "Jason and I have talked about it. We can pay more rent for the guest house, help with utilities."

Jack had been both counting on and dreading this part of the conversation. "I've factored that in," he admitted, turning to another page where he'd written their names with a question mark beside a figure. "But I don't know if it's fair to ask you—"

"You're not asking. I'm offering."

Jack nodded, relief mingling with discomfort. His sister shouldn't have to support his family, but pride was a luxury he couldn't afford anymore. "I've estimated what's reasonable based on what you're paying now, minus what you'll save by sharing utilities." He showed her the number.

Ruby studied it, then took the pen from his hand and increased the amount by two hundred dollars. "We can manage this."

"Ruby—"

"It's not a discussion, Jack." She met his gaze steadily. "You'd do the same for me. You have done the same for me."

The unspoken reference hung between them. How many times had he stepped in, taken care of things, made sure she was safe after what happened with Brad? And now here he was, going to prison for making sure he would never hurt Ruby—or anyone else—again.

His hands were numb from writing, but a different sensation spread through his chest—a mixture of gratitude and something harder to name. "Thank you," he said simply.

Ruby nodded once, acknowledging but not lingering on the sentiment.

"What about selling the house?" Ruby asked, her tone carefully neutral. "You have equity. Tabby could move somewhere smaller, more manageable."

He'd considered it, run the numbers, but something in him rebelled at the thought. "This is our home. Simon's home. I don't want him growing up in some apartment because I—" He stopped, recalibrating. "The market's not great right now anyway. We'd lose money."

Ruby didn't push, just made another note. "Too bad Tabby's parents are...." Ruby shrugged, leaving her thought unfinished.

Jack regarded her for a moment before speaking. "Deadbeats?" he offered, meeting her gaze.

"Well, yeah," she confirmed. "What about Mom and Dad?" Ruby asked redirecting.

Jack dismissed the suggestion immediately. "No. I've caused them enough trouble."

Ruby gave a slow nod, smirking faintly. "Yeah, you'll definitely lose your golden child status when you tell them you killed Brad and buried his body on their land."

Jack ignored the jab.

Ruby took another sheet of paper and began writing. "So, we're looking at Tabby's income, our rent, whatever small savings can be preserved." She looked up. "What about her getting a second job?"

Jack shook his head immediately. "She'll have a newborn, Ruby. She's already planning to go back to work after just eight weeks for financial reasons." The thought made his stomach twist. "I can't ask her to work a second job on top of that."

"You might not have to ask," Ruby said quietly. "Tabby's stronger than you give her credit for. She might make that choice herself."

Jack stared at the ultrasound picture on the refrigerator. "That's what I'm afraid of."

The silence that followed was broken only by the ticking of the kitchen clock and the distant sound of a lawnmower from a neighboring yard. Life continuing its normal rhythms while his own had been fundamentally altered.

"There's one more thing," Jack said finally, reaching for a thin file folder he'd kept separate from the others. "My commissary account and phone calls."

Ruby's expression tightened. "What about them?"

"They cost money. It adds up fast." Jack opened the folder to reveal a sheet with weekly and monthly projections. "I've calculated a minimum amount to maintain basic communication, but even that will be around eighty dollars a month."

"We'll handle it," Ruby said firmly.

"I don't want to be another expense."

"Too bad." Ruby's tone brooked no argument. "Simon needs to hear his father's voice. Tabby needs to talk to her husband. That's not negotiable."

Jack nodded, unexpectedly grateful for his sister's stubbornness. "I've set aside enough for six months of calls in a separate account. After that..." He trailed off.

"After that, we'll figure it out," Ruby finished for him. "One day at a time."

Jack smiled faintly.

Ruby gathered the papers into a neat stack. "So, what's the bottom line here, Jack? With everything factored in—my rent, Tabby's income, the current savings—what are we looking at"

Jack pulled out his most recent calculation, the one he'd been working on when Ruby arrived. "We're short. About three hundred a month, give or take." He tapped the paper. "And that's assuming nothing unexpected happens. No major repairs, no medical emergencies, no car trouble."

Ruby studied the numbers, her expression thoughtful. "Three hundred isn't insurmountable."

"It is when you're already stretched thin," Jack countered. "It's the difference between making ends meet and falling behind on the mortgage."

"There are options we haven't explored," Ruby insisted. "I could pick up extra shifts at work. Jason might get that promotion he's been talking about."

"I can't build a financial plan on maybes," Jack said, frustration edging into his voice. "I need certainty. I need to know they'll be okay."

"You can't have certainty," Ruby said, her voice gentle but firm. "Not with this. Not with anything."

The truth of her words settled over him like a weight. Jack had always been the fixer, the planner, the one who made things right. But there were limits to his control now, boundaries he couldn't cross from behind prison walls.

He gathered the papers mechanically, organizing them into folders with labels written in his neat block letters: MONTHLY EXPENSES, SAVINGS, CONTINGENCY PLANS, FUTURE PROJECTS. Each one a desperate attempt to extend his protection beyond the physical constraints that awaited him.

"I'll scan all of these," he said finally. "Email copies to you and Tabby, store backups in the cloud." His voice sounded distant to his own ears. "You'll need to check in regularly, make sure the numbers are tracking correctly."

Ruby reached across the table and placed her hand over his, stilling his movements. "Jack. Look at me."

He raised his eyes to meet hers.

"We will figure this out," she said, each word deliberate. "Tabby is capable. I am capable. Jason is stepping up. We're not helpless without you."

"I know that," Jack said, though part of him didn't, couldn't accept it.

"Do you?" Ruby squeezed his hand once before releasing it. "Because sometimes I think you believe if you don't control every variable, everything will fall apart."

Jack closed the last folder, aligning its edge perfectly with the others. "I'm just trying to take responsibility."

"There's a difference between responsibility and control." Ruby stood, taking her coffee cup to the sink. "You're responsible for your actions. You're not responsible for protecting everyone from every possible hardship."

The words struck closer to home than Jack wanted to admit. Wasn't that exactly what had led him here? The belief that it was his responsibility to protect Ruby, to ensure Brad could never hurt her again?

"I just want them to be okay," he said quietly.

Ruby turned from the sink, leaning against the counter. "They will be. Not because you calculated every penny or predicted every scenario, but because you've built relationships with people who care. That's worth more than any financial plan."

Jack nodded, not entirely convinced but too exhausted to argue. He stacked the folders neatly, this physical manifestation of his need to bring order to chaos. The morning light had shifted, no longer falling directly on the table but casting longer shadows across the kitchen floor.

"Tabby will be home soon," he said, checking the time. "She has the afternoon off today."

Ruby nodded. "I should get going then. I've got work in an hour." She hesitated. "Do you want me to take any of these files for review?"

Jack considered this, then selected one folder. "This one has the main summary. Look it over when you have time." He paused. "And Ruby? Thank you."

She accepted the folder with a small smile. "What are sisters for if not to help their brothers obsess over spreadsheets"

The attempt at levity didn't quite reach her eyes, but Jack appreciated it nonetheless. He walked her to the door. Through the open doorway, he could see the oak tree in the yard, its branches moving gently in the breeze, roots hidden deep beneath the surface, anchoring it against whatever storms might come.

Jack closed the door and returned to the kitchen, to the folders and calculations that represented his last attempt to provide certainty in an increasingly uncertain future.

He placed his hand on the ultrasound picture, his son's ghostly image beneath his fingertips. "I'll figure it out," he promised quietly. "Somehow."

Ruby's hand tightened around her coffee mug, as her brother's eyes watched her intently. "You're serious?" she asked, setting the mug down with a quiet thud that seemed to stretch into the charged air.

Jack nodded, swallowing against the anxiety tightening his throat. "I can't think of anyone else who'd see her through like you would."

Jack's fingers traced absent patterns on the tabletop—a silent map of his uncertainty. "It's a lot to ask," he murmured.

Ruby held his gaze, surprise lingering in her eyes before it settled into something else—something harder to read. She glanced down at the mug as if expecting an answer from its depths, then back at him, her expression cautiously neutral.

Jack felt the weight of his request press against the air between them. The refrigerator hummed softly, a background of domesticity to a conversation that felt anything but ordinary. "I just need to know Tabby's not alone," he continued. "That she has someone who'll be there through all of it."

Ruby breathed in, a measured intake of air that seemed to steady her. She met his gaze again, searching for any sign of hesitation. "You really think I'm the right person for this?"

Jack nodded again, feeling the tightness in his chest as he spoke. "There's no one else I trust like you."

They sat in silence, the clock's ticking marking the seconds with unrelenting precision. Jack's pulse quickened with each passing moment, anticipating his sister's response. The urgency of his situation—of Tabby's situation—seemed to close in around him, narrowing his world to the kitchen, the table, Ruby's deliberating eyes. She finally broke the silence, her voice tentative.

"Jack, this isn't just labor coaching. This is... everything, isn't it?"

He exhaled, relieved to hear her putting words to the enormity of what he couldn't fully articulate. "Everything," he echoed. "I want you to be there for the labor, but also for what comes after. The hard parts. The middle-of-the-night parts."

Ruby's fingers tapped against the mug, absorbing the impact of his request. The sound was small, but it carried in the quiet room. "You're asking me to be Tabby's partner while you're gone."

He didn't deny it. How could he, when that was exactly what he needed, what he was desperate enough to admit? Jack's voice was lower now, the vulnerability breaking through his usual control. "She'll need someone, Ruby. I need someone I can count on to get her through."

The words hung in the air, heavy with implication. Jack held his breath, waiting.

"And you don't think Tabby can do this on her own?" Ruby asked, not accusing but seeking clarity.

"I think she can do anything," Jack said quickly, defending Tabby's strength even as he questioned his own ability to leave her. "But that doesn't mean she should have to. Especially not with me... especially not now."

Ruby nodded slowly, absorbing what he was saying. The gravity of his situation—of Tabby's situation—seemed to settle over her like a tangible thing, reshaping the contours of their conversation.

Jack leaned forward, his arms resting on the table, the words coming faster now. "I know how much I'm asking, Ruby. I know it's a huge responsibility. But I can't stand the thought of her facing it alone."

His eyes were wide with unspoken fears; the fears of a man used to controlling his world and now forced to relinquish control to others. Ruby saw the way he gripped the table's edge as if it might anchor him through the storm he was about to weather. She took a breath, then another, the seconds stretching out as she considered the promise she was about to make.

"You want me there for every contraction," she said finally, her voice gaining steadiness with each word. "And every two a.m. feeding."

Jack swallowed hard, nodding. His controlled breathing was the only sign of the relief he felt.

"And every meltdown, every moment when she thinks she can't do it," Ruby continued, her words becoming a promise.

"Yes," Jack said, the word escaping on an exhale. His eyes met hers, and in that moment, he saw the understanding he hoped for. The acceptance.

Ruby reached across the table, her hand covering his. "I'll be there," she said simply, her voice strong. "I'll be there for everything."

The tension in the room eased, the heavy air shifting as Jack released the breath he'd been holding. His relief was palpable, an unspoken gratitude that softened his features and loosened the tightness in his shoulders.

"You have no idea what this means," Jack said, his voice rough with emotion he couldn't quite contain.

"I think I do," Ruby replied, a hint of a smile tugging at the corner of her mouth. "You're trusting me with your family, Jack. I know exactly what that means."

After a beat, she added, "So, I'm getting the full husband experience—minus the fun part that got her pregnant," unable to resist teasing him.

Jack let out a dramatic eye roll. "I'm really going to miss that sweet, innocent humor of yours," he shot back.

Ruby's smile faded into something more resolute. "Let's make a schedule. You love schedules."

"I've already started," Jack confessed, pulling a small notebook from beneath the stack of papers. His hands were steady, but the tension in his shoulders belied the calm he tried to project.

Ruby's eyes softened as she watched him. "You've really thought this through."

"I have to," Jack said, opening the notebook to reveal pages filled with neat, precise handwriting.

Ruby reached for the notebook, scanning its contents. "Childbirth classes?"

Jack's mouth curved into a reluctant smile. "I figured you'd want to be prepared."

"Doula training, even," Ruby said, her voice lighter now. "You've really outdone yourself."

Jack watched her closely, his eyes following every flicker of her expression. "So, you'll do it?"

Ruby handed the notebook back to him, a hint of admiration in her gaze. "I'll do it. If we're committing, let's commit. I want you to know I'm taking this seriously, Jack."

He exhaled, the relief almost visible as it passed through him. "Thank you. I know how much I'm asking."

"You always ask a lot," Ruby said with a shrug. "It's what makes you Jack."

He accepted the words without argument, his focus returning to the pages in front of them. "I think the hardest part for Tabby will be the last few weeks of pregnancy. That's when things might really hit her."

Ruby nodded, considering. "And you'll be...?" She let the question hang, knowing the answer.

"I'll be gone," Jack said, the words heavy with resignation. "I want you to be there for the delivery. Make sure she gets to the hospital."

"You know I will be," Ruby said, her confidence unshakable.

The room was silent except for the ticking clock and the distant sounds of the neighborhood outside—a barking dog, a car driving past, the ordinary rhythms of a life he wouldn't know for much longer.

It wasn't the plan he'd wanted, but it was the plan he had. And maybe, just maybe, it would be enough.

The door closed softly behind Ruby as she left, leaving Jack alone in the kitchen with the clock's steady ticking and the quiet strength of her promise.

The bedroom held its breath, the weight of unsaid things dense as the late afternoon light filtering through the curtains. Jack's pacing etched the floor with the gravity of what he couldn't yet say. He'd been rehearsing this moment all day, the words worn from repetition but still tight in his throat. When Tabby entered, easing herself onto the edge of the bed, Jack sat beside her, leaving space, leaving room for all he needed to tell her.

He took a deep breath, his voice a study in calm even as his hands betrayed him, smoothing the sheets with restless energy. "I think we should get married," he said, the directness of it hanging in the air between them.

Tabby blinked, her hand moving instinctively over the swell of her belly. "What? now?"

"Before I go in," Jack continued, the words coming faster now, propelled by necessity. "It makes sense. You'll have insurance coverage, hospital visitation, legal protection."

She watched him with a mixture of emotions playing across her face. "You've really thought this through."

Jack nodded, grateful she didn't need more convincing. He paused, watching her carefully, the silence filled with the soft rasp of fabric as his fingers moved against the bed sheets. He knew the proposal wasn't romantic, knew it wasn't how either of them had imagined this moment. But what mattered now was urgency and the specter of separation looming over them. What mattered was making sure they were a family, despite the circumstances.

Tabby met his gaze, a soft understanding in her eyes. "When are you thinking?"

"As soon as possible," Jack replied, his voice a mix of practicality and something more vulnerable. "Before Simon comes. Before I..." He let the sentence hang unfinished, trusting her to fill in the gaps.

Tabby absorbed this, her own thoughts turning visibly behind her eyes. "And after?" she asked, the question small and cautious. "You'll be gone. We'll be—"

"Married," Jack finished for her. "And ready for whatever comes."

She nodded slowly, her hand resting protectively over her belly, the weight of his words settling in. "I never thought this would be how our wedding planning would go."

Jack gave a faint smile. "I didn't either."

Jack's breath caught in his throat. "I want this, Tabby. I want us to be a family. I just..."

He hesitated, then continued, the words raw and unguarded. "I just don't know how to give you everything you deserve right now."

"We can do the paperwork," Tabby said, her voice firmer now, moving into planning mode. "At the courthouse. What about witnesses?"

"Ruby and Jason," Jack said without hesitation. "They'll be there."

"And the timing?" she asked, ever practical. "Before I'm too huge to fit into a dress?"

"Next week, if you're up for it." Jack tried to read her reaction, to measure her happiness against the sadness that crept in at the edges. "Are you okay with that?"

"I'm okay with whatever it takes," Tabby said, echoing the resolve that had carried them this far.

Jack let out a breath he didn't realize he'd been holding. "I know it's not how we pictured it."

"How did you picture it?" Tabby asked, a hint of wistfulness in her tone.

He thought of the plans they'd once made, the future they'd imagined before everything changed. "Not like this," he admitted. "But still us. Still together."

"That's all I need," Tabby said, conviction and emotion mingling in her voice.

Jack took her hand, holding it as if it might anchor him against the tide of uncertainty. "There's one more thing."

Tabby's curiosity mixed with cautious hope. "What is it?"

Jack reached into his pocket, feeling the cool metal against his fingertips. "I wanted to wait for the right time to make our engagement official," he said, his voice lower now, thick with what he couldn't quite articulate. "But with everything that's happening..."

He brought out the simple ring, the silver catching the light, and saw Tabby's eyes widen with surprise. "It was my grandmother's. I've been saving it for—"

"For this?" Tabby asked, her voice catching, eyes filling with tears that reflected both joy and the weight of all that lay ahead.

"For a more romantic proposal," Jack said, smiling despite himself. "But I guess we're not working with that timeline anymore."

He turned the ring in his fingers, watching her as he spoke. "I know this isn't how either of us planned it. But I love you, Tabby. I love you and Simon. I want us to be a family, no matter what it takes."

Tabby's tears spilled over, her hand reaching out to touch the ring, then resting against his cheek. "I love you, too," she said, the words thick with emotion, their shared truth carrying them.

She let him slip the ring onto her finger, both of them watching as it settled into place, a physical promise amid the chaos and uncertainty that surrounded them. The moment was heavy with significance, with the understanding that their lives were about to change in ways neither could fully comprehend.

Jack placed his hand over hers, feeling the warmth of her skin, the delicate circle of metal now a part of their shared history. He moved closer, until their foreheads touched, the silence around them profound and complete.

"I'm scared, Jack," Tabby whispered, the vulnerability in her voice echoing the thoughts he'd kept buried.

"Me too," he admitted, his own fear tempered by the strength he found in her. "But we'll get through it. Together."

They stayed like that, eyes closed, breathing in the closeness that would soon be a memory to sustain them. The ring felt foreign and familiar on Tabby's finger, its presence a small but significant comfort. A reminder of what they were building even as so much slipped beyond their control.

"This isn't the end," Tabby said, her words a fragile bridge over the distance they would face.

"No," Jack agreed, his voice gaining certainty as he spoke. "It's the beginning. For us."

The room around them seemed to exhale, the weight of their decision lightening as they embraced it fully. It wasn't the wedding they'd dreamed of, but it was the marriage they needed. And as long as they were committed, as long as they believed in each other, that would be enough.

"Next week, then?" Tabby asked, the question a hopeful whisper against his skin.

"Next week," Jack confirmed, the words solid and sure.

He pulled back slightly, looking into her eyes and seeing both the love and the resilience that had drawn them together in the first place. "I won't lose you, Tabby. No matter what."

"You won't," she promised, sealing it with a kiss that held all their faith, all their determination.

The future loomed vast and uncertain, but they faced it with renewed strength, their resolve an invisible thread binding them together across time and distance.

6
Interrogations

Jason anchored himself with arms crossed, hoping it came across as tough instead of terrified. The sterile interrogation room seemed to conspire with the detective against him. "Tell me what you know about Jack's actions." The voice cut like a saw through Jason's pretense of calm. He shrugged, though the effort seemed Herculean. "He confessed, didn't he? You know everything." The detective flipped through his file, a methodical hunt. "How long did you know before Jack confessed?" Jason's mouth was dry, his thoughts more so. "What difference does it make?" The detective met Jason's eyes, pinning him to the chair like an insect.

Detective Brooks leaned back, the wooden legs creaking against the floor. "It makes a big difference, Mr. Michael." His voice carried a weariness that spoke of a thousand similar conversations, a thousand failed defenses. Jason tried to focus on anything to distract from the sense of being flayed open by the questions. "Your friend was quick to confess," Brooks continued, his words precise. "But we think there's more to it. We think you're the missing piece in understanding Jack's real motivations."

Jason's throat closed around a quick denial, but he forced himself to breathe. "I told you," he said, the words like sandpaper on his tongue. "I didn't know. Not until he confessed." He wished he could still cross his arms, but they felt too heavy, useless by his sides.

"You didn't know?" Brooks repeated, letting the question hang in the air, thickening the room's chill. Jason felt the walls pressing in, the ceiling dropping like a slow avalanche. He wanted to bolt, to escape the detective's relentless gaze, but he held himself in place through sheer will.

Brooks didn't break eye contact, didn't give Jason a moment's reprieve. "Did Jack ever talk about hurting Brad beforehand?"

Jason flinched, a flicker of movement he couldn't control. He cursed himself silently, knowing the detective would latch onto that like a hawk. "No," he said, trying to inject steel into the denial, but his voice betrayed him with its faint quiver.

"No?" Brooks echoed, and Jason could see the wheels turning, feel the screws tightening. The detective leaned forward, making the room shrink even more. "Let me be clear. If you knew what Jack planned and said nothing, we can bring you up on accessory charges. Is that sinking in?"

Jason's heart pounded like a fist against his ribs. He could almost hear the echoes bouncing off the stark walls, could almost feel them ricochet through his mind. He swallowed hard, the dryness cracking through him.

"Look," Jason started, his voice tightrope thin. "I didn't help him. I didn't cover anything up."

"But you knew." Brooks' tone was as certain as a closed case, as damning as a gavel.

Jason hesitated, his entire being fighting the admission. He felt his resolve crack, felt the confession bleed through. "Yeah," he said finally, a whisper of defeat. "He told me that night. The night he turned himself in." Jason said, the admission heavy on his conscience. Jason's accusations that night came back with vivid clarity. He'd demanded that Jack take accountability for what he did. He hadn't realized how far Jack would take that accountability.

The detective gathered his file as if already done with Jason. "We'll see how that plays out. Right now, you're not on trial." He stood, his chair scraping loudly against the tension-filled air. "But this is far from over."

Jason remained in the chair as he watched Brooks leave, the door clicking shut with a finality that echoed in his mind, leaving him alone with the weight of what he'd set in motion.

Tabby sat with hands folded, composure masking fatigue in the coldly lit room. The lights buzzed insistently overhead, like gnats swarming a porch lamp. Detective Brooks opened the file with slow, deliberate motions, watching for her reaction. She gave him nothing, offered no Jason-like fidgets. "Thanks for coming in," he began, voice betraying expectation of hostility. Tabby simply watched him. "I'd rather not be here," she replied, composed even in defiance. Brooks nodded, acknowledging the strain that should have cracked her. "We know Jack told you months ago." She held his gaze with unfaltering precision. "He told me," she said, vagueness cloaked in certainty.

Brooks' chair groaned as he leaned back, eyes still fixed on her. "You know it's important we get the timeline right." His statement seemed rehearsed, as though it had worked a hundred times before.

Tabby raised an eyebrow, considering her response with deliberate calm. "Jack told you what happened. Isn't that enough?"

"It would be," Brooks replied, "if we didn't have evidence you knew well before he came in." He paused, letting the implication dangle, hoping it would provoke some crack in her resolve.

But Tabby remained unmoved, her voice as steady as her hands. "I found out," she said, a deliberate non-answer.

"Months ago?" Brooks pressed, the edge of impatience creeping into his voice.

"When he told me," Tabby repeated, as if patience were infinite, her precision cutting through the air like a taut wire. Brooks studied her, then flipped a page in his file.

"Can I ask you something?" Brooks shifted tactics, his tone softening. "How do you see your future? You know, without Jack."

Tabby took a slow breath, as if absorbing the question. The room's sterile chill seemed to sharpen, an accomplice to Brooks' attempt to undermine her defenses. "I'm not sure what you're asking," she replied, feigning confusion.

"He's facing serious time," Brooks said, a faint frown playing across his lips. "It might be easier if you opened up now, rather than later."

Tabby met his gaze, refusing to look away. "This isn't about making things easier."

Brooks held his silence, letting it thicken between them, letting it work to unsettle. But still, she didn't waver, didn't give him the satisfaction of seeing her shift or squirm.

"I asked Jack to tell me everything," Tabby said finally, cutting through the pause with measured words. "So, he did."

"And you just accepted it?" Brooks sounded almost incredulous, as though her calm were a trick he couldn't quite figure out.

Tabby's voice was soft but unwavering. "It wasn't my decision to make."

"Most women would have a harder time letting something like this go," Brooks said, studying her with a hint of disbelief.

Tabby gave a small, humorless laugh. "Most women aren't in this situation."

The detective nodded slowly, as if reassessing her entirely. "I guess I expected more emotion."

"Emotion doesn't fix anything," she said, the words carrying both the weight of experience and the lightness of practiced acceptance.

Brooks watched her for a moment longer, then closed the file with a deliberate click. "That's all for now."

Tabby rose smoothly, her movements as controlled as her answers. She walked to the door, her steps unhurried, her figure casting an unwavering shadow against the stark walls. She didn't wait for an escort, didn't look back as the door shut behind her with a sound that seemed more liberating than final.

Ruby sat rigid, shoulders squared like a soldier in formation, eyes fixed and unblinking. The fluorescent lights turned the room into an interrogation theater, casting shadows that performed silent dramas on the walls. Detective Lyons broke the stillness, his voice both script and stage direction. "You knew Bradley Torres." A statement, not a question. She nodded, a puppet's movement. "He assaulted you," Lyons added, observing her with scientific precision. Ruby swallowed but didn't flinch, the reflex nearly imperceptible. "That gives you motive," he suggested.

"Motive for what?" Her words shot back like darts, more than willing to play this game.

Lyons sat with arms crossed, his expression unreadable, while Detective Carter leaned in with aggressive energy. The table seemed to grow smaller, a battlefield where space and silence were both weapons and defenses. "You know what we're getting at," Carter said, his voice a verbal shove.

Ruby held his gaze, refusing to give an inch. "Jack already confessed," she said, her tone carefully controlled. "Why am I here?"

"We're interested in the why," Lyons said, his calm contrasting sharply with Carter's forward momentum. "Jack confessed, but we're not convinced that's the whole story."

"You think I'm lying?" Ruby's eyes flicked between them, assessing the situation with quick, precise movements.

"More like we're missing something," Carter replied, leaning back but keeping his eyes locked on her. "Like why Jack would confess to killing a man who assaulted his sister, if his sister was the one with the real motive."

Ruby took a breath before speaking. "He acted on his own. I didn't ask him to do anything."

Lyons uncrossed his arms and leaned forward, his face all seriousness and scrutiny. "How can we be sure? Jack loves you. We think he might be protecting you."

The suggestion hung in the air like a smoke plume, twisting and turning, but Ruby refused to let it choke her resolve. She kept her voice steady, her gaze level. "You're wasting your time."

"We think," Carter interrupted, his tone implying authority and certainty, "you might have convinced him to do this for you. Maybe even helped him."

A flash of anger sparked in Ruby's eyes, quickly extinguished by the same discipline that kept her sitting so impossibly still. "You're wrong," she said. "And you're not listening. I had nothing to do with it."

Lyons and Carter exchanged a glance, a silent conference of doubt and decision. Ruby remained motionless, though inside she felt her pulse quicken.

"If you had motive," Carter pressed, leaning forward again, his body language as aggressive as his words, "wouldn't you want Bradley dead?"

Ruby's stare turned glacial, freezing out any trace of doubt. "I would," she said, her words slow and deliberate. "Which is why I'm sitting here talking to you. Because I didn't act on it."

The room fell silent, the buzz of the fluorescent lights like a whisper in the tense atmosphere. Ruby watched them, seeing the gears turn behind their scrutinizing eyes, knowing they wanted her to crack, to break under pressure.

"Why did Jack do it then?" Lyons asked, his tone a mixture of curiosity and accusation.

"Because he's Jack," Ruby replied, the words a cryptic truth she wouldn't elaborate on. They wouldn't understand anyway.

Lyons tapped his pen on the closed file, a measured rhythm of dissatisfaction. "We can keep this up all day, Miss West."

"And so can I," Ruby said, her voice never faltering. "You want to charge me? Go ahead. Otherwise, I'm leaving."

Carter started to say something, but Lyons stopped him with a gesture. They exchanged another look; a signal Ruby couldn't read but took as resignation.

Lyons sighed, frustration woven into the sound. "That's all for now."

Ruby rose with a grace that belied the tension coiled within her. She walked to the door, her back a wall against any further questioning. She was almost out when Carter's voice stopped her. "If Jack's covering for you, he can't do it forever."

She turned slightly, giving them her profile, a silhouette of defiance. "He's not. But thanks for your concern."

The door clicked shut behind her, leaving the two detectives in the web of their own suppositions, and she let herself exhale only when she was clear of the building.

Jack's fists rested like small fortresses on the table. His pulse thrummed visibly in his neck, a metronome of controlled panic. Ruby sat opposite, composed yet tightly wound. The room was an echo chamber of their unspoken fears. "They questioned me," she said, detonating the silence.

Jack nodded, trying to contain the implosion. "I figured they would." He almost smiled, a futile attempt at reassurance.

Ruby leaned in, her voice a scalpel. "They think you're covering for me."

Jack froze, the truth a cold draft through his intentions. Shadows fell across his face, as though knowing what came next. The visitation room felt vast and indifferent, its institutional corners swallowing Jack's assumptions about his ability to protect. He looked at Ruby, who met his gaze with a firmness that refused to break. "I thought confessing would be enough," Jack said, the words a strained confession in themselves.

Ruby shook her head, her eyes dark and unyielding. "They're convinced I was involved," she replied. "That you're taking the fall."

Jack absorbed the impact; felt it shift the foundations of all he'd planned. He sat motionless, his physical stillness a stark contrast to the chaos churning inside. The confession that was meant to shield her had only ensnared her further.

"The detectives are looking for anything," Ruby continued, her voice steady but laced with urgency. "They don't believe it was all you."

The lights above hummed in accusatory harmony, casting long shadows across Jack's features. He breathed deeply, slowly, each inhale a fight against the panic trying to claw its way out.

"They'll keep pushing," Ruby warned, watching him carefully. "On everyone. Jason, Tabby—"

Jack's expression tightened, a fissure of concern that quickly solidified into resolve. He took in the room, the bars, the guards, and finally Ruby's face. All of it refocused him, turned his despair into something harder, more unyielding.

"They can't pin this on you," he said, breaking the silence with the clarity of a vow. His fists uncurled, but his determination did not.

Ruby watched him, and in the measured rhythm of his pulse, the deliberate cadence of his breathing, she saw what was coming. She recognized the shift in his eyes, the unmistakable moment when Jack West decided to solve everything.

His voice was low but unwavering. "I'll fix it."

It wasn't just a promise; it was a plan forming, a strategy that crystallized in the space between them. Ruby searched his face, reading the change as clearly as a chapter in a book she knew by heart.

She nodded, an acknowledgment not of agreement but of understanding. "You're sure?" she asked, knowing the answer even as she posed the question.

Jack's look said it all. He was past doubt, past deliberation.

"Even if they find everything?" Ruby pushed, wanting to test the strength of his new resolve.

"Especially then," Jack said, his words as firm as the hands he'd uncurled. "I'll tell them everything."

The room seemed to shrink around their certainty, the institutional walls and lighting unable to erode the commitment that had taken shape at the visitation table. They sat without speaking, letting the magnitude of what came next settle over them like the unrelenting buzz of the overhead lights.

When the guard finally came to take Jack back to his cell, he stood with the quiet grace of a man who knew his next move, the tension transformed into the kind of purpose that no amount of time or questioning could break.

7

Jack Gives Police the Evidence

The light from the corridor sliced through the darkness of Jack's cell, casting rigid bars of shadow across his face as he lay motionless on the narrow bunk. Three in the morning, and sleep remained as elusive as freedom. His mind raced with the precision of a stopwatch, ticking through possibilities and consequences.

Jack's foot tapped against the metal frame of the bed, a small rebellion against the stillness enforced by the walls around him. The mattress beneath him might as well have been stuffed with gravel—thin, unforgiving, a constant reminder of his current reality. From another holding cell a man coughed, the sound echoing like a ghost wandering the corridors.

The rhythm of his foot increased, matching the acceleration of his thoughts. He released the mattress only to begin drumming his fingers against his thigh, a silent percussion that accompanied the cacophony in his mind.

Jack's jaw clenched and unclenched, a silent grinding that matched the tension building in his chest. He'd seen the signs during his own interrogation—the way the detectives exchanged glances when he mentioned Ruby, the pointed questions about her whereabouts on the night of Brad's disappearance. He'd thought his confession would be a shield, an impenetrable barrier between his sister and further pain.

Instead, he'd unwittingly made her a suspect.

His partial confession—admitting to the killing but withholding the location of the body—had only fueled their suspicion. In their eyes, he was either protecting someone or leveraging his confession for a better deal. And Ruby, with her obvious motive, became the logical accomplice.

The answer was simple, really. Almost elegant in its clarity. He had to tell them everything. The location of the body, the gun, the full details of what had happened that night. A complete confession that would leave no room for Ruby's involvement, no space for the detectives to squeeze her into their narrative.

Jack's foot stopped its tapping. His fingers stilled their drumming. His breathing slowed and deepened as certainty replaced anxiety. He knew what he had to do, and the decision, once made, brought a strange calm.

He rose from the bunk and moved to the small sink in the corner of his cell. The metal was cold against his palms as he leaned forward, studying his reflection in the scratched mirror above it. The harsh lighting caught the angles of his face, casting shadows that made him look older, harder. He splashed water on his face, the shock of cold clarifying his thoughts further.

Ten years minimum, probably more. That's what he was looking at with a full confession, with physical evidence to back up his words. The thought should have terrified him, should have sent him spiraling back into the restless anxiety of moments before. Instead, he felt his shoulders relax, releasing a tension he hadn't realized he'd been carrying.

A life for a life. Brad's for Ruby's. It seemed fair somehow, this exchange. He would give up his freedom to ensure hers. Jack dried his face on the rough towel hanging beside the sink, then returned to sit on the edge of his bunk.

In the morning, he would ask to speak with his lawyer. He would tell Campbell his decision, weather the inevitable argument, and then he would face the detectives again. He would tell them about the oak tree at the north end of his parents' property, about the grave he'd dug beneath its sprawling branches, about the gun left with Brad's body.

And then it would be over. Ruby would be safe. The price was high, but Jack would pay it without hesitation.

He lay back on the bunk, hands folded across his chest, and for the first time since his arrest, he felt something close to peace. The shadows continued their slow dance across the ceiling of his cell, but Jack no longer saw them. His eyes closed, and at last, sleep came.

Jack sat across from Michael Campbell in the precinct's interview room, a space designed to strip away all comfort and privacy while maintaining the illusion of both. The table between them bore the scars of countless similar conversations—scratches, initials, and the faded ghosts of coffee rings telling stories neither man cared to hear. Campbell's leather portfolio lay closed before him, a barrier of professionalism against the raw emotion that permeated such places.

Campbell looked tired—the kind of bone-deep weariness that came from decades of watching clients make decisions that would irreversibly alter their lives. His salt-and-pepper hair was neatly combed; his tie straightened with the precision of habit rather than vanity.

"I'm telling them where the body is," Jack said without preamble, his voice low but clear in the confined space.

Campbell's fingers, which had been reaching for his portfolio, stilled. His expression remained neutral, but something flickered behind his eyes—surprise, perhaps, or resignation. "I see," he said, his professional tone wavering almost imperceptibly. He completed the motion, opening the portfolio with methodical care that seemed at odds with the bomb Jack had just dropped.

"You understand what this means," Campbell continued, retrieving a pen from his breast pocket. Not a question but a statement, a lawyer's careful probing.

Jack nodded once, his gaze steady. "I do."

Campbell tapped his pen against the legal pad, creating a soft rhythm that filled the silence between them. "This changes everything, Jack. Right now, they have nothing but your word. Give them a body, and you're looking at a minimum of ten years." His voice remained even, but the pen tapped faster, betraying his concern.

"I know the consequences," Jack replied, his hands resting flat on the table, steady and certain.

Campbell leaned forward, his professional distance slipping as genuine concern broke through. "They can't prove anything without physical evidence. Your confession alone isn't enough for a conviction—not one that would stick, anyway." He shook his head, exasperation leaking into his voice. "We had options. Reasonable doubt. Mitigating circumstances. Self-defense, even."

"It wasn't self-defense," Jack said quietly.

"That's not the point." Campbell's wedding ring clicked against the table as he set his pen down with more force than necessary. "The point is that right now, we have leverage. The moment you tell them where to find Torres' body, that leverage disappears."

Jack's expression didn't change, but his eyes tracked Campbell's movements with the focus of a man who had measured every angle, calculated every risk. "They're looking at Ruby," he said, the words falling between them.

Campbell's brow furrowed. "What do you mean?"

"They questioned her." Jack's fingers curled slightly against the table's surface. "They think she might have been involved. That I'm covering for her."

Understanding dawned on Campbell's face. He sat back, a small sigh escaping him. "And this is your solution? To bury yourself deeper?"

"To protect my sister," Jack corrected, his tone brooking no argument. "I won't let Ruby pay for what I did."

Campbell studied him for a long moment, taking in the set of his jaw, the resolute calm in his eyes. "There are other ways to handle this," he said finally. "We can prepare her for questioning. Make sure she has representation. Establish her alibi."

"And let her live under suspicion? Let her face their questions every time they decide they need to push?" Jack shook his head. "No."

The two men fell silent, the space between them charged with unspoken arguments and predetermined outcomes. Campbell's fingers drummed against the leather of his portfolio, a nervous gesture at odds with his usually composed demeanor. Jack remained still, a counterpoint to Campbell's agitation.

Campbell nodded, accepting the answer while clearly still frustrated by the situation. He flipped to a fresh page in his legal pad. "Tell me exactly what you plan to disclose, so I can at least prepare for the fallout."

Jack leaned forward, his voice steady as he outlined the details of his confession. Campbell took notes, his handwriting growing progressively tighter as the implications of Jack's decision became unavoidable.

When Jack finished speaking, Campbell set his pen down and looked up, his expression a mixture of professional concern and personal regret. "For the record," he said quietly, "I think this is a mistake."

"Noted," Jack replied, the ghost of understanding passing between them.

Campbell closed his portfolio with a finality that echoed through the room. "I'll arrange for you to speak with the detectives. But Jack," he hesitated, then continued, "once this is done, there's no taking it back. Make sure this is what you want."

Jack met his gaze without wavering. "It's not about what I want. It's about what needs to be done."

Campbell's shoulders sagged slightly, the posture of a man who recognized defeat. He gathered his things and stood, signaling the end of their meeting. "I'll be present for the interview," he said, a final professional courtesy.

Jack nodded, accepting the gesture for what it was—not agreement, but respect for his choice. As Campbell knocked for the guard, Jack remained seated, his decision as immovable as the concrete walls surrounding them.

The interrogation room felt smaller than Jack remembered, as if the walls had inched closer overnight, conspiring to compress the space around the metal table where he now sat. Detectives Lyons and Carter occupied the chairs opposite him, their expressions carefully neutral, professionally distant. The overhead light cast harsh shadows across their faces, turning the lines of fatigue into deeper crevices of suspicion. Jack's lawyer, Campbell, sat beside him—a silent, reluctant witness to what was about to unfold.

Lyons opened his notepad with methodical precision, the pages crinkling under his weathered fingers. Carter leaned back in his chair, arms crossed over his chest, a posture of skepticism etched into every line of his body. The air conditioning hummed a monotonous tune, the room's only soundtrack besides the occasional click of Lyons' pen.

"You requested this meeting," Lyons began, his voice carrying the weight of decades spent listening to confessions both true and false. "We're all ears."

Jack glanced briefly at Campbell, who gave him a barely perceptible nod—not approval, but acknowledgment. Jack returned his gaze to the detectives, his hands resting loosely on the table, neither clenched nor fidgeting.

"I buried him near the old oak at the north end of my parent's farm," Jack said. "The gun is there too."

Carter's mouth twitched into something close to a smile, though it held no warmth. "You realize we'll need to verify this information."

"I expect you will," Jack replied.

Lyons glanced at Campbell, who sat with a carefully controlled expression that nevertheless communicated his professional frustration. "Counselor, I assume you've advised your client of the implications of this confession?"

Campbell cleared his throat. "I have. At length."

Jack nodded, the gesture calm and decisive. Campbell closed his portfolio with a soft thud that seemed to echo in the tension-filled room.

"Detective," Campbell said, rising to his feet, "I'd like to be notified immediately of anything you find."

"Of course, counselor," Lyons replied, professional courtesy masking the triumphant undercurrent that now charged the air.

An officer entered at Lyons' signal, handcuffs at the ready. Jack stood without being prompted, turning to present his wrists with a practiced motion that spoke of his acceptance. The metal closed around his wrists with a click that seemed to release something within him—a tension he'd been carrying since the partial confession that had inadvertently endangered Ruby.

As the officer led Jack toward the door, his shoulders relaxed slightly, the rigid set of his back easing despite the weight of the handcuffs. He'd done what needed to be done. Ruby would be safe now, free from suspicion, free to live her life. The price was high—years of his freedom, years away from his child—but in that moment, it felt like a fair exchange.

Behind him, he could hear Lyons and Carter already discussing logistics, their voices fading as the distance grew. Campbell followed a few steps behind, his leather shoes clicking against the floor in a rhythm that sounded like reluctant acquiescence.

Jack kept his gaze forward, moving toward his cell with the same calm determination that had carried him through his confession. Whatever came next—the recovery of Brad's body, the formal charges, the sentencing—he would face it with the same resolve. He had protected Ruby in the only way he knew how, and that knowledge would sustain him through whatever followed.

8
The Grave

Jack positioned the backhoe at the edge of the field, the massive oak tree looming above him like a silent witness. The late afternoon sun slanted through its branches, dappling the ground with shifting patterns that would soon be disturbed. His fingers tightened around the controls, familiar yet foreign in this context. He'd operated this machine a hundred times before—clearing land, digging irrigation—but never for this purpose.

He surveyed the area one final time, confirming what he already knew—no houses visible from this spot, no roads cutting through the distant tree line, no reason for anyone to venture this far into the northern edge of his parents' property. The isolation that had always felt peaceful now seemed complicit, a natural ally in his grim task.

The key turned with a mechanical growl, and the backhoe shuddered to life beneath him. The vibrations traveled up through the seat, into his spine, settling in his chest like a second heartbeat. Jack engaged the hydraulics, testing the controls with short, precise movements. The yellow arm rose obediently, its giant metal scoop hovering momentarily before he directed it toward the earth.

The first bite into the soil broke the field's undisturbed surface, tearing a dark wound in the ground. Jack worked methodically, each movement calculated, each scoop of dirt placed in a neat pile to the side. The engine's roar drowned out the evening birds, the distant farm sounds, even the thoughts trying to claw their way to the surface of his mind. But not all of them.

Sweat beaded on his forehead despite the cool autumn air, rolling down his temples and the back of his neck. He didn't wipe it away. The physical discomfort was almost welcome, a tangible distraction from the weight pressing against his ribcage. Jack's breathing remained steady, controlled, a conscious effort that required almost as much concentration as the precise movements of the backhoe.

The backhoe's engine changed pitch as he adjusted the depth, a mechanical protest that briefly punctuated the monotonous roar. Jack checked his progress, mentally measuring the hole against the dimensions he needed. Not too shallow—the spring thaw and rain could expose what lay beneath. Not too deep—he didn't want to hit the water table, didn't want Brad's remains floating where they might be carried elsewhere.

Just deep enough to stay hidden. Just deep enough to contain what had happened.

The late afternoon sun hung low on the horizon now, casting long shadows that stretched across the field like dark stains. The oak tree's silhouette had grown massive, swallowing the ground beneath it in premature darkness. Jack worked on, the backhoe's headlights cutting yellow swaths through the gathering dusk.

The pit reached its final dimensions as the first stars appeared in the eastern sky. Jack maneuvered the backhoe back, surveying his work with a critical eye. The hole gaped back at him, a perfect rectangle of darkness cut into the earth, approximately seven feet long, three feet wide, and six feet deep. Enough to contain a man and the weapon that had ended him.

Jack cut the engine, and the sudden silence rang in his ears. The evening sounds rushed in to fill the void—crickets beginning their night chorus, a distant owl, the soft rustle of leaves in the oak tree above. Ordinary sounds, continuing as if nothing had changed, as if the world hadn't shifted irreversibly on its axis.

He climbed down from the backhoe, his boots hitting the ground with a soft thud. Standing at the edge of the pit, Jack looked down into the darkness he'd created, his shadow falling across it like a partial cover. The cool evening air chilled the sweat on his skin, raising goosebumps along his arms.

Jack stood at the rear of the old pickup truck, its rusted blue frame barely visible in the deepening twilight. His breath formed small clouds in the cooling air as he steeled himself for what came next. The canvas tarp inside the truck bed lay still and oblong, containing what had once been Brad Torres—college athlete, sister's tormentor, now reduced to dead weight.

He lowered the tailgate, its hinges protesting with a screech that pierced the evening quiet. Jack paused, listening for any response—a distant voice, an approaching engine—but only cricket song and wind answered. The property's vastness had always seemed excessive to Jack, until now, when its sprawling isolation served as a perfect accomplice.

The tarp shifted slightly as the truck bed tilted, and Jack found himself holding his breath. He knew Brad wasn't going to sit up, wasn't going to speak, yet some primal part of his brain remained alert to the possibility of movement. He reached for the bundle, his fingers meeting rough canvas still cold from the hours in the truck bed. Jack had wrapped the body meticulously—first in plastic sheeting to contain any fluids, then in the heavy canvas tarp secured with baling twine, the kind his father kept in spools in the equipment barn.

Jack positioned himself, bending his knees as he'd learned from years of lifting hay bales and feed sacks. With a controlled heave, he hoisted the wrapped body over his shoulder in a firefighter's carry. The burden settled across his frame, and Jack took a moment to find his balance.

The first steps away from the truck were the hardest. Jack's boots sank slightly into the soft earth of the field, making each stride an exercise in determined forward motion. The wrapped body shifted with each step, forcing Jack to adjust his grip, to redistribute the weight. His breathing came in measured pulls, deliberately calm despite the exertion.

The oak tree stood sentinel, its massive form blotting out a section of the emerging stars. Crickets fell silent as Jack passed, resuming their chorus once he moved beyond their immediate vicinity, as if even they recognized the gravity of what transpired.

His mind remained strangely clear, focused entirely on the physical task—the placement of each foot, the strain across his shoulders, the cooling evening air against his face. There was no room for the chaotic thoughts that had plagued him since the shooting, no space for questions or doubt. There was only this moment, this burden, this necessity.

When he reached the edge of the pit, Jack knelt slowly, maintaining his balance as he lowered the body to the ground beside the grave. His muscles trembled slightly from the exertion, but his movements remained controlled, deliberate. He straightened, rolling his shoulders to release the tension, and looked down at the wrapped form at his feet.

The weight pressing against him was more than physical—it was the burden of finality. What lay before him wasn't just a body but the sum of everything that had transpired: Brad's choices, Ruby's suffering, his own actions.

Jack bent and gathered the tarp-wrapped bundle in his arms, no longer carrying it but cradling it, almost tender in his approach. He stepped to the edge of the grave and knelt, lowering Brad's body into the darkness with unexpected care. The bundle settled at the bottom with a soft thud, slightly off-center. Jack frowned at the imperfection.

He stood, considering for a moment, then made his decision. Using the shovel he'd brought from the truck, Jack lowered himself into the grave. The earthy walls rose around him, damp and close. The smell of fresh soil enveloped him, primal and clean, a counterpoint to the knowledge of what the canvas contained.

Jack adjusted the position of the body, centering it in the grave with the precision of someone making a bed. He smoothed the wrinkles from the tarp, his hands passing over the canvas in long, deliberate strokes. There was no one to witness this strange care, this respect offered to a man he'd killed, yet Jack continued until the surface was as neat as possible under the circumstances.

Standing in the grave beside Brad's body, Jack reached to his waistband and removed the gun. The metal felt unusually heavy in his palm, its presence both familiar and alien. It was no longer a tool or a safeguard but a murder weapon.

Jack placed the gun on top of the wrapped body, positioning it carefully over what he estimated was Brad's chest. The gesture felt ritualistic, meaningful in a way he couldn't articulate. The gun belonged to Brad now—not as evidence to be hidden but as a companion piece in this burial. The weapon and the wound it created, together in the earth.

His breath visible in the cooling air, Jack stood motionless for a long moment, looking down at the tableau he'd created. No words came to him—no prayer, no apology, no justification. There was only silence, the weight of his actions, and the certainty that this moment would live within him forever, buried but never truly gone.

With a deep breath, Jack hoisted himself out of the grave, his boots leaving indentations in the soft earth beside the body. Standing at the edge of the pit, he looked down one last time at the wrapped form and the gun resting atop it. The stars had fully emerged now, their cold light barely reaching into the depths he'd created.

Jack turned to the pile of excavated soil and picked up the shovel. It bit into the mound of excavated earth with a dull thunk, and Jack lifted the first full load. It hung suspended for a moment—dark, damp soil caught between sky and grave—before he let it fall. The dirt hit the canvas with a soft patter, like distant rainfall, partially obscuring the gun that lay atop Brad's wrapped body. Jack watched the soil spread and settle, then dug the shovel in again. The second load followed the first, and then a third, each one falling with the same quiet finality, each one making Brad a little less real and a little more memory.

The oak tree stood silhouetted against the night sky, its familiar shape rendered alien by the harsh floodlights surrounding it. Three months had passed since Jack had stood beneath its branches alone; now he returned in handcuffs, surrounded by a forensic team whose methodical movements mirrored his own from that autumn evening. Detective Lyons stood slightly apart, his weathered face impassive as he watched both Jack and the excavation team with equal intensity.

Jack's breath formed small clouds in the frigid night, dissipating before they reached the shoulders of the officer standing guard beside him. The handcuffs bit into his wrists, a constant reminder of his new reality, though he needed none. His eyes tracked the movements of the forensic technicians as they marked off the area with yellow tape, establishing a grid over the spot he'd indicated with unsettling precision. Their white Tyvek suits caught the floodlights, making them appear ghostly against the dark field.

Detective Lyons moved closer, his shoes crunching on the frost-hardened ground. "Cold night," he remarked, his voice neutral, giving away nothing of his thoughts.

Jack nodded but offered no reply. Words seemed superfluous here, in this place where actions—past and present—spoke with perfect clarity. He watched as a female technician photographed the undisturbed surface, documenting it from multiple angles before the excavation began. The thoroughness might have seemed excessive for a voluntary confession, but Jack understood the protocol. Evidence required documentation, regardless of how it was discovered.

Lyons studied Jack's profile, searching for something—remorse, perhaps, or fear. But Jack's expression remained composed, his eyes steady as they followed the technicians' movements. The detective had interrogated countless killers over his twenty-three-year career, had seen every variation of denial and justification. Jack West presented something different—a man who had made a decision and accepted its consequences with a clarity that Lyons found both admirable and unsettling.

"We'll need to verify the weapon's registration," Lyons said, breaking the silence again. "Serial number should still be intact, assuming you left it as you described."

"It's there," Jack replied, his voice as even as his gaze. "Registered in my name. Purchased legally three years ago."

Lyons nodded, filing away the information though he'd already confirmed it. The technicians began the excavation, removing the first layer of soil with careful, measured movements. Each shovelful was placed on a tarp for later examination, a reversal of Jack's burial process that struck him with its strange symmetry.

The leaves and natural debris Jack had scattered were incorporated into the soil, but the ground still bore subtle signs of disturbance—a slight depression, a texture different from the surrounding area. The technicians worked methodically inward from the perimeter, their movements precise and unhurried. Time had ceased to matter in this field; there was only the steady progression toward what everyone knew they would find.

Jack watched the earth being removed in layers, memories surfacing with each one. He had stood in this same spot, under this same tree, making a choice that would alter the course of multiple lives. There had been no witnesses then except the oak and the stars; now there were officers, technicians, and the unblinking eye of the law. Jack felt strangely calm, as if he'd been waiting for this moment since he'd first lifted the shovel to cover Brad's body.

"You buried him deep," Lyons observed after thirty minutes of excavation.

"Six feet," Jack confirmed. "It seemed appropriate."

Lyons' eyebrow raised slightly at the response. Most killers didn't concern themselves with propriety when disposing of bodies. Most didn't calculate depth with such precision. The detective made a mental note, another piece in the puzzle of understanding Jack West.

As the dig progressed, the conversation lapsed into silence. The only sounds were the scrape of tools against soil and the occasional murmur between technicians. The night grew colder, but no one suggested pausing. The momentum of discovery carried them forward, a current that could not be diverted once set in motion.

Two hours into the excavation their efforts revealed a corner of canvas. "We've got something," she called, her voice professionally detached despite the significance of the find. The team's movements became even more meticulous, brushes replacing shovels as they worked to expose the tarp without disturbing its contents.

Jack felt a strange tightness in his chest as the canvas emerged from the earth, still remarkably intact despite the months underground. The plastic sheeting beneath had done its job, containing what remained of Brad Torres. The forensic team worked with painstaking care, documenting each stage of the revelation with photographs and notes.

When they uncovered the gun, placed precisely where Jack had described, Lyons turned to study him again. The deliberate positioning of the weapon struck the detective as significant—not hidden separately or discarded but placed with intent on the victim's chest. It wasn't the act of someone trying to conceal evidence but of someone making a statement.

"Why leave the gun?" Lyons asked, genuine curiosity breaking through his professional detachment.

Jack considered the question, his eyes still on the partially exposed canvas. "It belonged with him," he said finally. "After what happened, they were connected."

Lyons nodded slowly, understanding dawning in his eyes. This wasn't a panicked cover-up or a calculated deception. It was a solemn, intentional act—a killing followed by a burial that bordered on ceremonial. The detective had expected to find confirmation of Jack's confession; instead, he found insight into the man himself.

The forensic team continued their work, carefully extracting the wrapped body from its resting place. They lifted it with a coordinated effort that reminded Jack of pallbearers, though this procession led not to a final rest but to examination and evidence. The gun was placed in a separate evidence bag, its metal surface catching the floodlights as it passed from earth to human hands.

Jack watched as Brad's remains were carried to the waiting medical examiner's vehicle, his expression unchanged. What he felt wasn't regret for his actions but a recognition of their finality. The burial had been a pause, a holding pattern between the act itself and its consequences. Now that pause was ending, and what followed would unfold with the same inevitability as the excavation he'd just witnessed.

The officer guided Jack into the backseat, the handcuffs clinking against the door frame. Through the window, Jack caught a final glimpse of the oak tree, standing tall against the night sky, no longer a guardian of secrets but a marker of truth revealed. The floodlights were being dismantled, returning the field to darkness, but there would be no going back to what was before. The evidence that would seal his fate was already being processed, cataloged, prepared for court.

As the vehicle pulled away, Jack felt the certainty that comes with seeing a path through to its end. He had protected Ruby in the only way he knew how. Whatever price he would pay, he would pay it without regret.

9

Jack's Sentencing

Silence hung over the courtroom like a gavel waiting to fall. Jack stood next to Michael, his presence as steady as the decision he'd already made. A stern-faced woman with silver-rimmed glasses called the court to order, the gavel finally striking. Jack rose, his voice a calm echo of his earlier resolve: guilty to voluntary manslaughter, guilty to evidence tampering, guilty to unlawful disposal. The prosecutor, posture sharp as a verdict, painted the premeditated nature of his crime in precise strokes. Michael countered, his words an urgent plea for leniency. Cooperation, confession, an extraordinary surrender.

The courtroom felt cold and efficient, a machine that turned people into cases and lives into files. Jack sat motionless at the defendant's table, while Michael worked tirelessly beside him. Papers rustled like dry leaves, the only sound before the gavel demanded order. The prosecutor watched, eyes narrow, knowing he held the stronger hand.

The prosecutor stood, thin and precise. "The state argues this was a premeditated act," he began, his voice carrying the authority of a man who believed in the maximum. "Mr. West took months to come forward. He buried the body, disposed of the weapon. He acted with deliberate intent."

Michael leaned in, his presence urgent against the prosecutor's clinical distance. "Your Honor," he interjected, "Mr. West has shown extraordinary cooperation with law enforcement. He provided the location of the body and weapon voluntarily, saving the state considerable resources."

The prosecutor didn't flinch. "He also deliberately took a man's life," he countered, his voice growing sharper. "And he concealed the evidence for months. The state recommends the maximum sentence."

Michael's tone grew more insistent. "His actions following the incident demonstrate remorse, not calculation," he argued. "His confession was not coerced. It was a conscious decision to take responsibility. We ask the court to consider the unique circumstances and show leniency."

The judge watched, her gaze sweeping over the courtroom, taking in every nuance, every argument. Her presence was as solid as Jack's resolve, her authority unchallenged. She sat with an air of patience that demanded precision, leaving all parties to wonder how her verdict would align with the careful architecture of Jack's sacrifice.

Jack sat, a study in composure, as the judge began her pronouncement. Her words fell into the courtroom's expectant silence. Ten years in state prison. Eligible for parole after eight. Michael's frustration cut through the air like a blade, his grip tightening around his legal pad. Jack absorbed the sentence, shoulders relaxing under the weight of its finality. The gallery murmured, a chorus of shifting bodies and whispers. He turned to where Tabby and Ruby sat, their eyes meeting his with a gravity that spanned the courtroom.

The judge continued, her tone measured and firm, each word a deliberate mark against the charged atmosphere. She acknowledged Jack's cooperation, a nod to the defense's plea, but emphasized the gravity of the crime. "The severity of your actions cannot be overlooked, Mr. West. While this court recognizes your admission and assistance, it cannot disregard the premeditated disposal and concealment. You will serve ten years."

Jack remained steady, letting the sentence settle over him, a weight he had already borne in his mind. The reality of it was now simply an echo, a confirmation of the path he'd chosen. His shoulders, instead of sagging under the weight, seemed to ease, as though finally released from a burden of uncertainty.

The bailiff approached, a figure of procedure amid the courtroom's drama. Jack rose to meet him; his movement as deliberate as everything else about him. He turned once more to Tabby and Ruby, one last glance before the bailiff led him away, a final, silent exchange that said more than words ever could.

As Jack was escorted from the room, his composure remained intact, an unbroken testament to his resolve. The whispers and the weight of the sentence echoed behind him, but he moved forward with the same certainty that had carried him through every step of this ordeal. The world might have seen his fate as sealed, but to Jack, it was a beginning—a chapter he'd authored with the only ink he had: his choice.

10

Public Perception

Tabby sat at her kitchen table, a stack of assorted newspapers before her. Her glasses perched precariously on the bridge of her nose as she separated each article, placing them into piles—supportive, neutral, hostile—each headline more garish than the last. Her belly, rounded with six months of pregnancy, pressed against the table's edge, the child within occasionally shifting as if sensing the tension in the room.

Ruby sat opposite her, fingers wrapped around a mug of tea gone cold. "They shouldn't be allowed to print this stuff," she said, but her voice lacked conviction, as if already resigned to this new reality where her pain was public property.

Behind them, Jason paced the length of the kitchen, his footsteps marking an irregular rhythm against the linoleum. He stopped occasionally to read over Ruby's shoulder, his jaw clenching visibly before he resumed his restless circuit. The sleeves of his dress shirt were rolled to the elbows, tie loosened at his neck—the uniform of a man who started his day with intentions of normalcy that had since unraveled.

"Tree Warden Buries Body on Family Farm." Tabby read aloud, her finger tracing the bold lettering. She paused, eyes narrowing behind her glasses. "Vigilante Justice: Man Kills Sister's Rapist." The last headline hung in the air, heavier than the others.

Ruby's fingers tightened around the mug. "Do they have to use that word?" She set the mug down with deliberate care, but her hand trembled. "And they keep using my name. Not directly, but 'the sister' this, 'the victim' that. It's pretty obvious who they mean."

Jason halted his pacing, placing both hands on the back of Ruby's chair. His fingers dug into the wooden frame. "We should sue them. There have to be laws about this kind of thing. They're dragging all of you through the mud for what? Papers to sell?"

"It wouldn't make a difference," Tabby said, removing her glasses and rubbing the bridge of her nose. Dark circles beneath her eyes suggested nights spent staring at the ceiling rather than sleeping. "And it would just keep the story going longer." She replaced her glasses and reached for another article, her movements methodical despite her exhaustion. "They're calling him a vigilante hero in one paper and a cold-blooded killer in another."

Ruby looked up, her eyes meeting Tabby's across the table. "Neither is true. They don't know him at all." Her voice softened on the last words, a private grief threading through them. "Jack isn't some avenging angel or a monster. He's just...Jack. My brother who's always tried to fix everything."

Jason's hand moved from the chair to Ruby's shoulder, a gentle pressure. "That's the problem. He tried to fix something that couldn't be fixed. Not that way."

Tabby added another article to the "hostile" pile, her movements becoming sharper. "What bothers me is how they dug up every detail. How did they find out about your suicide attempt, Ruby? That wasn't in any court records."

"Someone talked. Maybe one of the nurses at the hospital, maybe someone at the counseling center." Her voice was flat, depleted of emotion. "Nothing's private anymore. I had a woman come up to me at the grocery store yesterday, telling me how brave I am. A complete stranger."

Tabby looked down at her rounded belly, her hand moving to rest protectively over it. "I worry about what this means for the baby. Growing up with everyone knowing his father is in prison."

Ruby reached across the table, her fingers briefly touching Tabby's arm. "We'll make sure he knows the truth. Who Jack really is."

"And what is that?" Jason asked, his voice carrying an edge that he immediately seemed to regret. "Sorry, I just mean—how do we explain it to him? That his father killed someone but had his reasons?"

Tabby's expression hardened. "We tell him his father protected the people he loves. That life isn't always clean-cut." She glanced down at a newspaper—Jack's burial method detailed in forensic detachment. "They keep harping on how he used his knowledge of soil acidity. Like that somehow makes it colder."

"It wasn't like that," Ruby said firmly. "That stretch of land's useless—nothing grows there. Our parents avoid it. Would it have been better if he dumped Brad in the cornfield?" She let out a bitter laugh.

Tabby scanned the headlines, a slow ache blooming in her chest. It hit her then—Jack hadn't concealed his crime to avoid prison. He'd done it to shield them from this: the tidal wave of public scrutiny, the relentless replays of Ruby's pain. He hadn't been dodging consequences. He'd been trying to protect them from the fallout.

Jason stopped by the window, looking out at the neighborhood where nothing appeared to have changed despite how dramatically their lives had. "You should both get away for a while. My parents have that lake house in Vermont. No one would bother you there."

"Running away won't solve anything," Tabby said. "Besides, I have work. Ruby has the garden center. We can't just disappear because things are hard."

Tabby gathered the newspapers back into a single stack, as if physically consolidating the scattered narratives of their lives. "The reporters will move on eventually. Some new tragedy will catch their attention, and we'll just be old news." She spoke with certainty, though her eyes betrayed doubt. "In the meantime, we keep our heads up. We don't hide, but we don't engage either."

The three sat in silence, the stack of papers between them on the table—a physical manifestation of the narrative they couldn't control but must somehow live with. Outside, a neighbor mowed his lawn, the distant buzz of normalcy continuing despite everything that had changed within these walls.

Tabby pushed through the heavy door of Leveret Municipal Library, the familiar scent of books and wood polish greeting her like an old friend. It was the people whose welcome felt foreign now. The morning chatter at the circulation desk died as she entered, her coworkers suddenly finding urgent reasons to look down at their computer screens or reorganize already-neat stacks of return slips. Tabby adjusted the strap of her bag across her shoulder, lifted her chin a fraction higher, and walked toward her desk in Technical Services with measured steps that betrayed nothing of the knot tightening in her stomach.

The library had been her sanctuary for five years, a place where order prevailed and knowledge was cataloged into neat decimal systems. She had loved the predictability of it, the quiet purpose of connecting people with information they sought. Now the tall shelves felt like they were closing in, the spaces between them narrower than before, the eyes of patrons following her with newfound interest as she passed.

"Morning, Tabby!" Ellen from Children's Services called out, her voice pitched higher than usual, a forced cheerfulness that rang false in the hushed atmosphere. "Beautiful day, isn't it?"

Tabby nodded, offering a faint smile. "Yes, lovely." The small talk felt absurd, a thin veneer over the obvious. She noticed Ellen didn't ask how she was doing, didn't mention Jack or the sentencing that happened just three days ago. None of them did. Her name badge might as well read "Tabby West, Cataloging Specialist, Wife of Convicted Killer."

At her desk, Tabby powered on her computer and set to work on the stack of new acquisitions awaiting cataloging. Her fingers moved efficiently over the keyboard, entering data, assigning call numbers, processing items for shelving. The familiar routine soothed her, offering a momentary escape from the weight of being observed. Her pregnancy made her more visible than she'd like; at six months, her condition was impossible to disguise and seemed to add another layer to her colleagues' discomfort—as if they weren't sure whether to offer congratulations to a woman whose husband would be in prison when the baby was born.

"Tabby?" The voice startled her from her concentration. Margaret Davis, the library director, stood by her desk, her thin frame rigid with what Tabby immediately recognized as administrative discomfort. "Could I see you in my office for a quick check-in?"

The words "check-in" hung between them, weighted with unspoken meaning. Tabby saved her work and stood, smoothing her blouse over her rounded belly. "Of course."

Margaret's office was meticulously organized, bookshelves lined with professional texts and framed degrees hanging on the wall behind her desk.

She had been director for twelve years, her silver-streaked brown hair cut in the same practical bob since Tabby started working here. She motioned to the chair across from her desk, her smile forced.

"How are you holding up?" Margaret asked as Tabby sat. "I can't imagine how difficult this must be for you."

Tabby clasped her hands in her lap, fingers interlaced to keep them still. "I'm managing, thank you." She didn't elaborate, unwilling to turn her private struggles into workplace conversation.

Margaret nodded, fidgeting with a pen on her desk. "That's good. You've always been so professional, so... capable." She paused, eyes dropping briefly to Tabby's belly before meeting her gaze again. "I'm sorry to have to bring this up, but there have been some concerns raised by patrons."

The knot in Tabby's stomach tightened. "What kind of concerns?"

"It's nothing you've done," Margaret said quickly, setting down the pen and folding her hands on the desk. "Some patrons have expressed... discomfort about your continued presence in public-facing roles. Given the circumstances of your husband's conviction."

Tabby's back straightened, her shoulders squaring slightly. "My husband's actions have nothing to do with my ability to catalog books or assist patrons."

"I know that," Margaret said, her discomfort more evident now. "And I've made that clear to everyone who's raised concerns. But perception matters in public service, and we need to be sensitive to community feelings."

"Community feelings," Tabby repeated, the words tasting bitter. "Which part of the community? The ones who think Jack is a monster, or the ones who think he's a hero? Because I've heard both, and neither is accurate."

Margaret's expression softened slightly, a glimpse of genuine sympathy breaking through her professional demeanor. "This is precisely why it's complicated, Tabby. Your family's situation has become very public, very polarizing. The library needs to remain neutral territory."

"And I compromise that neutrality by doing my job?" Tabby asked, her voice controlled despite the heat rising in her chest.

"It's not about your job performance," Margaret said, reaching for the pen again, rolling it between her fingers. "It's about minimizing distractions and maintaining a comfortable environment for all patrons." She took a breath, visibly steeling herself. "The city council is discussing whether to temporarily reassign you to a less public-facing position. Technical Services backroom, perhaps, or database management."

"I see." Her voice was quiet but steady. "So I'm to be hidden away until... when? Until people forget? Until my husband serves his sentence? Until my child is grown?"

Margaret looked genuinely pained now. "It would just be temporary, until the media attention dies down. I advocated for you, Tabby. I told them you're one of our most valuable employees."

"But not valuable enough to stand behind when it's inconvenient," Tabby said, the words escaping before she could temper them. She drew a deep breath, regaining her composure. "I apologize. That was unprofessional."

"It's understandable," Margaret said. "This isn't a decision I agree with, but I have to consider the library as a whole."

Tabby nodded, her face settling into a mask of professional acceptance. "When will this reassignment happen?"

"It's still being discussed," Margaret said, her relief at Tabby's apparent acceptance visible. "I'll let you know as soon as I hear anything definitive."

"Thank you for being direct with me," Tabby said, rising from her chair. Her tone was even, her posture dignified. "I appreciate knowing where things stand."

Margaret stood as well, looking like she wanted to say more but couldn't find the right words. "Tabby, if there's anything you need..."

"I'll be fine," Tabby said, the phrase worn smooth from repetition. "Is there anything else?"

"No, that's all for now."

Tabby nodded and turned to leave, each step carefully measured as she walked through the door and down the hallway. It was only when she reached her desk, settling back into her chair, that the tremor appeared. Her hands hovered over the keyboard, fingers shaking slightly as she attempted to return to the catalog entry she was working on. The screen blurred momentarily, and she blinked rapidly, refusing to give anyone the satisfaction of seeing her cry.

The cursor blinked on the screen, waiting for her input. Call numbers, subject headings, publication details—all fitting neatly into their designated fields. If only life could be so easily categorized, so cleanly organized. Tabby flexed her fingers, willing them to steady, and began typing again. Each keystroke was an act of defiance, a refusal to disappear even as the world seemed determined to make her invisible. The trembling in her hands gradually subsided, replaced by the precise, deliberate movements of someone who had decided that composure was its own form of resistance.

11
Transfer to State Prison

Jack sat in the holding area's hard plastic chair; his tan prison uniform a perfect match for the institutional walls that hemmed him in. He kept his cuffed hands resting in his lap, the metal warm now against his skin, no longer a shock but a familiar weight he'd chosen to bear.

The clock on the wall ticked through another minute, its mechanical precision a mockery of the time stretching before him. Other inmates shifted nervously in their seats, their anxieties rippling through the room like current through water. Jack remained still, letting the minutes wash over him without resistance. Inmate #4872. The number had settled on him now, a designation he'd accepted with the same deliberate calm as everything else.

The door swung open with a metallic groan, admitting two corrections officers whose expressions suggested they'd left their personalities at home. One tall and broad, the other compact and wiry, they moved with the synchronized efficiency of men who had done this a thousand times before.

"West," the taller one called, consulting a clipboard with cursory attention. "Time for transfer."

Jack rose without hesitation, his movements measured and compliant. He stepped forward, the soft shuffle of his institutional shoes barely audible against the concrete floor. The officers flanked him, their presence less a threat than a formality. Jack had no intention of complicating the process.

"Procedure says leg restraints for transport," the second officer stated, kneeling to apply the shackles. His hands moved with practiced efficiency, the metal cool and unyielding as it circled Jack's ankles. The chain between them rattled, a percussive reminder of his new limitations. "Standard twelve-inch chain. You'll need to take short steps."

Jack nodded, accepting this additional constraint without comment. The officer stood, checking the restraints with a quick tug that was neither gentle nor deliberately rough – simply procedural.

"Department policy requires full restraint during transit," the first officer recited, his tone suggesting the words had lost all meaning through repetition. "You will remain seated at all times. Any attempt to communicate with other prisoners or to interfere with the vehicle's operation will result in disciplinary action. Medical needs or emergencies should be communicated clearly to the transport officers."

Jack absorbed these instructions with a slight nod; his attention caught momentarily by the gleam of his wedding ring as he shifted his weight. The gold band caught the harsh fluorescent light, transforming it into something warmer, more human. It was the only personal item they'd allowed him to keep, a small circle of his previous life that had survived the systematic stripping away of his identity.

"Let's move," the second officer directed, gesturing toward the door with a tilt of his head.

They emerged into a covered loading dock where the transport van waited. The vehicle sat heavy on its wheels, white with "Department of Corrections" stenciled in dark blue along its side. The windows were covered with mesh, and the doors reinforced with additional locking mechanisms. It resembled an ambulance's utilitarian cousin, designed not to save lives but to contain them.

"Step up," the first officer instructed, opening the rear door of the van to reveal the austere interior.

Metal benches ran along either side, bolted securely to the floor. A wire mesh divider separated the prisoner compartment from the officers' area in front.

"Sit there," the second officer directed, pointing to a spot on the left bench.

Jack complied, lowering himself onto the cold metal. The surface was unyielding, designed for security rather than comfort. The officer secured an additional restraint through a ring on the floor, connecting it to Jack's existing handcuffs. The system of chains and locks created a web of metal that held him firmly in place while allowing minimal movement.

"Transport restraints secured," the officer reported to his colleague, who made a notation on the clipboard.

The officers performed their final checks, moving through a verbal checklist with the dispassionate efficiency of long practice.

"Prisoner secured?"

"Affirmative."

"Paperwork in order?"

"Transfer documents signed and sealed."

"Vehicle inspection complete?"

"All systems operational."

The doors slammed shut with a heavy finality, sealing him into this moving cell. Through the mesh-covered windows, Jack caught a last glimpse of Morris County Correctional Facility – a transitional space now giving way to something more permanent.

The van rumbled along the highway, each mile drawing Jack closer to South Woods State Prison. Through the mesh-covered window, he caught fragmented glimpses of a world continuing without him – commuters in cars, trees swaying in the breeze, billboards advertising lives he would no longer live. The journey passed in silence, the officers in front occasionally exchanging terse comments about traffic or schedule, their voices barely audible over the engine's persistent growl. Jack measured time by the subtle shifts in landscape, suburban sprawl giving way to stretches of forest that signaled their approach to the prison.

"Five minutes," the driver announced, more to his colleague than to Jack.

The van slowed as it turned off the main road, following a narrow access route that cut through stands of trees before opening onto a cleared perimeter.

South Woods emerged in full view, resembling a sealed city more than a prison. Buildings clustered in rigid formation—orderly, impersonal. Six medium-security housing units stood identical, cold, their windows mere slits conceding light. The maximum-security unit loomed heavier, its silence weightier.

Jack's gaze locked onto the warehouse—vast, industrial—and the minimum-security building, a dormitory-style housing unit he recalled from his research.

Observation towers pierced the skyline, two stark silhouettes rising above all else.

The van circled toward a receiving area at the side of the complex, a separate entrance designed specifically for the processing of new inmates. A gate opened, another closed behind them, the sequence repeating until they reached a covered loading dock similar to the one they'd left at the county facility. The engine died, leaving a sudden silence that felt unnaturally heavy.

The officer announced, turning in his seat. "Wait for the processing team."

Jack nodded, his eyes still taking in what details he could see through the limited view of the van's windows. The receiving area was all concrete and steel, designed to process human cargo with maximum efficiency and minimum risk.

A knock on the van's rear doors preceded their opening. Two South Woods corrections officers stood waiting, their expressions professionally neutral as they assessed their new charge.

"Prisoner transfer, Jack West," the county transport officer announced, handing over a thick folder of paperwork.

One of the South Woods officers nodded, taking the paperwork while his colleague kept eyes fixed on Jack. "We'll take him from here," he said, his voice carrying the flat authority of someone who expected immediate compliance.

The county officer moved to release Jack from the van's restraints, unclipping the chain that secured him to the floor. "Stand up, West," he directed. "Exit slowly."

"Those restraints stay with us," the county officer said, producing a key.

The South Woods officers nodded, one of them producing their facility's restraints – similar in design but older, the metal more worn from repeated use. Jack stood patiently as they performed the exchange, one set of cuffs coming off only long enough for another to replace them. Jack remained silent throughout this exchange, understanding his role as object rather than participant.

The county officers retreated to their van, their responsibility ended. The engine started again, and they pulled away, leaving Jack in the custody of strangers who would become his daily regulators.

"This way," the first South Woods officer said, gesturing toward a heavy metal door. "Reception and Orientation." The name lent the procedure an air of voluntary employment, masking the reality of intake and processing."

Inside Jack took in his surroundings with methodical attention, filing away details that would matter in the days to come. The lighting fixtures and their coverage, the blind spots in camera placement, the rhythm of guard rotations – all of it information he might need. Not for escape – Jack had no interest in breaking the sentence he'd chosen – but for survival within the system.

The officers led him through another door; into a processing room lined with benches bolted to the floor. "Wait here," one directed, securing Jack's restraints to a metal loop embedded in the concrete.

Jack counted the tiles on the opposite wall—twelve across, eight down—while men came and went. Some entered with bravado that crumbled under the processing officers' indifference. Others arrived already broken, shoulders hunched as though trying to disappear inside themselves. Jack noted every detail with methodical attention, filing away observations that might prove useful later.

The bench's cold metal had long since leached the warmth from his body when two officers finally approached. The taller one—narrow-faced, with eyes that never quite landed on Jack's—unlocked the restraint connecting him to the floor.

"Up," the officer commanded.

Jack rose without hesitation, finding his balance with the practiced ease of someone who'd spent days learning to move in chains. The officers flanked him, guiding him toward a counter where a third officer waited, fingers poised over a keyboard, face set in an expression of bureaucratic detachment.

"Name," the seated officer demanded, not looking up.

"Jack West," he replied, his voice calm and precise.

The officer's fingers clacked across the keyboard, the sound brittle in the hard-surfaced room. "Date of birth."

Jack provided it without inflection, watching as the information appeared on the screen in neat, digital rows. The processing continued with mechanical efficiency—questions asked, answers recorded, each exchange as impersonal as if between machines rather than men.

"Stand here," the narrow-faced officer directed, pointing to a spot against a white wall marked with height measurements.

Jack moved to the designated spot, turning to face the camera without being told. He knew the procedure. The camera clicked, capturing his composed expression, neither defiant nor defeated. Just present. Just here.

"Turn right."

Click.

"Turn right again."

Click.

"Last time."

Click.

The profile shots completed, they led him to the fingerprinting station. Though his prints had already been taken at the county jail, South Woods required its own records. Jack placed each finger against the scanner as directed, watching the swirled patterns of his identity appear on the monitor.

"Palm flat," the officer instructed. Jack complied, pressing his hand against the cold glass.

Next came physical description for the record. Height. Weight. Eye color. Hair color. Identifying marks.

"Tattoos, scars, birthmarks," the officer recited, scanning Jack's file.

"No tattoos," Jack answered. "Scar on left forearm, approximately five inches. Result of work accident."

The officer noted this without comment. Jack's history as an arborist was reduced to a single notation about a scar—a life of skilled labor compressed into five inches of damaged skin.

They moved him to property inventory, where the few items he'd been allowed to bring from county were recorded again. Comb. Toothbrush. Toothpaste. Basic hygiene items, prison-approved. His wedding ring gleamed under the harsh light as the officer inspected it.

"Religious item?" the officer asked, the first question that wasn't purely procedural.

"Wedding ring," Jack answered simply.

The officer hesitated, then made a notation. "Permitted item," he said, neither approving nor disapproving. Jack felt a small measure of relief. This last connection to Tabby would remain with him.

The processing continued, each step stripping away another layer of his former self, replacing it with institutional identifiers. Medium security. Unit 4. Cell 217. These would be his coordinates in the prison universe.

"Rules orientation," another officer announced, sliding a thin booklet across the counter. "Read it. Know it. Violations mean discipline."

Jack nodded, accepting the booklet with steady hands. He'd already researched South Woods extensively before his confession, had already memorized most of what would be expected. But he took the booklet anyway, another piece of his new identity to be absorbed.

"Daily schedule," the officer continued, indicating a printed sheet. "Count times, meal times, yard times, work detail. Be where you're supposed to be when you're supposed to be there."

Jack nodded again, his eyes scanning the schedule and committing it to memory. The routine would become his anchor in the years ahead—a framework within which he could maintain some semblance of control over his days, if not his circumstances.

The final step was the issuing of his prison ID—a plastic card with his photograph, number, and housing assignment. The officer handed it to him without meeting his eyes.

"Display ID at all times," he instructed. "Lost or damaged ID means disciplinary action."

Jack took the card, studying his own face looking back at him. The photo showed a man composed, contained, deliberate. It was still him, despite everything. The hard knot of certainty in his chest hadn't diminished through the processing. If anything, it had solidified. This was exactly where he had chosen to be, every step mapped out to protect Ruby, to give her the chance to heal without the shadow of suspicion hanging over her.

"Processing complete," the narrow-faced officer announced, turning to another officer who had approached to take custody of Jack. "217, medium security, general population."

The exchange was efficient; Jack's personhood reduced to a location and classification. The new officer nodded, gesturing for Jack to follow. "This way," he said.

The medical examination room was small enough that Jack could touch both walls if he extended his arms. Mint-green paint peeled at the corners, revealing layers of institutional history beneath. A metal examination table dominated the center, its paper covering crackling as Jack sat upon it at the nurse's direction.

The nurse—a woman with cropped gray hair and efficient movements—positioned herself at a small metal desk in the corner. Her scrubs were the same mint-green as the walls, as if she were designed to blend into this environment of clinical detachment. The clipboard in her hands contained forms with tiny boxes, each waiting to be filled with the data points of Jack's physical existence.

"Current medical conditions?" Her pen hovered over the form, ready to document his deficiencies.

"None," Jack answered, his voice clear and even.

"Past medical conditions requiring hospitalization?"

"No."

Her pen made small, precise marks on the paper, each stroke documenting his health with the same detachment she might use to inventory supplies. Jack watched her methodical movements, recognizing in them a reflection of his own careful precision.

"Allergies to medications, foods, or environmental factors?"

"No."

The questions continued—a rapid-fire inventory of potential medical complications. Asthma? No. Diabetes? No. Seizures? No. Heart conditions? No. Each negative response seemed to irritate rather than please her, as though his health were somehow an inconvenience to the form's design.

"Height," she stated, directing him to stand against a wall-mounted scale. "Six-one," she noted, before pointing to the base. "Step on."

Jack complied, watching the digital numbers settle at 189 pounds. The nurse recorded this without comment, while Jack reflected on how he'd lost weight during his time in county, though his frame remained strong.

"Return to the table," she instructed, turning to a new page on her clipboard. "Drug use history."

"None," Jack replied.

Her eyes flicked up briefly, skepticism evident in the slight narrowing of her gaze. "Alcohol?"

"Socially. Not to excess."

"Tobacco?"

"No."

"Prescription medications? Past or current."

"No."

Each answer was met with the same small, precise marks of her pen. Jack wondered how many men sat where he now sat, offering different answers—longer lists of substances, more complicated medical histories. His simplicity seemed to confuse the system designed to catalog human complexity.

"Communicable diseases," she continued, moving down her list with mechanical precision. "Tuberculosis?"

"No."

"Hepatitis?"

"No."

"HIV or AIDS?"

"No."

"Sexual history?"

Jack paused, the question more invasive than those about his internal organs. "Monogamous," he answered finally, the wedding ring on his finger suddenly heavy with meaning.

The nurse made another mark, neither judging nor acknowledging the life behind his answer. She was recording data, not stories. Facts, not feelings. The system had no column for the weight of Tabby's absence, no checkbox for the ache of separation.

A knock preceded the doctor's entrance—a tall man with thinning hair and glasses that magnified eyes already enlarged by years of scrutiny. He nodded to the nurse, took the clipboard, and glanced over the information without acknowledging Jack's presence.

"Dr. Mercer," he introduced himself finally, looking up with the detached interest of someone examining a specimen. "Remove your shirt."

As Jack complied the cool air raised goosebumps on his skin, but he showed no reaction. The doctor approached with a stethoscope, pressing it against Jack's chest and back in various locations.

"Breathe deeply," he instructed.

Jack inhaled and exhaled as directed, the sound of his own breathing amplified in his ears. The doctor listened, his expression unchanged, before moving on to examine Jack's eyes, ears, and throat with the same cursory attention.

"Arms out," the doctor ordered.

Jack extended his arms. The doctor examined the scar on his left forearm—the result of a chainsaw that had slipped while clearing storm damage years ago. Five inches of raised tissue, a permanent reminder of a moment's inattention.

"How did this occur?" the doctor asked, the first question that required more than a one word answer.

"Work accident," Jack replied. "I was an arborist."

The doctor nodded, making a notation before moving on to check Jack's reflexes with a small hammer that tapped against his knee. Jack's leg jerked appropriately, his body responding as designed despite the circumstances.

"Stand," the doctor directed, waiting as Jack rose from the table. "Turn around."

Jack complied, feeling exposed as the doctor examined his back, checking for any signs of injury or illness that might complicate his incarceration. The examination continued methodically—a physical inventory that reduced Jack to his component parts, each deemed acceptable or requiring note.

"Any pain or discomfort?" the doctor asked, the question feeling like an afterthought.

"No," Jack answered.

The doctor made a final notation, then handed the clipboard back to the nurse. "Medical clearance approved," he stated, addressing her rather than Jack. "General population, no restrictions."

With that, he exited, the encounter concluded in less than fifteen minutes. The nurse placed the clipboard on her desk and retrieved a small plastic cup from a drawer.

"Urine sample," she explained, holding it out to Jack. "For drug screening."

Jack took the cup, his face betraying nothing of the indignity. This was simply another step in the process, another reduction of his humanity to measurable components. The nurse pointed to a small bathroom attached to the examination room.

"Leave the door open," she instructed. "Security requirement."

Jack nodded, understanding without needing explanation. Privacy was a privilege he'd surrendered, one of many. He provided the sample with the same composed efficiency that characterized his responses to the examination, neither rushing nor hesitating.

When the medical intake was complete, the nurse sealed various samples in labeled containers and signed the final forms. Jack stood waiting, his clothes restored to order, his restraints once again secured. His body had been cataloged, examined, and approved for the system that would contain it for years to come.

The psychologist's office existed in defiance of personality—a room stripped to functional essence. A metal desk, two chairs, a filing cabinet.

Dr. Ellis was a woman of perhaps fifty, her gray-streaked hair pulled back in a severe bun that emphasized the sharp angles of her face. Her eyes were dark and evaluating, trained through years of separating truth from performance. Her lips formed a perpetually crooked line of disinterest, as though she'd heard every possible human story and found none of them particularly compelling.

"Mr. West," she began, her voice neutral yet penetrating. "I'm Dr. Ellis, staff psychologist. This evaluation determines your mental health classification and potential need for services during your incarceration." She glanced down at the file open before her. "I see you've been quite forthcoming with law enforcement about your crime."

It wasn't a question, so Jack offered no answer. He waited, hands resting lightly on his thighs.

Dr. Ellis looked up, noting his silence with a slight narrowing of her eyes. "How would you describe your current mental state?"

"Stable," Jack replied, the word selected for its precision.

Dr. Ellis made a brief notation. "Are you experiencing any symptoms of depression? Feelings of hopelessness, worthlessness, persistent sadness?"

"No."

"Anxiety? Racing thoughts, panic, excessive worry?"

"No."

Her pen moved across the pad in small, tight strokes. Jack couldn't see what she wrote, but he recognized the rhythm of documentation—the translation of a human being into clinical language.

"Do you have any thoughts of harming yourself?" she asked, her tone unchanged despite the weight of the question.

"No," Jack answered, meeting her gaze directly.

"Have you ever attempted suicide in the past?"

"No."

Dr. Ellis studied him for a moment, as if searching for cracks in his composure that might reveal something his words did not. Finding none, she continued.

"What about thoughts of harming others? Are you experiencing any urges toward violence?"

The question hung in the air, heavy with implication. They both knew why he was here—the violence that had brought him to this point.

"No," he said simply.

Dr. Ellis made a more extensive notation, her pen moving rapidly across the page. When she looked up again, her approach shifted.

"Do you have family support during your incarceration?"

"Yes," Jack answered, the gold band on his finger catching the fluorescent light. "My wife, Tabby. My sister, Ruby. A friend, Jason."

"And how do you imagine they're coping with your incarceration?"

Jack's expression softened almost imperceptibly. "They're strong."

"That doesn't answer my question," Dr. Ellis pointed out. "I'm asking how you think they feel about this situation."

Jack's jaw tightened slightly, the first visible sign of tension. "They understand why I'm here."

"Understanding and accepting are different things," she observed.

"Yes," Jack agreed, offering nothing more.

Dr. Ellis seemed to recognize the boundary he'd drawn. She changed direction again. "Let's discuss your history with controlling behaviors. Would you say you need to be in control of situations in your life?"

The question struck closer to home than the others. Jack took a measured breath before answering. "I prefer order to chaos."

"That's not quite what I asked," Dr. Ellis noted. "Many people with controlling tendencies struggle in prison, where almost all control is removed from them. Do you anticipate that being a problem for you?"

Jack met her gaze directly. "No."

"Why not?"

"Because I chose this," he said simply. "This was my decision."

Dr. Ellis's eyes narrowed slightly as she made another notation. "An interesting perspective. Most inmates don't view their incarceration as a choice."

"Most inmates didn't confess voluntarily," Jack countered, his voice still calm.

This seemed to satisfy something in Dr. Ellis's assessment. She nodded, writing several more lines before looking up again. "One final question, Mr. West. What do you hope to accomplish during your time here?"

Jack hadn't expected this question. He considered it carefully, weighing his response. "To serve my sentence without causing additional harm," he said finally.

Dr. Ellis studied him for a long moment, her expression unreadable. Then she closed her notepad with a definitive movement. "Based on this evaluation, I'm classifying you as low-risk for self-harm or suicide." She paused, her gaze direct. "However, I'm noting your controlled responses and tendency toward emotional containment. These are traits that bear monitoring in a prison environment."

Jack nodded, accepting her assessment without comment.

"You'll have access to mental health services should you need them," she added, the statement more procedural than compassionate. "Regular check-ins will be scheduled during your first month."

She pressed a button on her desk, signaling the end of their session. The door opened almost immediately, the corrections officer waiting to escort Jack to his next destination.

"Thank you for your cooperation, Mr. West," Dr. Ellis said, her tone suggesting the words were as much a formality as the clipboard she now set aside.

Jack rose, his movements neither hurried nor reluctant. "Thank you," he replied, the courtesy as measured as everything else about him.

As he followed the officer from the room, he could feel Dr. Ellis's gaze on his back, still evaluating, still assessing the man who had walked voluntarily into a cage and showed no visible regret for the choice. Her notes would follow him through the system, a psychological profile to complement his inmate number: stable but controlled, accepting but watchful, present but revealing little beyond the surface. Jack West, a man who had built his own prison long before the state provided one.

A stocky officer with a military-precise haircut gestured Jack forward. "Stop here," he commanded, his voice pitched to carry without shouting. Jack complied, positioning himself exactly where indicated, neither too close to the officer nor too far away. The officer assessed him with a practiced gaze, taking in Jack's restraints, his county-issue uniform, his composed demeanor.

The officer produced a key for his restraints.

"Arms forward," he directed.

Jack extended his arms, watching as the officer unlocked his handcuffs with practiced efficiency. Their fingers brushed momentarily, and Jack felt a spark – static from the dry air, but it jolted him nonetheless, a brief reminder of human contact in this process of systematic depersonalization.

"Step out of your shoes," the officer instructed next, kneeling to remove the leg shackles.

"Turn to face the wall," the officer instructed. "Hands against the wall, feet back, legs spread."

Jack complied, placing his palms flat against the cinder blocks, positioning his feet as directed. The wall felt cool against his hands, its rough surface a concrete reality to focus on as he prepared for the search to come. He heard the officer approach; the subtle sound of latex gloves being adjusted.

"Remain still during the search," the officer said, his voice now closer.

The search was thorough and impersonal, hands moving across Jack's body with practiced efficiency. The officer's movements were neither rough nor gentle – simply procedural, a physical inventory conducted with mechanical precision. Jack remained motionless, his breathing steady, his focus fixed on a small crack in the wall before him. The officer continued downward, examining each leg, each foot, leaving no area unchecked.

"Turn around," the officer directed when the first half was complete.

Jack pivoted as instructed, keeping his back to the wall, hands still raised. The search continued, the officer's expression never changed, his eyes focused slightly away from Jack's face, maintaining the professional distance that made this invasion bearable for both parties.

"Search complete," the officer announced finally, stepping back. "Proceed to uniform issue."

Jack lowered his arms and moved toward the indicated counter, where a third officer waited with a stack of prison-issued items. This officer was older, with the weathered face of someone who had spent decades watching men come and go through the system. He consulted a clipboard, then looked up at Jack with tired eyes.

The officer pushed the stack toward him – a tan top and pants with "NJ DOC" stenciled across the back in black letters. Beneath it lay white underwear, white socks, and a new pair of canvas shoes. A thin blanket, sheet, and towel completed the pile.

"Standard issue," the officer explained, tapping each item. "Two uniforms, three sets of undergarments, one jacket for yard time, one pair of shoes. Bedding exchanged weekly. Hygiene kit."

Jack examined the small clear plastic bag containing a toothbrush, toothpaste, soap, and a comb – the bare essentials of human maintenance reduced to their most basic forms.

"Change area is there," the officer continued, pointing to a small alcove with a half wall. "Remove all county items and change into facility uniform. Fold and return transport clothing."

Jack gathered the stack and moved to the indicated area. The half wall provided minimal privacy – enough to change without being fully exposed but designed to prevent concealment of contraband. He began undressing with methodical precision, removing the county uniform and folding it neatly despite knowing it would likely be discarded or recycled into the system.

He set aside the county-issued clothes and undergarments, creating a precise stack that reflected his inner need for order amid the chaos of transition. The concrete floor was cold beneath his bare feet as he stood momentarily exposed before reaching for the South Woods uniform. The fabric felt stiff and unyielding, not yet softened by wear and washing. He pulled on the underwear and socks, then stepped into the new attire, feeling the rough material settle against his skin like a new layer of identity.

With careful attention Jack adjusted the collar and sleeves to fit as well as the generic sizing allowed. The tan fabric hung slightly loose on his frame, but the overall fit was adequate.

He slipped on the canvas shoes, their institutional design as anonymous as everything else he now wore. Only his wedding ring remained as a connection to his former life, the gold band a small circle of warmth amid the cold standardization of prison issue. Jack ran his thumb across it once, a private gesture of remembrance, before gathering his folded county clothes and returning to the counter.

The officer accepted the stack without comment, checking off another box on his clipboard. "Uniform compliance acceptable," he noted, the words flat and colorless.

Jack stood before them now, transformed in appearance yet unchanged in essence. His physical presence still commanded attention, his posture still reflected the disciplined control that defined him. But the tan uniform marked him unmistakably as property of the state, his individual identity subsumed beneath the number that would follow him through the years ahead.

"Walk straight, don't talk, don't stop," the officer instructed, his voice pitched low enough that only Jack could hear. The man wore authority like a well-fitted uniform, his posture and movements suggesting years of navigating this controlled environment. His name badge read "Wilson," though Jack doubted the opportunity to use it would arise.

"General population begins here," Wilson explained without turning. "Eyes forward, no interaction."

As they entered the next section, the human presence of the prison revealed itself more fully. Inmates moved along designated paths in small groups, their tan uniforms identical to Jack's, their movements constrained by both visible and invisible boundaries. Some walked with purpose, others with the aimless shuffle of men killing time that refused to die. All of them noticed Jack—the new arrival, the unknown quantity.

Their gazes held the weight of assessment. Jack felt himself being categorized, evaluated, measured against a complex social hierarchy. He maintained his forward focus as instructed, but his peripheral awareness captured the reactions. Some eyes held curiosity, others indifference, a few the predatory calculation of men seeking weakness. Jack kept his pace steady, his posture neither challenging nor submissive, presenting a blank canvas that revealed nothing while absorbing everything.

They passed through a day room where inmates sat at bolted-down tables, playing cards or talking in low voices. The television mounted high on the wall played a daytime talk show, its vibrant colors and animated host a surreal contrast to the muted environment below. Activity paused momentarily as Jack passed, conversations suspended mid-sentence as attention shifted to assess the newcomer. Jack noted the alliances visible in seating arrangements, the territorial divisions invisible to outsiders but clear to those who lived within them.

"Cell 217," Wilson announced, stopping before a door standing open. "This is you."

12
Incarceration

The cell was smaller than Jack had imagined, though he'd never wasted much time imagining prison cells before. Six paces long, four wide. The walls were institutional beige, painted over countless times, revealing their history in the small chips near the floor. Two bunks, metal frame. A steel toilet without a seat. A sink with a mirror made of polished metal, not glass. Nothing to break, nothing to weaponize.

Jack stood in the center, his state-issued items clutched in a bundle against his chest – sheets, a thin blanket, toiletries in a clear plastic bag that hid nothing. The guard had left moments ago, the echo of his boots still reverberating down the corridor. Jack had been told his cellmate was at work detail. For now, he had these few minutes alone to absorb his new reality.

His fingertips brushed against the concrete wall, finding it cool and slightly rough. Everything here was designed to remind you that you were contained, managed, reduced to your most basic form. Even the light from the small window cast geometric shadows across the floor, bars within bars.

The sounds of the prison filtered through the solid door – distant shouts, the metallic clang of doors, the squeak of shoes on polished floors, and beneath it all, a constant murmur of voices. Never silence.

He was setting his thin mattress on the upper bunk when the door opened. Jack didn't turn immediately, taking the extra second to steady himself, to prepare his face for whatever was coming.

"You West?"

Jack turned. The man filling the doorway was broad-shouldered, solid like an oak stump. His head was shaved close to the scalp, not bald but nearly there, with just enough growth to show it was dark. Arms roped with muscle extended from a short-sleeved uniform shirt; every inch of visible skin covered in a complex network of tattoos – faded blues and blacks that had settled deep into his skin years ago. His face carried the weathered look of someone who'd spent too many years indoors under artificial light, skin pale but somehow tough-looking, like leather left too long in the sun and then stored in a dark place.

But it was the eyes that Jack noticed most – neither friendly nor hostile, just measuring, calculating. They took in Jack's stance, his bundle of belongings, the way he held himself, all in one sweep.

"Yes," Jack said, keeping his voice neutral. "Jack West."

The man nodded once and moved into the cell. He sat on the lower bunk, the mattress compressing under his weight.

"Cameron Walsh," he said. "Cam."

The name came with no additional information, no story, no question about what Jack was in for. Just a name, offered without expectation.

After a moment's consideration, Cam stood again and stepped forward. Jack remained still, waiting. Cam extended his hand in a motion that seemed deliberate, practiced. Jack took it, feeling the callused palm against his own work-hardened hand. The handshake was firm but brief – a single up and down movement that communicated strength without challenge. It wasn't friendly, exactly, but it wasn't threatening either. It was functional, a necessary acknowledgment between two men who would be sharing eight-by-ten feet of space for the foreseeable future.

"There's no privacy in here," Cam stated, releasing Jack's hand and stepping back to his bunk. His voice was flat, matter-of-fact, like he was explaining that water was wet. "Everything's somebody's business."

Jack nodded, understanding the warning beneath the simple statement. Watch what you say, what you do, how you react. Everything is currency.

"I figured," he replied, turning back to his bunk to finish making it up. The sheets were thin, rough against his fingers, but clean. Small mercies.

As if on cue, a shadow passed across the small window in the door – a guard peering in for the routine check. The intrusion was brief but pointed, underscoring Cam's words with perfect timing.

"They do rounds every hour," Cam said, stretching out on his bunk, hands behind his head. "More often if they're bored or suspicious. You'll get used to it."

Jack tucked the corners of his sheet under the mattress with precise movements. His mind cataloged the interaction so far: Cam was established, respected enough to have information, controlled enough to share it without seeming eager. Not a threat, at least not an immediate one, but not a friend either.

"How long have you been here?" Jack asked, smoothing the blanket over the sheet.

"This cell? Six months. South Woods? Going on nine years." Cam's eyes tracked Jack's movements without seeming to. "You're lucky you got assigned here. Last guy they put me with lasted three weeks before he got himself sent to solitary."

Jack didn't ask what happened. Some questions were better left unasked until you knew the terrain better.

"How much time did you get?" Cam asked, the question casual, as if inquiring about the weather.

"Ten years, possibility of parole after eight." Jack folded his uniform and placed it at the foot of his bunk. "Voluntary manslaughter."

Cam nodded, absorbing the information without visible reaction. "First time inside?"

"Yes."

"Thought so. You're too careful, watching everything. Old-timers stop noticing." Cam sat up, swinging his legs over the side of his bunk. "Got people on the outside waiting for you?"

The question hung in the air between them. Jack paused in arranging his few belongings, aware that his answer would reveal more than just facts. He nodded once; eyes fixed on his task.

"Family," he said simply, offering nothing more.

Something shifted in Cam's expression – not softening exactly, but a slight alteration, like a door opening just a crack to let in a sliver of light.

"I don't have anyone anymore," Cam said, followed by a dry chuckle that contained no humor whatsoever. The sound was hollow, practiced, a shield against whatever story lay behind those words.

Jack recognized the sound for what it was – not an invitation to ask questions, but a deliberate closing of a topic even as it was introduced. The subtext was clear: We all lose things in here. Be prepared.

Jack climbed onto his bunk, feeling the thin mattress compress under his weight. From this vantage point, he could see most of the cell without having to move his head. He watched as Cam returned to his prone position, noting how the older inmate positioned himself – back to the wall, feet toward the door, eyes able to track any movement in the cell or at the door without appearing to be watching.

"You worked outdoors before," Cam observed, not a question but a statement.

Jack raised an eyebrow, curious about the deduction.

"Your hands," Cam explained. "Calluses in different places than factory work. The way you squint sometimes, like you're used to stronger light. The tan lines."

Jack nodded. "Arborist."

"Trees," Cam said, nodding as if confirming something to himself. "You'll miss that. Sky, mostly. Wind. Rain that doesn't come with guards watching you get wet."

A silence fell between them, not uncomfortable but watchful, each man taking the measure of the other.

"There are rules here," Cam said eventually, his voice low enough that it wouldn't carry beyond their cell but clear enough that Jack wouldn't miss a word. "The ones the guards tell you, those are just the surface. The real rules are the ones nobody writes down."

Jack waited, saying nothing, understanding that this was valuable currency being offered.

"Mind your own business but never look like you're not paying attention. Don't get involved in other people's beefs unless you're sure which side has the numbers. Don't borrow, don't lend, don't owe favors unless you're prepared to pay them back at interest. In the shower, keep your eyes up. In the yard, keep your back to a wall. In the mess, eat what's on your tray and nothing else."

Each sentence was delivered like a separate bullet point, distinct and precise. There was no embellishment, no storytelling, just pure information distilled from experience.

"Never tell anyone the whole truth about why you're in. They'll find out anyway, but what you say first sets the tone." Cam continued. "Don't make friends your first month. Watch who talks to who, who sits where, who the guards treat different."

Jack absorbed the advice, recognizing it for what it was – not kindness exactly, but a practical investment. A stable cellmate was valuable; one who understood the unwritten codes even more so.

"The gangs will approach you eventually. White guy, strong, first offense, long sentence – you're a good recruit. When they do, be respectful but non-committal. Say you're still finding your feet. Buying time is better than making enemies your first week."

Cam fell silent then, having delivered what he deemed necessary. Jack didn't thank him – that would have cheapened the exchange, turned it into something it wasn't.

Instead, he said, "I don't sleep much."

It was an offering of his own – practical information that Cam could use. I won't keep you awake with tossing and turning, but I'll be alert, aware, even at night.

Cam nodded once. "Most don't, at first. Gets better. Or worse. Depends."

The distant sound of a bell rang through the block, followed by increased activity in the corridor.

"Dinner in twenty minutes," Cam said, sitting up again. "They'll open the doors soon for movement to the mess hall."

"One more thing," Cam said, his voice even lower now. "Whatever kept you going on the outside – family, hope, anger, whatever it is – hold onto it. But keep it close. Don't let anyone see it. That's how they get to you in here."

Before Jack could respond, the buzzer sounded, and the cell doors opened. Cam stepped out into the corridor, already part of the flow of movement, and after a moment's hesitation, Jack followed, stepping into the stream of his new reality.

The phone bank stretched along the wall like a row of confessionals, each booth separated by thin metal dividers that offered the illusion of privacy rather than the reality. Jack stood fifth in line, his state-issued prison garb identical to those of the men before and behind him, all of them waiting for their allotted minutes of connection to the world beyond concrete and steel.

Three days since intake. Three days of orientation, of learning to walk with his eyes down but aware, of memorizing the timing of meals and counts and lights-out. Three days of Cam's silent, watchful presence and terse advice. And now, finally, his first phone call home.

A guard stood at the end of the row, arms crossed, expression bored but attentive. On the wall beside him, a large industrial clock marked the passage of time with an audible tick that somehow cut through the ambient noise – the murmur of conversations, the metallic clang of a distant door, the squeak of a guard's boots on the polished floor. Each sound bounced off the concrete walls and floor, creating a persistent background hum that never quite faded.

Jack shifted his weight, rolling his shoulders slightly to ease the tension building there. His jaw remained tight, teeth pressed together behind closed lips. He watched as the inmate at the first phone booth hunched forward, one hand cupped around the mouthpiece, voice low but urgent. The man's other hand gripped the receiver with white knuckles, as if holding onto a lifeline.

Four inmates ahead of him. Then three. Then two.

Jack's fingers twitched at his sides. What would he say? How could words possibly bridge this new reality? He'd rehearsed this call in his mind for days, but now the carefully planned sentences seemed inadequate, hollow.

The inmate directly in front of Jack finished his call, hanging up the receiver with a gentleness that contrasted sharply with his tattooed knuckles and scarred face. Their eyes met briefly as the man turned away, and Jack caught a glimpse of something raw and unguarded before the prison mask slipped back into place.

Then it was his turn.

The booth smelled faintly of sweat and desperation. Jack picked up the receiver, feeling its weight and the slight stickiness from previous users. He wiped it quickly against his shirt before bringing it to his ear. His fingers hovered over the keypad for a moment before dialing, each number precise and deliberate. He'd memorized the collect call procedure during orientation, the sequence of buttons to press, the automated prompts to follow.

Then came the ringing – once, twice, three times. Jack's breathing grew shallow as he waited, each ring stretching into eternity.

On the fourth ring, a click, and then – her voice.

"Hello? Jack?"

He closed his eyes briefly, his free hand coming up to press against the metal divider for support. The sound of Tabby's voice hit him like a physical force, simultaneously grounding and destabilizing.

"Yes." His voice emerged rougher than he'd intended. He cleared his throat. "It's me."

A small inhale on the other end of the line. "How are you?"

Such a simple question. In the before, he might have answered with a casual "fine" or a detailed account of his day's work. Now, the question carried the weight of everything between them.

"I'm here," he said finally, the words inadequate but honest.

The silence that followed felt laden with all they couldn't say. Jack's breathing filled the space – in through his nose, out through his mouth, a technique he'd used when scaling dangerous trees, when the only thing between him and a fatal fall was his own steady hand and focused mind.

"We're already preparing," Tabby said eventually. "For visitation."

Jack nodded, then remembered she couldn't see him. "Good. That's good." His fingers tightened around the receiver. "The first visit can be scheduled after two weeks. You can download the paperwork."

"I'll fill it out right away."

Another silence. In the background, Jack could hear the familiar sounds of home over speakerphone – the soft hum of the refrigerator, the distant ticking of the clock in the hallway. Ordinary sounds that now seemed impossibly precious.

"The house feels empty," Tabby said, her voice catching slightly.

Jack pressed his forehead against the cool metal divider, eyes squeezed shut. His throat tightened, making speech difficult.

"Ruby's been staying over," Tabby continued, filling the silence he couldn't break. "She's helping with the nursery. We painted it yesterday – that soft green you liked. The one that reminded you of new leaves."

The image struck him with unexpected force – Tabby and Ruby with paintbrushes, preparing a room for a child he wouldn't hold for years. His breath hitched, almost imperceptibly.

"That's good," he managed, the words scraping against his throat. "You shouldn't be on ladders now."

A small laugh, watery but genuine. "That's exactly what Ruby said."

Jack's eyes opened, fixing on the blank wall in front of him. He became aware again of his surroundings – the inmate in the next booth speaking rapidly in Spanish, the guard checking his watch, the constant background noise of the prison continuing around him despite the momentary escape the phone call had provided.

"And the doctor's appointment?" he asked, grasping for the practical matters, the safe topics that wouldn't unravel him.

"Everything's normal. Right on schedule for June."

June. He would be four months into his sentence when his child was born. Four months out of one hundred and twenty. The math was simple, devastating.

"Jack?" Tabby's voice pulled him back. "Are you still there?"

"Yes." He straightened his shoulders, pulled himself together. "I'm still here."

"Ruby's here. She wants to talk to you too," Tabby said, calling Ruby closer to the phone.

In the next booth, the Spanish-speaking inmate hung up his phone with more force than necessary, his face twisted with some private pain as he walked away.

Jack drew a deep breath, preparing for Ruby's voice, for the next test of his composure. The guard at the end of the row caught his eye and tapped his wrist – a reminder that time was passing, that this tenuous connection to home would soon be severed.

Time enough, Jack thought. It would have to be.

"Hey, Jack!" Ruby's voice came through the line, her cheerfulness almost convincing. "How's the food? As bad as they show in the movies?"

Jack's grip on the receiver tightened, knuckles whitening against the black plastic. The question was so deliberately normal, so carefully chosen to be both light and answerable, that he felt a surge of gratitude for his sister's strength.

"Worse," he replied, allowing a hint of dry humor to color his voice. "Mystery meat that stopped being mysterious decades ago."

Ruby's laugh came through clearly – a bit forced, but genuine in its effort. "Well, I've seen what you consider cooking, so maybe it's an improvement."

Jack leaned his shoulder against the metal divider; eyes fixed on a small scratch in the paint before him. This exchange of banter felt both essential and surreal, a familiar rhythm performed on unfamiliar terrain.

"Jack?" Tabby's voice returned. "We need to talk about June. About the birth plan."

He swallowed hard, nodding reflexively before remembering again that they couldn't see him. "Yes. Tell me."

"Dr. Winters says everything looks good for a natural delivery. Ruby's agreed to be my coach."

Jack closed his eyes briefly, picturing the scene – Tabby in a hospital bed, Ruby beside her in the space where he should be standing.

"Thank you," he said, the words directed to Ruby but encompassing so much more than could be expressed.

"Of course," Ruby replied immediately. "What else would I do? Besides, I've been reading all the books. Did you know the partner is supposed to massage the lower back during contractions? I've been practicing on Tabby."

"She's terrible at it," Tabby interjected, and Jack could hear the smile in her voice. "All elbows."

"I'm getting better," Ruby protested. "Jason says my technique has improved dramatically."

The mention of Ruby's boyfriend brought a fleeting smile to Jack's face. The four of them had spent so many evenings together, planning for the baby's arrival, before... before everything changed.

"Ruby moved the rocking chair to the nursery yesterday," Tabby continued. "The one from your parent's house. It fits perfectly in the corner by the window."

Jack's free hand formed a fist at his side, then slowly relaxed, finger by finger. The chair had been in storage. He'd planned to refinish it himself before the baby came.

"That's good," he said, his voice calm despite the ache in his chest. "It needs to be by the window. For the late-night feedings."

"That's exactly what I said," Ruby chimed in. "Great minds."

In the background, Jack heard the shrill whistle of the kettle, followed by the soft pad of footsteps moving away from the phone. He pressed the receiver harder against his ear, hungry for these domestic sounds, for the auditory glimpse into the life continuing without him.

There was a slight rustling on the line, the sound of a chair creaking, Tabby shifting her weight. He could picture her at the kitchen table, one hand resting on her growing belly. The image was so clear it made his throat tighten.

"Oh, and I made an appointment with that lawyer friend of Jason's," Ruby said, her tone deliberately casual but underlaid with significance. "The one who specializes in family law. For the guardianship paperwork we talked about."

Jack straightened, understanding immediately. They had discussed this before his sentencing – legal guardianship arrangements for Ruby in case anything happened while he was inside. Not that they expected anything to happen to Tabby, but preparation had always been Jack's way of controlling the uncontrollable.

"Thank you," he said simply, knowing Ruby would understand all that lay behind those two words.

The metallic jingle of keys filtered through the line – Ruby's distinctive keychain with its collection of small tools and trinkets. The sound was so familiar, so ordinary that it felt almost surreal to hear it from within these concrete walls.

"I'll see you soon, Jack. First visiting day, I'll be there." Ruby said, her voice suddenly thicker.

"Ruby—" He started, then stopped, unsure what he wanted to say, what he could say with the guard watching, with time ticking away.

"I know," she said, saving him from having to find the words. "Me too."

Jack drew a deep breath, steadying himself.

"Jack?" Tabby's voice again, closer to phone now. "I miss you."

The simple declaration hit him with unexpected force. His knuckles whitened again around the receiver, his jaw clenching against the surge of emotion those three words released.

"I miss you too," he replied, the words inadequate but necessary.

A brief silence stretched between them, heavy with all they couldn't say. In that moment, Jack became acutely aware of the plastic receiver in his hand, the unyielding floor beneath his feet, the ever-present background noise of the prison – all the physical reminders of the barrier between them.

"How are you really?" Tabby asked, her voice lower now, more intimate.

Jack swallowed, considering his answer carefully. The truth – that he felt hollowed out, that he startled awake each night disoriented and reaching for her, that he measured his days in survivable increments – would only cause her pain.

"I'm adjusting," he said instead. "Following the rules. Keeping my head down."

"Are you safe?" The question held all her fears, distilled into three words.

"Yes," he answered firmly, giving her this certainty at least. "My cellmate is... experienced. Respectful. The kind who minds his own business."

He heard her exhale, a small release of tension. "Good. That's good."

"Ruby snores," Tabby added. "Did you know that? How did I not know that about your sister after all this time?"

"She always has," Jack replied, grateful for this moment of normalcy. "Like a chainsaw with a loose muffler."

Tabby's laugh came through the line, warm and genuine this time, bridging the distance between them for just a moment. Jack closed his eyes, holding onto the sound, storing it away to retrieve during the long nights ahead.

"The baby moved this morning," she said softly. "While I was having breakfast. Strong kicks, right under my ribs."

Jack's free hand lifted unconsciously, as if to reach across the impossible distance and feel those movements for himself. He let it fall back to his side, fingers curling inward.

"June will be here before you know it," Tabby continued, her voice gentle but firm. "And then you'll meet him."

"One minute, West." The guard's voice cut through Jack's consciousness like a blade, severing the momentary connection he'd felt to home. He straightened immediately, shoulders squaring, mind shifting gears.

"We're running out of time," he said, his voice dropping lower, words coming faster. "Listen carefully."

"We're here," Tabby replied, her own tone shifting to match his urgency. Ruby's breathing was audible in the background, both women clearly bracing for whatever he needed to say.

Jack pressed the receiver harder against his ear, turning slightly toward the wall to create even the illusion of privacy. His voice became steady, controlled, each word selected with precision.

"I'm physically safe. The routine here is predictable, which helps. Three meals, work assignment starting next week. I'm following every rule." He paused for half a second, then continued. I'm not involved in anything. I stay aware but uninvolved."

He heard Tabby's small intake of breath, understanding what he wasn't saying – that danger existed but he was navigating it carefully. Ruby remained silent, but he could picture her nodding, absorbing his subtext.

"The baby fund," Jack continued, referring to the savings account they'd established months ago. "Use it if you need to. Don't try to save it all for later."

"Jack—" Tabby began to protest.

"No," he cut her off, gentle but firm. "Your health and the baby's come first. Ruby knows where the emergency cash is if anything happens with the bank accounts."

Ruby's voice came through, closer to the receiver now. "I've got it covered, Jack. The money, the house, everything. I promise."

Jack closed his eyes briefly, a surge of gratitude threatening his composure. When he opened them again, his gaze fixed on a specific point on the wall, anchoring himself.

"The most important thing," he said, voice dropping even lower, "is that you both know I'm handling this. I'm steady. I'm present. This is just time we have to get through."

He could almost feel Tabby's nod through the phone line, the way she would be pressing her lips together to maintain control, a gesture so familiar he could see it without seeing.

"We're going to be fine," she said, her voice carrying that quiet determination he'd always admired, even as it wavered slightly at the edges. "All of us."

The guard moved closer, tapping his watch. Jack nodded acknowledgment without looking at him.

"Visiting forms," he said quickly. "Fill them out immediately. First possible date is the 29th. Bring your ID. Ruby will need to be on the approved visitor list too."

"We'll be there," Ruby assured him.

"Jack," Tabby said, her voice suddenly urgent. "I love—"

The line went dead with a mechanical click, the automated system cutting off the call at exactly fifteen minutes. The silence was so abrupt, so complete, that for a moment Jack remained frozen, the receiver still pressed to his ear as if he might catch one last echo of her voice.

Three seconds passed. Four. Five.

With deliberate care, he placed the receiver back in its cradle, his movements controlled and precise. His face remained expressionless as he turned away from the booth, eyes focused on the middle distance, seeing neither the guard nor the other inmates waiting for their turn at the phones.

He walked away with measured steps, neither rushing nor dawdling, maintaining the careful neutrality he'd observed in the more experienced inmates. His back was straight, his arms relaxed at his sides, nothing in his posture to suggest vulnerability or distress. Only his hands, curled into tight fists, betrayed anything of his internal state, his mind replaying fragments of the call.

Tabby's voice saying, "I miss you." The kettle whistling in the background. Ruby's careful optimism. The sound of his family continuing without him, the life he should be living carrying on just beyond his reach.

He continued through the cellblock, a cavernous space with two tiers of cells lining both sides, the center area below currently filled with inmates in recreational time – some playing cards at metal tables bolted to the floor, others watching a small television mounted high on the wall, a few simply sitting alone, staring at nothing in particular.

Jack climbed the metal stairs to the upper tier, footsteps echoing slightly on the grating. Cell 217 – his assigned home for however many years stretched ahead – waited with its door currently open for rec time. He entered the small space, noting that Cam was absent, likely still at his work assignment.

The momentary privacy was a gift. Jack sat on the edge of his bunk, the thin mattress barely yielding beneath his weight. His eyes fixed on the blank wall opposite, seeing not the institutional beige but the green walls of the nursery Tabby had described, the rocking chair positioned by the window.

His controlled exterior remained intact, nothing in his face or posture to suggest anything beyond ordinary contemplation to any passing guard. But beneath that careful mask, something shifted and settled – the full weight of his separation from his family, the reality of all he would miss, all he had sacrificed.

Minutes passed, marked only by the distant sounds of the cell block and the steady rhythm of his breathing. Eventually, Jack's right hand uncurled from its fist. His fingers spread wide, then slowly closed again around nothing, a gesture reminiscent of how he might have touched Tabby's belly to feel the baby's movements, how he might have held his child's tiny hand.

The motion complete, he returned his hand to his lap, palm flat against his thigh. His face remained impassive, his breathing steady. To anyone observing, he appeared to be simply sitting, perhaps thinking of nothing in particular. Just another inmate adapting to confinement.

Only Jack knew that behind that composed exterior, he was carefully filing away every detail from the call – Tabby's voice, Ruby's determined optimism, the domestic sounds of home – storing them like precious artifacts to be taken out and examined during the long nights ahead. Only he knew that he was mentally constructing a bridge across the chasm that now separated him from his family, building it word by word, memory by memory.

Only he knew that while his body sat contained within these walls, his mind was already planning for the next call, the first visit, the thousands of small connections that would have to sustain them all through the years of separation to come.

Footsteps approached – Cam returning from his work detail. Jack didn't turn his head, didn't acknowledge the other man's entrance. He remained still, present yet distant, physically confined but mentally reaching toward home.

Seconds ticked by, measured by the institutional clock visible through the cell door. Each one carrying him further from the sound of Tabby's voice, closer to the moment when he would meet his child for the first time – and begin the impossible task of being a father from behind these walls.

13

The Wedding Ring

The recreation yard sprawled beneath a cloudless sky, a rectangle of cracked concrete surrounded by chain-link fencing topped with coils of razor wire that glinted like jewelry in the afternoon sun. Jack stood with his back against the fence, cataloging the invisible boundaries that divided the yard into territories as clearly as property lines on a surveyor's map. One week in South Woods had been enough to identify the patterns – which benches belonged to which groups, where the guards focused their attention, and where their gaze rarely reached. He rotated the wedding band on his left hand with his thumb, a habitual gesture that had become more deliberate since intake, each turn a silent connection to Tabby.

The yard hummed with contained energy – men lifting weights at the far end, a basketball game in constant motion on the cracked court, clusters of inmates huddled in conversation, their voices deliberately low. Jack kept his eyes moving, never lingering long enough to appear interested, never shifting so quickly as to seem nervous. Cam's advice echoed in his mind: "In the yard, keep your back to a wall." The fence wasn't a wall, but it served the same purpose – nothing could approach from behind.

The wedding band caught the light as he twisted it again. An intake officer had considered confiscating it – metal items with potential value were contraband in many facilities – but South Woods allowed wedding rings provided they were simple bands without stones. Jack had watched the officer consider the plain titanium ring, assessing its value against the hassle of forcing its surrender. In the end, the officer had simply offered a casual warning: "Might want to keep this out of sight. Some guys in here haven't seen their wives in years."

Jack had nodded but made no effort to hide the ring. It remained on his finger, a small circle of resilience in a place designed to strip away identity.

He'd made two promises the day he slipped it on his finger – one to Tabby, spoken aloud in their small ceremony, and one to himself, silent but equally binding. The first was to love and protect her; the second was to never remove the ring, no matter what came. He intended to keep both.

Across the yard, a man detached himself from a group near the weight bench. Jack noted the movement without appearing to, his peripheral vision tracking the man's approach while his face remained impassive, gaze directed at the basketball game as if mildly interested in its outcome. The man was tall, rangier than Jack but carrying the wiry strength of someone who relied on speed rather than pure power. His arms were heavily tattooed, blue ink crawling up his neck to lick at his jawline. His prison-issued clothing had been modified – sleeves torn off the tan shirt, pants hemmed shorter than regulation to show off elaborate ink on his calves. A sign of status, that alteration; it meant the guards didn't bother him about dress code violations.

The man approached with deliberate casualness, path angled to seem coincidental rather than targeted. But Jack recognized the intent in the movement, the way the man's eyes kept returning to him despite the seemingly random trajectory. Jack straightened slightly, weight shifting to the balls of his feet, body preparing while his face remained neutral.

Three other inmates watched from the sidelines, their conversation paused, attention fixed on the scene unfolding. Jack cataloged them briefly – potential backup if things escalated, though their posture suggested they were spectators rather than participants for now. The nearest guard stood by the entrance to the yard, attention focused on his clipboard, deliberately oblivious to the subtle currents of tension flowing through the space.

The tattooed man stopped a few feet away, leaning against the fence as if the spot had been his destination all along. He rolled his shoulders back, exhaling slowly, the gesture unhurried and deliberate. Only then did he turn his head to acknowledge Jack, the movement carrying a practiced nonchalance. "West, right?" The man's voice had a sandpaper quality, words rasping as if dragged across rough stone. "The tree man."

Jack gave a single nod, neither friendly nor hostile. His file listed his occupation – information freely traded in the prison ecosystem. That the man knew it was no surprise; that he'd opened with it indicated he'd been asking questions.

"Moss," the man introduced himself. "Been watching you. You keep to yourself. Smart move for a new fish."

Jack said nothing, maintaining eye contact without challenge. Silence was often more effective than speech.

Moss smiled, the expression not reaching his eyes. "Not much for conversation. That's alright. Actions speak louder anyway." His gaze dropped deliberately to Jack's left hand, to the wedding band catching sunlight. "Nice ring."

The comment hung in the air between them, its weight far greater than the two syllables suggested. Jack's thumb stilled its habitual rotation of the band, but otherwise he remained motionless, face revealing nothing of the sudden alertness that coursed through him.

"Titanium?" Moss asked. "Good choice. Doesn't bend easy. Most guys don't wear them in here. Too risky, you know? Easy to lose things that matter."

Jack met the man's gaze steadily. "Not planning to lose it."

Moss chuckled, the sound dry and without humor. "Plans change in here, tree man. Especially when you're looking at what, ten years? Long time to hold onto anything." He pushed off from the fence, moving closer, entering the invisible boundary of personal space. "What's her name? The woman on the other end of that ring?"

Jack felt his jaw tighten, a small betrayal of emotion that he immediately controlled. "My business," he said, voice level.

"Everything's everybody's business in here," Moss countered, echoing Cam's earlier warning with eerie precision. "Especially anything worth having." His eyes flicked to his companions, then back to Jack. "Like that ring. Worth something on the outside. Worth more in here."

Jack remained still, neither backing away nor advancing, measuring the distance between them, calculating angles and force and potential outcomes. He'd assessed risk professionally for years – which branches could bear weight, which might snap, how a tree would fall when cut. The principles weren't so different here.

"I collect things," Moss continued, voice lower now. "Souvenirs. Memories of conversations." He reached out slowly, deliberately, fingers extending toward Jack's left hand. "That would make a fine addition."

Jack didn't move, didn't flinch, didn't shift his gaze from Moss's face even as the man's fingers approached his hand. The yard seemed to quiet around them, the basketball game continuing but the ambient conversation dimming as attention shifted subtly toward their corner of the fence.

Moss's fingers stopped a centimeter from the ring, hovering in the space between them. "Question is," he said, voice dropping further, "how much is it worth to you? You willing to bleed for it?"

The question wasn't just about the ring – it was a test, carefully designed and publicly staged. How Jack responded would define his place in the prison hierarchy, would determine whether he would be seen as prey or as someone to be left alone. In the week since his arrival, he'd kept to himself, followed Cam's advice, observed and learned. But observation time was over. This was the moment Cam had warned would come.

Jack's hands were steady, his breathing controlled. The same calm that had served him eighty feet up a dying oak with a chainsaw settled over him now. His left hand remained at his side, neither withdrawn nor offered up, the ring gleaming in the sunlight.

"Not yours," he said simply. The words emerged without heat, without bravado, just a statement of fact delivered with absolute certainty.

Moss's eyes narrowed slightly, his hovering hand not retreating but not advancing either. The standoff stretched for three heartbeats, four, five – the yard around them holding its collective breath.

"You sure about that?" Moss pressed, fingers inching closer until they almost brushed the metal band. "Things change hands quick in here. One minute you're wearing it, next minute you're in the infirmary wondering what happened."

Jack's gaze remained unwavering, his voice steady when he spoke again. "It stays where it is."

A hint of something like respect flickered across Moss's face, quickly replaced by calculation. He glanced again at his audience of companions, aware of how this interaction would be perceived, how the outcome would reflect on his own status.

"Big talk for a new fish," he said, voice louder now, meant to carry. "Specially one who's never had to back it up."

Jack understood the escalation for what it was – Moss creating space to either press the challenge or withdraw without losing face. The tattooed man's fingers finally made contact with the ring, a deliberate touch that left no doubt about his intentions.

"Last chance," Moss said. "Give it up easy, or things get complicated."

Jack didn't look at the hand touching his ring. Instead, he maintained eye contact, his posture shifting almost imperceptibly – weight centered, balance perfect, ready. "It's not coming off," he said, each word distinct and measured. "Not today. Not any day."

The yard had gone almost completely silent, the basketball bouncing unattended as players paused to watch. Even the guards had noticed the tension, one of them straightening from his clipboard, hand drifting toward his radio.

Moss's fingers remained on the ring, neither retreating nor attempting to remove it. The standoff teetered on a knife-edge, the next move determining whether blood would spill on the concrete.

Jack had made his decision – the ring would stay, or he would bleed defending it. There was no middle ground. Jack didn't blink, didn't breathe, didn't shift his gaze.

Something in Jack's stillness, in the absolute certainty of his stance, communicated itself to Moss. The tattooed man's lips curled into a smile that contained a measure of genuine amusement mixed with assessment.

"Strong feelings about jewelry," Moss observed, withdrawing his hand with deliberate slowness. "Interesting."

The collective tension in the yard released slightly, like a cable pulled taut and then granted minimal slack. Jack remained motionless, waiting, aware that the confrontation wasn't necessarily over just because Moss had withdrawn his touch.

"You know," Moss said, taking a step back and regarding Jack with newfound interest, "most new fish would've either swung at me or handed it over by now. You did neither." He paused, estimating Jack. "Makes me curious what you'll do when words aren't enough."

The statement carried both a threat and an acknowledgment – this test had been passed, but others would follow. Jack gave a single nod, accepting both implications without comment.

Moss returned the nod, a businessman concluding an informative if inconclusive meeting. "We'll talk again, tree man," he said, turning to rejoin his companions.

Jack watched him go, maintaining his position against the fence, aware of the eyes still on him from around the yard. The confrontation had established something, though precisely what remained to be seen. He rotated the wedding band with his thumb once more, the metal warm against his skin.

In the distance, a whistle blew – recreation time ending. Inmates began moving toward the doors, the brief drama already fading into the constant flow of prison life. Jack pushed off from the fence, joining the steady stream of tan clad men, his face revealing nothing of the calculation happening behind it.

The ring remained on his finger, its presence both a victory and a vulnerability. Jack understood with perfect clarity that he had marked himself by refusing to surrender it – had declared something worth fighting for, worth bleeding for. In a place designed to strip away all value beyond survival, such declarations were dangerous.

But as he crossed the threshold from sunlight back into the institutional fluorescence of the corridor, Jack felt the weight of the band against his skin and knew he would make the same choice again tomorrow, and every day after. Some anchors couldn't be surrendered, no matter the cost. Some promises had to be kept, especially here, especially now.

14

The Invitation

The kitchen knife sliced through carrots with mechanical precision, each orange disk falling exactly the same thickness as the last. Jack guided the blade with the practiced rhythm of someone for whom tools were extensions of thought rather than merely objects in hand. Steam billowed from industrial pots nearby, the air heavy with the institutional smell of overcooked vegetables and bleach, but his focus remained unbroken – slice, slide, gather, repeat. He'd found unexpected comfort in the monotony of kitchen duty, a sanctuary of predictable motion in a place where predictability was otherwise scarce.

Three weeks into his sentence, and Jack had established a routine. Kitchen duty wasn't coveted work – the heat was oppressive, the noise constant, the supervision tight – but he'd requested it specifically. The kitchen offered structure, physical activity, and most importantly, time that passed with measurable progress. Each vegetable prepared, each tray assembled, each minute counted down was another small victory against the endless stretch of days ahead.

A cook shouted orders from the far end of the prep line, his voice barely rising above the cackling steam valves and clattering pots. Jack didn't look up. He'd learned the choreography of the kitchen, could anticipate the rhythm of commands without needing to see who was speaking. His station remained orderly – knives aligned when not in use, scraps collected in a designated container, cutting board kept clean with efficient wipes between ingredients. This precision hadn't gone unnoticed.

"Onions next," called the head cook, sliding a plastic container toward Jack's station. "Diced fine for the sauce."

Jack nodded once, transferred the carrot slices to their waiting container, and wiped down his board. The onions were firm, newly delivered, their papery skins crinkling as he peeled them with quick, practiced movements. The knife found its rhythm again – different from the carrots, adapted to the new texture and required cut. Slice, rotate, slice again, gather the pieces, chop with controlled force. His hands knew the work even as his mind remained vigilantly split – half on the task, half on the room around him.

Three guards stationed at intervals along the kitchen perimeter. Two cooks arguing about salt quantities by the steam table. Four inmates on serving line duty, arranging trays with bored efficiency. Six more at various prep stations. Two by the industrial dishwasher, their faces flushed from the heat. All accounted for, all tracked in Jack's peripheral awareness without ever looking directly at any of them.

The kitchen's clamor created a strange privacy, a curtain of noise behind which conversations could happen unheard by those more than a few feet away. Jack had noticed this pattern his first day – how inmates would time certain exchanges to coincide with the dishwasher's loudest cycle or position themselves near the exhaust fans when sharing information. He'd cataloged these behaviors without comment, added them to his growing mental map of South Woods' invisible currents.

A week ago, he'd heard his name mentioned between two inmates working the serving line. "West keeps to himself," one had said, voice low beneath the hiss of steam. "Smart fish." The other had nodded, eyes flicking briefly toward Jack before moving on. He'd given no indication that he'd heard, but the exchange confirmed what he already suspected – his reputation was forming, taking shape around his silence and self-containment.

The onions released their sharp, eye-watering compounds as Jack diced them with efficient precision. He didn't blink, didn't pause, didn't reach up to wipe away the involuntary tears that gathered at the corners of his eyes. The mild discomfort was almost welcome – a small, honest reaction in a place where every expression was measured and calculated for effect.

He sensed the approach before he saw it – a shift in the kitchen's energy, a subtle repositioning of bodies as someone moved against the established flow. Jack's hands maintained their rhythm as he tracked the movement in his peripheral vision: an inmate detaching himself from the serving line, crossing behind the head cook's station, angling toward the vegetable prep area with deliberate casualness.

One of the guards glanced up, noted the movement, then returned to his clipboard, apparently deciding the deviation wasn't worth intervention. Jack gathered the diced onions into a neat pile at the center of his cutting board, already reaching for the next one without looking up.

The inmate who positioned himself at the adjacent prep station was lean and wiry, with close-cropped hair and arms corded with the kind of muscle that came from bodyweight exercises rather than weights. Jack had seen him before – always surrounded by others in the yard, quick to laugh but with eyes that never shared in the amusement. A center of gravity. Someone with influence.

The man picked up a knife from the station, tested its edge with his thumb, and pulled a bell pepper toward him. He began to slice it with casual competence, not looking at Jack but positioning himself just close enough that they could speak without being overheard by the nearest guard.

For several minutes, they worked in silence side by side, the only sounds between them the rhythmic contact of knife on cutting board. Jack started on his third onion, maintaining the exact dimensions of his dice, neither slowing nor speeding up to acknowledge the other man's presence.

"You keep those tears in check pretty good," the man finally said, voice pitched low beneath the kitchen's constant din. "Most guys blink like crazy with the onions."

Jack continued working, his movements uninterrupted. He gave a slight nod – acknowledgment without invitation.

"Noticed you around," the man continued, quartering the bell pepper with quick, efficient cuts. "Three weeks in and you ain't said more than ten words to anybody except your cellie."

It wasn't a question, so Jack didn't answer. He finished the third onion and reached for a fourth, his hands steady and deliberate.

The man chuckled softly. "They said you were quiet. Wasn't sure if it was discipline or fear." He paused, watching Jack's knife work. "Way you handle that blade, I'm thinking it's not fear."

Jack sliced through the onion's core with a single clean stroke, separating it into perfect halves. The man beside him wasn't looking for conversation;

he was testing, probing, measuring responses against some internal standard.

"Name's Decker," the man said, setting down his knife and turning slightly toward Jack. "Run things on the east yard."

Jack continued working but inclined his head slightly – recognition without deference.

"Word is you stood up to Moss over that ring," Decker continued, eyes flicking briefly to Jack's left hand where the wedding band caught the fluorescent light. "That took balls. Moss doesn't usually walk away without taking what he wants."

The knife sliced through onion layers with mathematical precision. Jack maintained his focus on the task but offered a single word: "Noted."

Decker's mouth quirked into something almost resembling a smile. He leaned slightly closer, voice dropping further. "So, here's what I'm wondering, tree man. You keep to yourself. You don't make trouble. But you also don't back down when pushed." He paused, waiting until a guard passed behind them before continuing. "What I need to know is – you throw hands when it comes to it?"

Jack's knife didn't falter, its rhythm unbroken as it transformed the onion into perfectly uniform pieces. The question hung between them, weighted with implications beyond its simple phrasing. In the background, the dishwasher roared to life, creating a wall of sound that ensured their conversation remained private.

He considered his response carefully, aware that this moment, like the confrontation with Moss in the yard, would define something essential about his place here. His movements remained steady, controlled, betraying nothing of the calculation happening behind his eyes.

"Not talking about cheap shots in the shower block," Decker continued, his knife resuming its rhythm against the cutting board. He worked with the casual efficiency of someone used to kitchen duty, his eyes rarely leaving his task yet somehow missing nothing. "I'm talking about something organized. Structured. With rules." The pepper under his blade fell into neat strips, each cut deliberate and controlled like his words. "Something that gives men who need it a way to settle things without shanks or gang numbers."

Jack continued dicing onions, his hands maintaining their mechanical precision. His silence wasn't agreement or refusal – merely space, allowing Decker to continue without encouragement or discouragement. The kitchen's industrial fans whirred overhead, pulling steam and heat upward in a constant current that matched the pull of Decker's words.

"Happens during yard time," Decker explained, voice pitched just above the ambient noise of the kitchen. "Behind the maintenance shed. Guards know about it but look the other way long as nobody ends up in the infirmary." He glanced sideways at Jack, measuring his reaction. "No weapons. Just skill. No jumping in – fight stays between the two men who started it. Winner walks away with respect. Loser walks away with a lesson."

Jack gathered the diced onions into a neat pile, transferred them to their container with methodical sweeps of his knife. His movements revealed nothing of his thoughts, his face remained composed in concentration on his task. But beneath that composed exterior, calculations were running – risk assessments as precise as those he'd once made eighty feet up a diseased oak.

"Not everybody gets invited," Decker added, a subtle emphasis suggesting the exclusivity was significant. "Most guys in here, they're all emotion, no control. They fight dirty, they take things personal." He selected another pepper, aligning it carefully before his knife descended. "What we need are men who can separate the fight from the feeling. Men who understand it's about establishing order, not chaos."

The kitchen supervisor called for the onions, and Jack slid the container down the prep line without breaking rhythm, immediately reaching for the next ingredient – potatoes that needed to be quartered for roasting. The knife felt familiar in his hand, its weight and balance assessed automatically as he positioned the first potato on his board.

Decker watched from the corner of his eye, noting how Jack's hands moved with the same controlled precision regardless of the ingredient before him. "You've got discipline," he observed. "That much is clear. Question is whether you've got the stomach for what needs doing."

Jack quartered the potato with four precise cuts, each applied with exactly the force required – no more, no less. The parallel to what Decker was proposing wasn't lost on him. Fighting as a system of control rather than emotional release. Violence as currency in an economy where protection was the most valuable commodity.

"Some guys can't separate the two," Decker continued. "They either can't fight at all, or they can't stop once they start." His knife paused momentarily. "Which one are you, West?"

Jack considered his position. Three weeks in, and already the careful neutrality he'd maintained was being challenged. He had intended to serve his time quietly, to keep his head down and stay out of the power struggles that defined prison life. But Cam's advice echoed in his mind – some invitations couldn't be refused without consequences. Some battles had to be fought to prevent worse ones.

His thoughts turned to Tabby, to the child growing inside her. To Ruby, who visited weekly with updates about the garden and nursery. What would they want him to do? The answer was simple – they would want him to come home. To survive. To do whatever was necessary to return to them intact, not just physically but in all the ways that mattered.

The fighting circuit Decker described offered both risk and protection. Refusing would mark him as weak or uncooperative – either made him a target. Accepting meant physical danger but also integration into a system that might shield him from random violence. The calculation was clear, even as his conscience rebelled against the compromise.

"First rule of the yard," Decker said, breaking into Jack's thoughts, "is understanding where you stand. Not just physically, but in the order of things." He slid his sliced peppers into their container, his movements efficient and practiced. "Right now, you're undefined. That makes people nervous. Nervous people do stupid things."

Jack cut through another potato, the knife's edge meeting the cutting board with a decisive sound. The logic was inescapable – in a place defined by hierarchies, remaining outside them wasn't an option. One either found their place or had it assigned to them, usually in the most painful way possible.

"Some guys think you're soft because you're quiet," Decker observed, his tone suggesting he wasn't among them. "Others think you're something else entirely." His eyes flicked briefly to Jack's hands, to the precise way they handled the knife. "I'm in the second camp, but opinions only go so far. Eventually, things need proving."

Jack aligned the next potato, considering Tabby's voice on the phone last week, steady despite the strain he could hear beneath her words. "We're going to be fine," she had said. "All of us." He thought of the baby coming in June, of the years that would pass before he could hold his child. Survival wasn't just about making it through each day – it was about ensuring he remained the man his family believed him to be.

The knife descended, separating the potato into perfect quarters. Jack set it down carefully, wiped his hands on the cloth tucked into his waistband, and for the first time, met Decker's gaze directly.

"When?" he asked, the single word carrying both his decision and his understanding of what it meant.

Something like approval flickered across Decker's face – not quite a smile, but a confirmation of something suspected. "Saturday," he replied. "Yard time. Bring nothing but yourself." He paused, studying Jack's expression. "You won't be matched your first time. Just watching. Learning the rules before you step in."

Jack gave a single, measured nod, neither eager nor reluctant, then returned to his task, picking up the knife and resuming the quartering of potatoes as if the conversation had never happened. His acceptance had been delivered with the same economy and precision as everything else he did.

Decker's mouth quirked into that almost-smile again. "Smart," he said. "Keep it just like that. No different after than before." He finished the last of his peppers as a guard moved into their section of the kitchen, clipboard in hand, performing a routine check of the prep stations.

"Back to my station," Decker said loudly enough for the guard to hear, the casual announcement covering his previous conversation. "Bell peppers are done, Jackson." He moved away smoothly, returning to the serving line with unhurried steps that suggested nothing of importance had transpired.

Jack continued working, his knife finding the same measured rhythm it had maintained before Decker's approach. To any observer – guard or inmate – he appeared unchanged, focused solely on his assigned task. Slice, quarter, stack, repeat. His face revealed nothing of the decision he'd just made or its potential consequences.

But beneath that controlled exterior, Jack's mind was already calculating angles, assessing what this new development meant for his survival strategy. The fighting circuit represented a variable he hadn't anticipated, a potential path through the years ahead that offered structure amid chaos. His acceptance wasn't about violence – it was about establishing boundaries, about defining his place in a system that would otherwise define it for him.

The knife moved through another potato, clean and precise. Jack felt the wedding band against his finger with each movement, a constant reminder of what waited beyond these walls. What mattered wasn't the fighting itself but what it protected – his identity, his future, his way back to Tabby and their child. In a place designed to strip away choice, he had found a small measure of agency – not in refusing the system, but in choosing how to navigate within it.

The potatoes accumulated in neat piles, each piece exactly the same size as the last. Jack worked on, outwardly calm and focused, while inside, he prepared for Saturday with methodical thoroughness– assessing risks, calculating approaches, determining exactly how much force would be required.

The recreation yard baked under the afternoon sun, concrete radiating heat like a kiln set to low. Jack stood with his back to the fence, just as he had during his confrontation with Moss, his eyes making their usual sweep of the yard's invisible territories. Three weeks and four days in, and already the patterns had revealed themselves to him – which inmates traveled in packs, which moved alone, which ones the guards watched and which they pretended not to see. He rotated the wedding band on his finger, the metal warm against his skin, and waited for Saturday.

Decker's invitation lingered in his thoughts. The fighting circuit. The rules. The structure within chaos. Jack had accepted with the understanding that survival here required more than just keeping to himself. It required definition – a clear signal to others about where he stood in the prison's unwritten hierarchy. Saturday would be his first glimpse into this system, an observation-only introduction to what might become a necessary part of his life inside.

A basketball bounced off the rim nearby, followed by good-natured cursing from the players. The weight bench across the yard hosted its usual occupants, men with arms sculpted into weapons through years of disciplined repetition. Guards stood at strategic intervals, attention seemingly casual but missing nothing of consequence. Jack had mapped their line of sight, noted the blind spots they allowed to exist by unspoken agreement. The space behind the maintenance shed – invisible from the guard towers, afforded just enough privacy for the circuit Decker had described.

Jack shifted his weight slightly, keeping his back against the fence. His eyes tracked movement without appearing to stare, cataloging changes, noting deviations from established patterns.

One such deviation approached from the basketball court – a man Jack had seen before but never spoken with. Medium height, leaner than Jack but with the compact, balanced build of someone who understood his body as a precision instrument rather than a blunt force tool. His movements as he crossed the yard were fluid and controlled, weight centered, steps measured. He wore the standard prison-issue clothing but carried himself differently than most inmates – not with swagger or aggression, but with the quiet certainty of someone who knew exactly what his body could do.

Jack recognized the walk. He'd seen it in professional climbers, in martial artists, in men who had trained their bodies to respond with practiced precision rather than raw instinct. This was someone who had spent thousands of hours perfecting specific movements, building muscle memory that had become second nature.

The man approached directly but unhurriedly, nothing in his manner suggesting threat or challenge, yet Jack felt the attention of nearby inmates shift subtly toward them. This interaction was being watched, assessed, its outcome already the subject of speculation. Jack maintained his position, neither advancing nor retreating, face composed in neutral observation.

"West," the man said when he reached conversational distance. Not a question. He stopped precisely at the boundary of personal space, balanced on the balls of his feet without seeming to be. His head was shaved close to the scalp, emphasizing the clean lines of his face and the prominent scar above his right eyebrow – the kind left by a significant impact rather than a blade. His arms were heavily tattooed, the designs a mix of classical boxing figures and stylized waves, their detailed execution suggesting time and money spent on quality work.

"I'm Dante," he continued when Jack acknowledged him with a slight nod. His voice was controlled like his movements – deliberate, measured, revealing exactly what he intended and nothing more. "Heard Decker talked to you about Saturday."

Jack studied the man before him, taking in the details that told a story beyond words. The specific calluses on Dante's hands – different from the weight-lifters, from the yard workers, from men who fought without training. The way he held his jaw, slightly forward but relaxed. The scar above his eyebrow, clean and precise in a way that suggested a professional cut man had tended to it. A boxer. Not just street fighting, but trained, disciplined ring work.

"He did," Jack confirmed, his own voice equally measured.

Dante nodded, a single economical movement. "Word travels. You accepted the invitation to watch." His eyes – dark, observant, assessing – moved over Jack with professional interest, taking note of his build, his stance, the way he distributed his weight. "I've got a different invitation."

Jack waited, silent. In the background, the basketball game continued, players shouting and laughing with deliberate volume, but Jack sensed the attention directed toward this exchange, the sidelong glances, the conversations that had paused mid-sentence.

"Saturday," Dante said, "you don't just watch. You participate." He shifted his weight slightly, the movement subtle but revealing to someone who knew what to look for. "With me."

The challenge hung in the air between them, its implications clear. This wasn't Decker's gradual introduction to the system – this was an immediate test, a fast-track into the hierarchy through direct confrontation with someone established. Jack kept his face neutral, but his mind calculated rapidly – what this meant, why it was happening, what accepting or refusing would signal to those watching.

"Decker said first-timers observe," Jack replied, neither agreeing nor refusing yet, testing the waters.

Dante's mouth curled slightly at one corner, not quite a smile. "Usually, yeah. But you're not the usual fish, are you?" His eyes flicked briefly to Jack's hand, to the wedding ring that had already been the focus of one confrontation. "Moss, then Decker approaching you directly... you're getting attention. That means you get tested sooner rather than later."

Jack understood the subtext. In prison, attention was currency, and he'd accumulated too much too quickly to remain undefined. The standard path wouldn't be available to him – he'd either step directly into the circuit or be marked as unwilling to defend his place.

"You've got the look," Dante continued, his voice dropping slightly so that only Jack could hear. "You're not just strong – you're controlled. Makes people curious what happens when that control gets tested."

Several inmates had drifted closer, their movements casual but their attention fixed on the exchange. Jack noted their positions without appearing to look, cataloged their affiliations based on who stood with whom. This moment would be discussed in cells and meal lines, analyzed and interpreted as part of the prison's constant assessment of strength and vulnerability.

"Saturday," Jack said finally, his voice revealing nothing of the calculations behind it. A statement, not a question.

Dante nodded. "Behind the maintenance shed. Second half of yard time. He studied Jack's face for a moment longer. "This isn't personal. It's necessary."

Jack met his gaze steadily. "I understand."

And he did. This wasn't about Dante, wasn't about Jack. It was about the system they existed within, about establishing order in a place designed to strip away identity and replace it with numbers. The fighting circuit wasn't violence for its own sake – it was control, structure, a way to define boundaries without the chaos of random attacks or the escalation of grudges.

"Good," Dante said, then added with that same not-quite-smile, "Been watching you move. You've got discipline. Makes for a better fight than most of these amateurs."

It was both compliment and warning – an acknowledgment of Jack's potential skill and a statement that Dante had been observing him long enough to assess it. Jack gave a single nod in response, neither cocky nor intimidated.

Dante turned to go, then paused. "One more thing," he said, glancing back. "Whatever training you've had, this isn't that. Different rules here. Different stakes." His eyes held Jack's for a moment. "Show respect, fight clean, you walk away with your standing improved regardless of outcome. Try anything else..." He let the sentence hang unfinished.

"Understood," Jack said, the word carrying his acceptance of both the challenge and its terms.

Dante nodded once more, then walked away with the same balanced, controlled movements with which he'd approached. The inmates who had been watching began to disperse, conversations resuming with new material to dissect. Jack remained against the fence, his posture unchanged, his expression revealing nothing of the thoughts moving behind his eyes.

Saturday had just become something different – not an observation but a trial by fire. His place in South Woods would be defined not by gradual integration but by immediate demonstration. Jack rotated the wedding band on his finger, feeling its familiar weight. The stakes had just increased, but the calculation remained the same – survive, maintain identity, find a path through the years ahead that would lead back to Tabby and their child.

He pushed off from the fence and began walking the perimeter of the yard, his pace measured, his eyes forward. To anyone watching, he appeared no different than he had before Dante's approach – contained, aware, neither seeking attention nor avoiding it. But inside, his mind had already shifted into preparation, assessing what skills he could rely on, what vulnerabilities he needed to protect, what this challenge meant for his survival strategy.

The whistle blew for the end of recreation time. Jack moved with the flow of inmates toward the doors, his face composed, his thoughts already on Saturday.

Night in South Woods had its own soundtrack – the rhythmic clank of cell checks, the muffled conversations that traveled through ventilation ducts, the occasional shout or laugh quickly hushed by guards making rounds. Fluorescent lights dimmed to half-power cast the cell in shadows that turned the institutional beige walls to muddy gray. Jack sat on the floor beside the bunks, back straight against the cold concrete wall, legs extended before him in a stretch that pulled at muscles grown tight from kitchen work. Above him, the ceiling bore the marks of previous occupants – faint scratches arranged in groups of five, counting days or weeks or months.

Cam lay on his bunk, one arm tucked behind his head, the other holding a dog-eared paperback with its spine creased to submission through multiple readings. He hadn't spoken since lockdown two hours earlier, but Jack could feel the weight of unasked questions in the cell's compressed air. Cam wasn't one to pry directly – his advice came packaged in observations, offered without demand for response. But tonight, his silence carried expectation, as if waiting for Jack to introduce the subject they both knew hung between them.

Jack switched positions, drawing one knee to his chest, extending the other leg. The concrete floor pressed hard against his tailbone, its unyielding surface a constant reminder of where he was. He rolled his shoulders methodically, cataloging the small clicks and pops of joints settling into alignment. A decade of climbing trees, of holding his body in unnatural positions while wielding dangerous equipment, had taught him the importance of maintenance – a body neglected was a body that failed when most needed.

That lesson had long since transcended tree work. Since Ruby's assault, hyper-vigilance had seeped into his routines like muscle memory, each workout a quiet act of preparation. He'd adapted his workouts to the prison environment, making up for the lack of proper equipment with an abundance of spare time but trained with the same purpose: a safeguard against vulnerability.

"You're fighting Dante on Saturday," Cam said finally, not looking up from his book, the statement delivered with the same casual tone he might use to comment on the weather. "Skipping the observation period. Interesting."

Jack continued his stretch, neither confirming nor denying. Cam's network of information was extensive, his sources reliable. If he said it was happening, others knew it too.

Cam closed his book, using a finger to mark his place, and turned his head to study Jack directly. "You know who he is, right? Not just another muscle-head with something to prove."

"Former boxer," Jack replied, switching to rotate his torso, feeling the stretch along his obliques. "Amateur level but trained."

Cam nodded, a slight smile touching the corner of his mouth. "Good. Knowing that already puts you ahead of most who've faced him." He sat up, swinging his legs over the side of the bunk, his feet finding the floor with practiced precision. The movement brought his scarred knuckles into the dim light – a roadmap of past confrontations etched into skin that had healed imperfectly multiple times.

"Prison fights aren't like street fights," Cam continued, his voice dropping lower, though the concrete walls ensured their conversation remained private. He flexed his hands unconsciously, the knuckles whitening then returning to their normal color. "Different rules. Different objectives."

Jack paused in his stretching, giving Cam his full attention. The older inmate rarely offered extended guidance without good reason.

"Most guys think it's about winning – putting the other man down, making him submit," Cam said, leaning forward slightly, elbows on his knees. "That's amateur thinking. Gets them hurt worse than necessary."

"What is it about then?" Jack asked, genuinely curious.

Cam's eyes fixed on some middle distance, as if reviewing memories cataloged by pain and consequence. "It's about showing you can take it. That you won't break." His gaze returned to Jack. "Win or lose isn't the point. How you handle yourself is what they're really watching for."

Jack nodded once, absorbing this. It aligned with his own assessment – the fighting circuit wasn't about violence for its own sake but about establishing order, defining boundaries and capabilities. About showing what kind of man you were under pressure.

"Stand up," Cam said suddenly, rising to his feet. "Let me show you something."

Jack complied, unfolding from the floor with fluid economy. The cell was cramped with both men standing – barely enough room to extend arms fully without touching the opposite wall. Cam positioned himself in the narrow space, his movements precise despite his size.

"Dante's a boxer," Cam said, raising his fists in a classic guard position. "He'll come at you with combinations – jab, cross, hook. Standard patterns." His scarred hands demonstrated each punch in slow motion, the movements clearly familiar to his body. "But this ain't a ring. No referee, no rounds, no points for technique." He lowered his hands slightly. "What matters is showing you can absorb what's thrown at you and still stand."

Jack watched attentively, noting the subtle weight shifts that telegraphed each movement. Cam wasn't just talking about fighting – he was offering a philosophy of survival, distilled through years of hard experience.

"You got any training?" Cam asked, eyes narrowing slightly as he studied Jack's stance.

Jack considered. "Nothing formal."

Cam nodded, seeming to read more in the vague answer than Jack had explicitly offered. "Well, whatever you've done, remember this: first minute sets the tone. Take the first few hits, show you're still there, then respond." He demonstrated a blocking motion, forearms raised to protect his face. "Don't try to dodge everything – that just pisses them off. Block, absorb, pick your moments."

Jack mirrored the position, muscle memory responding to the familiar stance. His own hands bore calluses in different patterns than Cam's – not from fighting primarily, but from years of rope work, of controlling chainsaws against the unpredictable forces of gravity and wood tension. Still, there were similarities in how his body understood leverage, balance, the physics of force applied and redirected.

"The other thing," Cam continued, dropping his hands and sitting back on his bunk, "is that these fights have limits. Unwritten rules, but real ones. No weapons. No eye gouging or groin shots. No continuing once someone's clearly done." His face hardened slightly. "Break those rules, you'll have bigger problems than whoever you're fighting."

Jack resumed his position on the floor, beginning another series of stretches focused on his core and lower back. The sounds of the prison night continued around them – a distant argument in another cell block, the squeak of guard boots on polished floors during rounds, the hum of the ventilation system laboring against the perpetual staleness of recycled air.

"Dante's got technique," Cam observed, watching Jack's methodical preparation. "Clean fighter, respects the boundaries. Not the type to carry a grudge if you show well against him." He paused, considering. "That's why they're putting you against him first. It's an assessment, not a punishment."

Jack nodded, understanding the distinction. He moved through another stretch, testing his range of motion, feeling for any hitches or limitations that might become vulnerabilities. His body responded with the reliable precision he'd maintained through disciplined care – muscles flexible but strong, joints stable, movements controlled.

"What they really want to know," Cam continued, "is whether you're the type who breaks under pressure or the type who finds another gear." His eyes tracked Jack's movements with professional assessment. "Once they know that, they know where to place you in the order of things."

Jack rolled onto his back, legs raised, stretching his hamstrings. The position felt vulnerable – exposed, defensive – but he maintained it, recognizing the parallel to what Saturday would bring. Sometimes the most important training was in making yourself uncomfortable, in learning to function through positions of disadvantage.

Jack rose from the floor, rolling his shoulders one final time before climbing onto his bunk. The thin mattress yielded reluctantly beneath his weight; its familiar lumps and depressions having become almost comforting in their consistency. He lay on his back, eyes fixed on the ceiling, mind cycling through scenarios for Saturday – approaches, responses, contingencies.

"One more thing," Cam said, voice lower now as lights-out approached. "Dante's got a tell. Right before he throws his power hand, his left shoulder drops just a fraction. Most guys don't notice 'cause they're watching his fists." He turned a page in his book, the paper rustling softly. "Might be useful."

Jack absorbed this information without comment, filing it away with all the other observations he'd been collecting. In the corridor outside, a guard's flashlight beam swept past their cell – the ten-minute warning before full lights-out. The prison's night rhythm continued its predictable progression, minutes ticking away toward Saturday.

"It's not about winning," Cam repeated, his voice barely audible now. "It's about showing them who you are. Make sure what you show is what you want them to see."

Jack closed his eyes, beginning the mental preparation that would continue through the night. Not visualization of victory, but calibration of response – how much to reveal, how much to withhold, how to navigate this test in a way that served his longer strategy. In his mind, he mapped the space behind the maintenance shed, calculated angles and distances, rehearsed movements that his body knew but rarely displayed.

The lights clicked off entirely, plunging the cell into darkness broken only by the faint glow from the corridor. Jack's breathing slowed, deepened, but his mind remained active, plotting trajectories through the years ahead, with Saturday marking just one necessary point on that long journey home.

15
The Fight

The space behind the maintenance shed had been cleared of its usual debris – empty paint cans and coiled hoses pushed against the far wall, creating a rough circle approximately twelve feet in diameter. Inmates formed the boundaries of this makeshift arena, bodies pressed shoulder to shoulder, faces arranged in expressions ranging from hungry anticipation to calculated assessment. The afternoon sun cast long shadows across the packed dirt, the angle providing just enough coverage from the nearest guard tower to make this gathering possible. Jack stood at the edge of the circle, breathing deeply and steadily, his face revealing nothing of the calculations running behind his eyes.

On the opposite side of the yard, a carefully orchestrated distraction unfolded – an argument over a basketball game escalating just enough to draw guard attention without triggering a lockdown. Three inmates, selected for their history of minor infractions and loud voices, created a perimeter of noise and movement that pulled focus from the maintenance shed's shadow. Jack noted the precision of the arrangement, the evidence of an established system that functioned with or without any single participant.

He stepped into the circle, bare-chested like the other fighters before him had been, prison-issue pants rolled up to mid-calf. The concrete had absorbed the day's heat, radiating warmth against his bare feet. Around him, conversations hushed to murmurs, assessments and wagers exchanged in undertones. He caught fragments – "new fish," "tree man," "Dante's fight" – but kept his focus internal, cataloging his own state with detached precision.

Heart rate: elevated but controlled. Breathing: deep and even. Muscles: loose, responsive, ready. Mind: clear, present, aware of surroundings but not distracted by them.

Movement on the opposite side of the circle drew his attention. Dante approached with the same controlled grace Jack had observed during their first encounter, his lean frame similarly bare-chested, the elaborate tattoos now fully visible across his torso and arms. Classical boxing figures intertwined with Japanese-style waves flowed over muscles that spoke of thousands of hours of disciplined training. The scar above his right eyebrow stood out starkly against his skin, a reminder that even skill could be overcome by sufficient force.

They met in the center of the circle, neither speaking, eyes locked in mutual assessment. Jack noted the balanced stance, the slight callusing on Dante's knuckles, the way he carried his weight centered and ready to shift in any direction. A boxer's posture, but adapted to the uneven surface beneath them, to the absence of gloves, to the different stakes of this encounter.

Someone in the crowd – Decker, Jack realized without looking – spoke a single word: "Begin."

Dante moved immediately, not rushing but setting the pace, establishing the rhythm of the encounter. His left jab shot out – a probe, a test, a question asked with knuckles instead of words. Jack slipped it with minimal movement, just enough to let the fist pass his cheekbone by centimeters. Dante nodded slightly, approval in the gesture, and followed with a combination – jab, cross, hook – textbook in its execution.

Jack blocked the cross with his forearm, absorbing the impact rather than avoiding it entirely, letting Dante feel the solidity of his defense. The hook he ducked under, moving just enough to make it miss without overcommitting to the evasion. Cam's advice echoed in his mind: Take the first few hits, show you're still there, then respond.

Dante pressed forward, increasing the tempo, testing Jack's reflexes and endurance with a series of quick combinations. His technique was clean, efficient, each punch thrown with purpose rather than anger or ego. Jack maintained his defensive posture, blocking what he could, slipping what he couldn't, absorbing the occasional blow that found its target. A fist grazed his ribs – a reminder rather than a serious attempt to damage.

The crowd around them had gone nearly silent, the usual shouts and taunts replaced by attentive observation. These men weren't watching for blood or dominance – they were studying technique, assessing capability, measuring both fighters against the unspoken standards of the yard.

Three minutes in – what would have been a full round in a sanctioned bout – and Jack had yet to throw a single punch. He'd moved only as much as necessary, conserving energy while allowing Dante to establish his patterns. Now, as Dante launched another combination, Jack saw what Cam had described – the slight drop of the left shoulder before the power hand came forward.

This time, instead of merely blocking, Jack moved. His response wasn't the wild counterpunch of an angry amateur but the precise redirection of someone who understood the physics of force and momentum. He stepped slightly inside Dante's punch, deflecting it outward with his forearm while simultaneously delivering a short, sharp blow to the floating ribs – not enough to damage, just enough to register.

Dante's eyes widened fractionally, reassessment visible in his expression. He nodded once, acknowledging the shift, and reset his stance. The next exchange came faster, Dante adjusting his approach now that he understood Jack wasn't merely defensive. Punches flew between them with increased intention, the sound of impact against flesh and bone punctuating the heavy breathing of both men.

Jack's movements revealed his training – not in boxing specifically, but in something more adaptable, more pragmatic. His responses weren't the programmed counters of a ring fighter but the efficient solutions of someone who had learned to handle force and threat in variable circumstances. When Dante threw a particularly fast combination, Jack didn't attempt to match his speed – instead, he absorbed what he could, redirected what he couldn't, and found the small opening that appeared when Dante committed to his power hand.

A murmur ran through the watching inmates as Jack landed a precise strike to Dante's solar plexus – not with enough force to end the fight, but sufficient to demonstrate that he could have. Dante stepped back, reassessing, respect visible in the slight inclination of his head. When he came forward again, it was with renewed focus, his techniques more varied, less predictable.

They continued this dance of calculated violence – Dante with his trained precision, Jack with his adaptive efficiency. Neither man attempted to humiliate the other, to cause unnecessary damage, to extend the encounter beyond what was required to establish capability. This wasn't about anger or dominance – it was about definition, about establishing parameters, about showing what kind of men they were under pressure.

Sweat glistened on both their bodies, dirt from the ground mixed with small smears of blood where knuckles had split skin. Jack tasted copper in his mouth from a well-placed jab that had caught his lower lip against his teeth. Dante sported a rapidly swelling mark high on his cheekbone where Jack's elbow had connected during a close exchange. Neither man showed pain or fatigue in their expressions – only focused attention, mutual assessment, professional respect.

The decisive moment came eight minutes in. Dante, perhaps recognizing that time was limited before the distraction across the yard would lose effectiveness, committed to a powerful combination designed to end the exchange definitively. Jack recognized the setup – had been watching for it – and made his decision in the fraction of a second between recognition and impact.

As Dante's power hand came forward, Jack moved not away but toward it, stepping inside Dante's reach at precisely the angle that transformed the punch's force into rotational energy. His own counter wasn't a punch but a precise application of leverage against Dante's extended arm, using the boxer's momentum and weight against him. Dante found himself off-balance, his center of gravity compromised, his training suddenly irrelevant to the physics being applied to his body.

Jack could have followed through – could have taken Dante to the ground, could have established dominance through superior position. Instead, he controlled the movement, allowing Dante to catch himself before falling, while simultaneously delivering a single, precise strike to the side of his jaw – just enough force to demonstrate what could have happened, not enough to cause real damage or loss of consciousness.

They separated, both breathing hard now, eyes locked in mutual acknowledgment. Blood trickled from Dante's lip, matching the smear on Jack's. Neither man moved to wipe it away. Around them, the circle of inmates remained silent, witnessing not just the physical exchange but the unspoken communication between the fighters.

"Enough," Dante said finally, straightening to his full height, no defeat in his posture but clear recognition in his eyes. He extended his hand – not in surrender but in acknowledgment, fighter to fighter.

Jack took it without hesitation, the handshake firm but not challenging. Something passed between them in that contact – respect, understanding, a boundary established and accepted.

The crowd began to disperse immediately, trained by experience to break up before guards could redirect their attention from the now-concluding distraction across the yard. Conversations resumed at normal volume, the fight already being analyzed, assessed, incorporated into the prison's complex social calculations.

Jack caught sight of Cam at the edge of the circle, the older inmate's face revealing nothing to casual observers but communicating volumes to Jack. A slight nod, a fractional relaxation around the eyes – acknowledgment that something important had been established.

"West held his own," Cam said to no one in particular as he turned away, his voice carrying just enough to reach those nearby. The simple statement, coming from someone of Cam's standing, carried more weight than any shouted celebration could have.

Jack retrieved his shirt from where he'd left it folded, pulling it over his head with unhurried movements that revealed neither pain nor triumph. His body would feel the effects tomorrow – bruises forming beneath the skin, muscles protesting the sudden intensity of use – but his expression showed nothing but calm focus.

Dante approached as Jack prepared to leave, the circle now empty except for them. "Good fight," he said simply, his voice pitched for Jack's ears alone. "Not many surprises in here. You're one." He studied Jack's face for a moment. "Where'd you learn to move like that?"

Jack considered his answer carefully. "Trees," he said finally. "When you're eighty feet up with a chainsaw, you learn how things fall. How to direct force."

Dante nodded, understanding flickering in his eyes. "Makes sense." He touched his jaw where Jack's final strike had landed. "Next time won't be so straightforward."

The statement wasn't a threat but a promise – Jack had earned his place in the circuit, would be matched again, would be expected to continue proving himself. Jack nodded once, accepting this new reality.

As they walked together toward the yard's main area, rejoining the general population with deliberate casualness, Jack felt the subtle shift in how others looked at him – not with the assessing hunger reserved for new arrivals, but with the measured respect given to someone whose boundaries had been established. It wasn't friendship or safety, not exactly, but it was definition in a place where being undefined was the greatest vulnerability.

He touched his wedding band briefly, the metal warm against his skin. This fight, like everything else he did inside these walls, was about survival – about finding a path through the years ahead that would lead back to Tabby and their child. Today he had taken another step on that path, had secured another small measure of control in a place designed to strip it away.

The yard whistle blew, signaling the end of recreation time. Jack moved with the flow of inmates toward the doors, his face composed, his thoughts already turning to the next challenge, the next adaptation, the next necessary compromise in service of the only goal that mattered – making it home.

The visitation room hummed with muted conversations, each table hosting its own island of reunion - mothers clutching hands of sons, wives leaning forward to catch every word from husbands, children fidgeting under the watchful eyes of guards stationed along the walls. Jack sat with his back straight, hands resting on the scratched metal table, fingers spread wide as if to anchor himself to this moment of connection with the outside world. He had arrived early, as he did for every visit, using the extra minutes to compose himself, to prepare the version of prison life he would present to Tabby – honest enough to respect her intelligence, edited enough to spare her unnecessary worry.

A week had passed since his fight with Dante, but the evidence remained – a darkening bruise high on his left cheekbone, impossible to hide under the harsh fluorescent lights that turned everyone's skin sallow and unforgiving. Jack had considered the bruise that morning while shaving, his reflection in the polished metal mirror revealing what would be the first thing Tabby noticed. He hadn't tried to conceal it; such attempts would only draw more attention; make it seem as though he were ashamed. And he wasn't. The fight had been necessary, calculated, a deliberate step in establishing his place within South Woods' complex social hierarchy.

Around him, other inmates sat in identical plastic chairs, their bodies displaying varying degrees of tension or relief as they interacted with their visitors. A heavyset man three tables away cradled an infant in arms covered with faded tattoos, his weathered face transformed by wonder as he counted tiny fingers. Near the door, another inmate leaned toward an elderly woman – his mother, perhaps – their foreheads nearly touching as they spoke in whispers. Each visit represented a tether to the world beyond concrete and steel, a reminder of the lives waiting to be resumed when sentences ended.

Jack rotated his wedding band with his thumb, the now-familiar gesture centering him as his eyes tracked the door through which Tabby would enter. Saturday visits had become the axis around which his weeks revolved, the point toward which all other days either built or fell away from. In the months since his incarceration, he'd come to measure time differently – not in days or weeks, but in the intervals between seeing her face, hearing her voice unfiltered by phone lines and distance.

The door opened, and Jack's attention sharpened. Tabby entered first, her pregnant belly now prominent beneath a loose-fitting dress patterned with small blue flowers. Her hair was pulled back in a simple ponytail, her face free of makeup but glowing with the increased circulation of late pregnancy. Behind her came Jason, carrying what looked like a manila envelope, his expression open and relaxed until his eyes found Jack's face.

Jack stood as they approached, the automatic response of courtesy ingrained despite his surroundings. Tabby reached him first, her smile warm but her eyes immediately finding the bruise on his cheek, cataloging it with the quick assessment he'd come to recognize – her way of checking his overall condition without obvious scrutiny. She stretched up to kiss him, her belly creating distance between them that hadn't existed during earlier visits.

"Hi," she said simply, the word carrying layers of meaning beyond its single syllable.

"Hi," Jack replied, his hand briefly touching her face before they both sat down.

Jason remained standing a moment longer, his gaze fixed on Jack's bruise, his brow furrowing with concern that rapidly transformed into something harder to categorize – disappointment mixed with anger, perhaps. When he finally sat, it was with a deliberateness that suggested he was restraining himself from immediate commentary.

"How are you feeling?" Jason asked instead of a greeting, his voice tight with suppressed emotion. "That looks painful."

Jack met his gaze directly. "It's fine. Looks worse than it is."

Recognizing the tension, Tabby interjected. "The baby's been kicking like crazy," she said, a deliberate change of subject. "Especially at night. I think he's got your sleep schedule."

But Jason wasn't ready to be diverted. He leaned forward, lowering his voice just enough to keep the conversation private without drawing attention from the guards. "What happened to your face, Jack?"

The fluorescent light buzzed overhead, casting harsh shadows that emphasized the discoloration on Jack's cheekbone. He didn't flinch under Jason's scrutiny, his expression remaining calm, composed.

"I got hit," he said simply. "It happens."

"It happens?" Jason repeated, incredulity raising his voice enough that a nearby guard glanced in their direction. He immediately modulated his tone, leaning closer. "You're fighting? Is that what you're telling us?"

Jack's thumb continued its unconscious rotation of his wedding band. "Yes."

The single word hung between them, neither explanation nor apology. Tabby's hands tightened slightly, but her face remained composed, revealing none of the inner conflict that surely accompanied this confirmation.

Jason sat back, running a hand through his hair in a gesture of frustration. "Jesus, Jack. That's not—" He stopped, recalibrated. "I mean, I thought you were going to keep your head down, stay out of trouble."

"I am," Jack replied, his voice even. "This isn't trouble. It's the opposite."

Jason's eyes widened, disbelief evident in the set of his jaw. "Getting punched in the face is 'the opposite' of trouble? What kind of logic is that?"

A family at the next table laughed at something their visiting son had said, the sound jarring against the tension surrounding Jack's table. He waited for the moment to pass before responding, measuring his words with characteristic precision.

"The kind that keeps you alive in here," he said finally. "There are rules. Systems. Ways things work that don't make sense outside but are essential in here."

"So, what – you're just going along with whatever barbaric rituals they've got going on? Letting yourself get beaten up as some kind of initiation?" Jason's voice carried both concern and judgment.

"It wasn't an initiation," Jack corrected, his eyes steady on Jason's. "It was a test. And I passed."

Tabby had remained silent, her eyes moving between the two men, assessing the growing tension. Now she spoke, her voice calm but firm. "Maybe you could explain it to us, Jack. Help us understand what's happening."

Jack considered her request, weighing how much to reveal, how to translate the complex unwritten codes of prison life into terms they could comprehend without causing more worry than necessary. The bruise on his face throbbed dully, a reminder of what he'd gained through that controlled violence – not just respect, but definition, a place in the order of things that would make the years ahead survivable.

"There's a hierarchy here," he began, his voice low enough to ensure privacy. "Not the official one with guards and wardens, but the real one that determines day-to-day life. Where you sit in the mess hall, which shower you use, whether someone takes what belongs to you." His eyes met Jason's directly. "Whether you get targeted or left alone."

Jason's expression remained troubled, his idealism visibly battling with the harsh reality Jack was describing. "And you have to fight to establish your place in this hierarchy? That's what you're saying?"

"Sometimes," Jack acknowledged. "Not randomly. Not out of anger. It's... structured. It's survival," he said instead. "A way to establish boundaries without worse alternatives."

The fluorescent lights buzzed and flickered overhead, casting momentary shadows across the table before stabilizing again. In that brief dimming, Jack saw something shift in Jason's expression – not acceptance, exactly, but the first recognition that his outside perspective might not fully apply to Jack's current reality.

"So this," Jason gestured toward Jack's bruise, "was deliberate? You didn't just get jumped in a corridor somewhere?"

"No," Jack confirmed. "It was controlled. Consensual. With rules."

Jason shook his head slightly, struggling to reconcile Jack's willingness to become involved in the prison hierarchy. "I just never thought you'd be the type to—"

"To adapt?" Jack finished for him, a rare edge entering his voice. "To do what's necessary to survive until I can come home to my family?"

The words hung between them, heavy with implications neither man was ready to fully articulate. Jason leaned forward, his shoulders hunched as if physically bracing against Jack's words. His hand, resting on the table's edge, curled into a loose fist that tightened with each passing second. The fluorescent light caught the gold of his watch – a graduation gift from his father – creating a small beacon of outside prosperity that seemed almost obscene against the institutional drabness surrounding them. When he spoke again, his voice carried the particular strain of someone trying to contain emotion within the boundaries of public decorum.

"I mean, they must have programs, counselors – people whose actual job is to prevent this kind of thing." His voice rose slightly with each suggestion, as if volume could bridge the gap between his idealism and Jack's reality. "There have to be other ways, Jack," he insisted, his free hand gesturing emphatically. Something that doesn't involve getting your face rearranged."

Jack remained still, his posture neither defensive nor confrontational. A nearby guard glanced in their direction, his expression a practiced blend of boredom and assessment as he cataloged the interaction for potential trouble.

"Lower your voice," Jack said quietly, his eyes flicking briefly toward the guard. "Drawing attention doesn't help anyone."

Jason followed Jack's glance, noted the guard's scrutiny, and immediately modulated his tone, though the intensity remained. He leaned closer across the table, his gestures becoming more contained but no less urgent.

"I just don't understand how you, of all people, could buy into this." The disappointment in his voice was palpable. "You've got so much to lose. And now you're telling me that punching your way up some prison food chain is your best option?"

Tabby, who had been watching the exchange with growing concern, placed her other hand on her rounded belly as if protectively shielding the baby from the tension at the table. Her expression contained none of Jason's overt judgment, but her eyes betrayed her own worry as they lingered on Jack's bruised face.

"If you show up missing teeth next time," she said, her tone striking a delicate balance between humor and severity, "I'm revoking your visitation privileges." The corner of her mouth lifted in what almost passed for a smile, but her eyes remained serious. "I mean it, Jack. I need you in one piece when you come home."

The small joke defused some of the immediate tension, creating space for Jack to respond without direct confrontation. His eyes met Tabby's, something passing between them that Jason couldn't fully interpret – an acknowledgment, perhaps, of concerns that didn't need voicing to be understood.

"I'm not looking for fights," Jack said, his voice level. "But this place doesn't allow for passive existence." He spread his hands flat on the table, a deliberate gesture that revealed the scrapes across his knuckles – evidence that he'd given as well as received in the encounter that had marked his face. "There's no neutral ground here. You're either established or you're vulnerable. There's no third option."

Jason shook his head, frustration evident in the tight line of his mouth. "There's always another way."

"Not in here," Jack replied, the words carrying the weight of certainty born from direct experience rather than theoretical understanding. "Prison isn't about rehabilitation or justice or any of the things they tell society it's about. It's about containment. And within that containment, we create our own systems."

He leaned forward slightly, his voice dropping lower, compelling both Tabby and Jason to lean in as well. "The official rules mean nothing compared to the unwritten ones. Who sits where in the mess hall isn't random – it's a map of alliances and territories. Which work detail you get assigned to determines not just your daily routine but your access to resources, to information, to protection." His eyes held Jason's steadily. "And all of it – every interaction, every exchange, every conversation – happens within a framework of established respect. That respect isn't freely given," he explained. "It's earned or taken. The bruise you're so concerned about? It represents something valuable – recognition. I've been defined now. Categorized as someone who can handle himself, who has boundaries that should be respected."

Tabby's hand tightened slightly, her eyes never leaving his face. "And if you hadn't earned that recognition?" she asked, her question cutting directly to what concerned her most.

Jack's expression remained composed, but something darkened in his eyes. "Then I'd be having a very different experience here." He glanced briefly around the room, his gaze pausing on specific inmates – ones who sat hunched, eyes downcast, bodies angled to appear smaller, less noticeable. "See the guy three tables over? Brown hair, thin, keeps looking at the floor?"

Jason and Tabby both glanced over, careful not to stare.

"He's been here two months. Refused to engage with the system, thought he could just keep to himself, stay neutral." Jack's voice remained even, clinical almost, as if describing a case study rather than a human being. "Someone takes his commissary every week. He's been moved to three different cells because his cellmates complained to the guards. Last week, he 'slipped' in the shower. Broke his wrist."

Jason's expression shifted from frustration to something more complex – discomfort mingled with the first hints of reluctant understanding. "And you know this how?"

"People talk," Jack replied simply. "Information is currency here. Everything is observed, analyzed, traded." He ran a hand through his hair, a rare gesture that betrayed the emotional toll of this conversation. "I'm not saying it's right. I'm saying it's real. And pretending it isn't won't keep me safe until I can come home."

The contrast between them had never been more apparent –They sat less than three feet apart, separated by a metal table and a chasm of experience that seemed to widen with each exchange.

"The guy who did this to your face," Jason persisted, unable to fully concede the point, "he just gets away with it? That's the system working?"

A shadow of something almost like amusement crossed Jack's face. "Who says I didn't give as good as I got?"

Tabby made a small sound – not quite a laugh, not quite a sigh. "That's not as reassuring as you think it is, Jack."

"It wasn't about winning or losing," Jack explained, echoing Cam's words from before the fight. "It was about showing what kind of man I am under pressure. About establishing parameters." He looked directly at Jason now. "The guy who hit me? We nodded to each other in the yard yesterday. No animosity, no lingering tension. Just mutual respect. Because now we both know where we stand."

Jason shook his head again. His eyes moved from Jack's bruised face to his steady hands resting on the table, to the controlled way he held himself even in this moment of confrontation. The idealism that fueled his outrage was meeting the unyielding wall of Jack's lived experience. Jason said. "This place doesn't have to change who you are at your core. You can choose to be better than that." His eyes held a particular kind of righteousness that came from never having been tested beyond his principles, from believing that moral strength alone could overcome any circumstance.

Something flickered across Jack's face – a brief disruption of the composed mask he'd maintained throughout their conversation. His hands, which had been relaxed on the table, tensed visibly, fingers curling inward before he deliberately flattened them again. The muscles in his jaw worked beneath the skin as he stared at Jason with an intensity that hadn't been present before.

"Better," Jack repeated, the single word carrying a weight that transformed it from echo to challenge. For the first time since they'd sat down, true anger showed in his eyes – not the controlled irritation of their earlier exchange, but something deeper, rawer. He leaned forward, lowering his voice not just for privacy now but to contain the emotion that threatened to break through his carefully maintained control.

"You think I haven't considered what's 'better'?" His voice had dropped to just above a whisper, forcing Jason and Tabby to lean in to hear him. "You think I wake up every morning in that cell and don't immediately calculate every decision against what keeps me alive and what keeps me recognizable to myself? To my family?"

Jack's wedding band caught the light as his hand tightened into a fist, then deliberately relaxed again. The bruise on his cheekbone seemed to darken as blood rushed to his face, though his voice remained precisely modulated despite the emotion behind it.

"This isn't about moral high ground, Jason. It's not about being 'better' or 'worse' than the system. It's about surviving it with enough of myself intact to be a husband when I get out." His eyes flicked briefly to Tabby's rounded belly. "To be a father. Every decision I make in here is measured against that single goal."

He glanced quickly at the nearest guard, ensuring their conversation remained private, then continued. "You walk in here for one hour a week, look at my face, and think you understand what choices I have available to me. You don't. You can't." The words weren't delivered as an attack but as a statement of irrefutable fact. "I live twenty-four hours a day in a world designed to strip away everything that makes me human, and I'm finding ways to hold onto those things despite it."

Jason opened his mouth to respond, but before he could, Tabby interrupted, "Jack," she said softly, neither agreeing nor disagreeing with his position, simply acknowledging him. The single syllable of his name carried recognition of both his struggle and his strength.

Jack's eyes met hers, and something passed between them – an understanding that transcended the need for explanation or justification. His breathing slowed, the tension in his shoulders easing slightly as he accepted her silent support.

Jason watched this exchange, his expression shifting with the first hints of genuine comprehension. His hands, which had been gesturing emphatically throughout their conversation, now rested still on the table, his fingers curled loosely inward as if physically holding back further arguments.

"I don't want this place to change you," he said finally, his voice quieter than before. "None of us do."

"It will," Jack replied, the simple truth of the statement hanging between them. "That's inevitable. The question is whether those changes are ones I choose or ones that are forced on me. I'm choosing, as much as possible, which parts adapt, and which parts remain untouched."

Around them, other visits continued – reunions and arguments and silent communions playing out at identical tables, each one representing its own complex negotiation between inside and outside worlds.

After a moment of weighted silence, Tabby spoke. "The oak in the backyard is budding," she said, deliberately shifting the conversation toward neutral ground. "Ruby says it's going to be a good year for it. The branches look strong."

Jack accepted the change of subject with visible relief, his posture softening slightly. "Did she clear away the dead branches from the south side?"

"Jason helped her with that last weekend," Tabby replied, glancing at Jason with a small smile that invited him to join this less contentious conversation. "They filled almost three yard waste bins."

Jason nodded, accepting the olive branch. "That tree is massive. Ruby said you've been maintaining it?"

"Yeah," Jack confirmed. "The previous owners neglected it. It needed structural pruning, removal of crossed branches." As he spoke about trees, his expertise showed in the precision of his language, the confidence of his assessments. This was familiar territory, a reminder of the identity that existed beyond prison walls.

The conversation continued in this vein – mundane updates about the garden, questions about the nursery preparations, discussions of the changing neighborhood. With each exchange, the earlier tension receded further, though it never fully disappeared. It remained as an undercurrent, acknowledged but temporarily set aside by mutual consent.

As their allotted time neared its end, Jack looked directly at Jason again, his expression open but resolute. "I hear your concern," he said, returning briefly to their earlier discussion. "I'm not looking for fights. I'm not becoming someone else." He touched his bruised cheek lightly. "But I need you to understand that survival in here sometimes requires things that don't make sense outside."

Jason held his gaze for a long moment before nodding slowly. "I don't like it," he admitted. "But I'm trying to understand."

"That's all I'm asking," Jack replied.

Tabby placed both hands on her belly, a small smile touching her lips as she felt movement within. "Your son is doing somersaults," she said to Jack. "I think he's trying to remind us what's actually important."

Jack's expression softened as he looked at her rounded form, his eyes reflecting both longing and determination. "June isn't far away," he said, the calendar of his sentence momentarily recalibrated to measure time not in years remaining but in weeks until his child's birth.

"I'll bring him to visit as soon as they allow it," Tabby promised, her voice even despite the emotion visible in her eyes. "He'll know your voice, your face."

The overhead speaker crackled to life, a disembodied voice announcing that visiting hours would end in five minutes. The room filled with the sounds of hurried final exchanges, of chairs scraping back, of promises to return next week. The guard nearest to their table straightened, his posture indicating the imminent enforcement of the time limit.

"I'll be careful," Jack said, addressing both of them but looking primarily at Tabby. "I promise. But I'll also do what's necessary to come home to you. To him." His hand moved briefly toward her belly, aware of the rules against extended physical contact.

Jason stood, collecting the manila envelope he'd brought – paperwork for the nursery, forms that needed Jack's signature, the bureaucratic requirements of parenthood that continued despite incarceration. "We'll see you next Saturday," he said, his tone suggesting that despite their disagreement, his support remained unwavering.

Jack nodded, rising to his feet as well. "Thank you for coming. Both of you."

Tabby stood with more difficulty, one hand supporting her lower back as she shifted her weight to accommodate her changing center of gravity. The fluorescent lights cast harsh shadows across her face, emphasizing the tired circles beneath her eyes.

"I love you," she said simply, the words carrying more weight here than they might have in the comfort of their home.

"I love you too," Jack replied, his voice steady but his eyes revealing the depth of emotion behind the simple phrase.

The guard called time, ending their visit with the same impersonal efficiency that governed all aspects of prison life. As Jack watched them walk toward the exit, Tabby's hand resting lightly on Jason's arm for support, he remained standing until they had passed through the door. Only then did he sit, his back straight, his face composed, the brief window into his outside life closing as visibly as the heavy door through which they had departed.

Around him, other inmates were being led back to their respective blocks, their expressions ranging from the temporary lift of having connected with loved ones to the crash that often followed such moments of normalcy. Jack joined the line forming at the exit, his thoughts already shifting back to the careful navigation of prison life, to the calculations of survival that Jason could critique but would never truly understand.

The bruise on his cheek throbbed dully as he walked, a reminder of the boundaries he had established, the respect he had earned. It would fade in time, but what it represented would remain – his choice to adapt rather than break, to find a way through this place that would allow him to return to Tabby and their child not just physically intact, but recognizable as the man they needed him to be.

16
The Baiting Attempt

The mess hall gleamed with the particular dullness of industrial surfaces designed to be cleaned with minimal effort - stainless steel serving counters worn to a matte finish by years of wiping, tables bolted to the floor whose once-sharp edges had been rounded by thousands of arms and elbows. Jack moved through the lunch line with practiced efficiency, eyes scanning the room without appearing to, cataloging the invisible territories and alliances that shifted subtly from day to day like tectonic plates beneath the prison's surface. Six weeks into his sentence, and already the map had become second nature - which tables belonged to which groups, where the guards focused their attention, which corners offered the illusion of privacy amid constant surveillance.

His tray contained the usual Wednesday offering – a pale imitation of meatloaf, mashed potatoes that bore more resemblance to plaster than food, limp green beans floating in cloudy water. Jack accepted each portion without comment, his face maintaining the neutral expression he'd perfected since arrival – alert but not anxious, present but not provocative. The bruise on his cheekbone from the fight with Dante had faded to a yellowish smudge, visible but no longer the first thing anyone noticed about him.

Cam waved from their usual table. Jack nodded in acknowledgment but didn't immediately head in that direction. Instead, he paused, noting a subtle shift in the room's energy – the slight redirection of attention, the microscopic adjustments in posture among certain inmates, the way conversations dipped then resumed at a different pitch. Someone was watching him with more than casual interest.

He collected his utensils – plastic sporks that couldn't be fashioned into weapons without considerable ingenuity – and turned, identifying the source of that attention without appearing to look directly. Three tables away sat a man Jack knew by reputation but had never directly interacted with. Harlow – no first name ever used – occupied a complex position in South Woods' hierarchy. Not physically imposing like the weight-bench crowd, not connected enough to command a crew like Decker, but possessing a different kind of currency – information, gossip, the small details of inmates' lives that could be weaponized with precision. His lean face housed eyes that missed nothing, cataloging weaknesses with the methodical patience of someone who collected vulnerabilities the way others collected commissary items.

Jack moved toward Cam's table; his path deliberate and unhurried. As he passed within earshot of Harlow's position, he felt rather than saw the man's attention sharpen, like a predator noting the proximity of potential prey. Jack maintained his pace, revealing nothing in his posture or expression, though his senses heightened to the subtle threat emanating from that table.

"West," Cam greeted him as he set his tray down. "Kitchen duty again tomorrow?"

"Yeah," Jack confirmed, taking his seat with his back to the wall, a position that allowed him to observe most of the mess hall without obvious surveillance. "Prep for Thursday's dinner."

Their conversation continued in this vein – mundane exchanges about work assignments, a brief mention of yard time schedules, commentary on the meatloaf that managed to be both overcooked and undercooked simultaneously. But beneath this ordinary interaction, Jack remained aware of Harlow's periodic glances, the considering calculation visible in the man's expression even from across the intervening space.

"You've caught someone's interest," Cam observed quietly, his back to the room but his awareness no less acute for it. "Harlow's been watching you since you walked in."

Jack nodded slightly, neither concerned nor dismissive. "Noticed that."

"He collects things," Cam said, his voice dropping further. "Not physical items. Information. Pressure points." He took a bite of meatloaf, chewed thoroughly before continuing. "Been here nine years. Never been in a fight that anyone knows of. Doesn't need to be."

The subtext was clear – Harlow represented a different kind of danger than Moss or Dante had posed. Not physical intimidation but psychological manipulation. Jack filed this away, adding it to his mental map of South Woods' complex terrain.

"What's his angle?" Jack asked, eyes briefly meeting Cam's before returning to a neutral middle distance.

Cam shrugged one shoulder. "Hard to say. Sometimes it's commissary. Sometimes it's just amusement." He speared a green bean with his spork. "Sometimes it's proving he can get to anyone, even the steady ones."

Jack continued eating, his movements unhurried despite the new awareness that prickled along his spine. Harlow represented an inevitable test – different in nature from his confrontation with Dante but no less significant for his standing within the prison hierarchy. How he handled it would define yet another aspect of his identity here.

As if summoned by their conversation, Harlow appeared at the edge of their table, tray in hand, expression arranged in a careful approximation of casual interest.

"Mind if I join?" he asked, the question clearly rhetorical as he was already setting his tray down across from Jack. "Cam, West." He nodded to each of them in turn, a small smile playing at the corners of his mouth that never reached his eyes. Those remained coolly observant, taking in Jack's neutral expression, the fading bruise on his cheekbone, the wedding band on his left hand.

Cam's face revealed nothing of his thoughts, but Jack noted the slight tension that entered his cellmate's shoulders – not fear exactly, but heightened vigilance. Interesting. Cam had faced down men twice Harlow's size without visible concern, yet this lean, unimposing inmate with his careful smile warranted particular caution.

"Free country," Cam replied, the irony of the statement hanging in the air between them.

Harlow laughed – a practiced sound that contained no genuine amusement. "Figure of speech," he acknowledged, then turned his attention fully to Jack. "Been meaning to introduce myself properly. Heard a lot about you."

Jack met his gaze directly, neither challenging nor submissive. "That so."

"Your fight with Dante made an impression," Harlow continued, cutting his meatloaf into precise squares though he made no move to eat it. "Not many new arrivals get invited into the circle that quickly. Fewer still hold their own when they do." His eyes flicked to Jack's cheekbone. "Though I see you didn't come away unmarked."

Jack said nothing, recognizing the comment for what it was – not a genuine observation but a probe, testing for sensitivity, for pride, for any reaction that might reveal a vulnerability.

"Still," Harlow pressed on in the face of Jack's silence, "impressive debut. Established your physical credentials quite effectively." His emphasis on 'physical' carried clear implication – that other forms of testing remained.

Cam shifted slightly, the movement barely perceptible but communicating his assessment of the situation. This wasn't a random conversation. This was calculated, planned, a deliberate approach with specific intent.

"Heard you had a visit last weekend," Harlow said, his tone conversational but his eyes watchful. "Wife, wasn't it? And a friend?" The question carried a subtle emphasis on the word 'friend' that couldn't be accidental.

Jack took another bite of his food, chewed unhurriedly, swallowed. His face remained composed, but beneath the table, his hand tightened momentarily before deliberately relaxing.

"That's right," he confirmed, offering nothing more.

Harlow nodded as if Jack had provided some fascinating insight. "Pregnant, I hear. Pretty far along now, isn't she?" He pushed his food around his plate, gaze now directed downward as if the conversation were merely casual. "Must be difficult, missing all that. The changes, the preparations."

The mess hall's ambient noise seemed to recede as Jack focused on maintaining his composure. This wasn't just conversation – this was reconnaissance, probing for reaction, for weakness. Harlow hadn't randomly approached their table. He'd come with purpose, with a strategy in mind.

"Life continues," Jack said, his voice neutral. "Inside and out."

"Indeed it does," Harlow agreed, a new edge entering his voice despite the pleasant expression he maintained. "Though differently in different places, wouldn't you say? The rules change depending on which side of these walls you're on."

Jack felt rather than saw Cam's subtle shift – a minute tensing that suggested he recognized where this conversation was heading. Around them, lunch continued, inmates moving through their routines, guards maintaining their positions along the walls, but Jack sensed a bubble of focused attention forming around their table. Others were watching, assessing, waiting to see how this exchange would unfold.

"Your wife seems devoted," Harlow continued, the observation delivered with practiced casualness that didn't match the calculated gleam in his eyes. "Coming every visiting day, bringing updates about the home, the baby preparations. Admirable."

Jack took a sip of water, allowing himself that moment to maintain control. His wedding band caught the fluorescent light as he set his cup down, the metal warm against his skin.

"Some women find it difficult, though," Harlow added, his voice dropping slightly as if sharing a confidence. "The separation. The loneliness. Especially with a baby coming." He glanced around the mess hall before leaning forward slightly. "You know Morgan in Unit 3? His wife visited every week for the first three months. Then every other week. Then once a month. Now?" He shrugged eloquently. "Been six months since she's been seen."

Jack maintained his steady rhythm of eating, though the food had lost any semblance of taste. His jaw tightened imperceptibly beneath the skin, but his eyes remained level, revealing nothing of the heat building in his chest.

"Then there's Diaz," Harlow continued, warming to his theme. "Found out his girl was seeing his cousin two months after he got sent up. Eight years they'd been together." He shook his head in mock sympathy. "And Williams – remember him, Cam? Wife divorced him year two of a five-year stretch. Remarried six weeks later."

Cam grunted noncommittally, his eyes moving between Jack and Harlow with increased vigilance. The strategy was becoming clear now – not random cruelty but targeted provocation, designed to test Jack's emotional control, to find the pressure point that would crack his composed exterior.

"Of course," Harlow said, his voice taking on a confidential tone, "your situation's different. Strong relationship, baby on the way. Solid friend supporting her." His emphasis on 'friend' was unmistakable now. "What's his name again? The one who comes with her to visits?"

The question hung in the air between them, its barbed intent fully exposed. Jack felt a surge of heat rise from his chest to his throat – not just anger but a more complex emotion, a protective instinct tied to Tabby, to their unborn child, to the life he'd left behind. His fingers remained steady on his spork, but it took conscious effort to maintain that control.

"Jason," he answered, voice level despite the emotion building beneath it. He met Harlow's gaze directly, neither challenging nor retreating. "My wife's friend. My friend."

Harlow nodded, a small smile playing at the corners of his mouth. "Loyal friends are rare. Especially ones willing to step in when a man's... unavailable." He glanced meaningfully around the mess hall. "Ten years is a long time, West. A lot can change. Especially with a woman whose needs aren't being met."

Several inmates at nearby tables had gone quiet, their attention fixed on this exchange while pretending to focus on their meals. The confrontation with Dante had established Jack's physical boundaries; this interaction would define his psychological ones.

Jack's hand remained steady as he set down his spork, though beneath the table, his other hand had curled into a tight fist, knuckles white with the effort of restraint. His mind flashed briefly to Tabby – her face during their last visit, the quiet determination in her voice when she'd said "We're going to be fine. All of us." The memory anchored him, even as Harlow's insinuations threatened to unbalance his careful control.

"Interesting thing about control," Harlow continued, apparently encouraged by Jack's silence. "Most men in here think it's about controlling others. But the real test is whether you can control yourself when something that matters gets threatened." His eyes flicked to Jack's wedding band. "When someone suggests your wife might be finding comfort elsewhere while you're in here. When you start to wonder who's going to be holding her hand in the delivery room. Who's going to be there for all those late-night feedings, those first steps, those..." he paused deliberately, "intimate moments when she needs a man's touch."

The provocation was naked now, the strategy clear – push until Jack broke, until he revealed the vulnerability that Harlow could exploit later. Around them, the mess hall had grown quieter, attention focusing on their table like a lens narrowing its field of view. Jack felt the weight of observation from inmates and guards alike, all waiting to see how he would respond to this most personal of challenges.

His hands were numb, but in his chest was a complex mixture of anger, fear, and something deeper – a certainty that transcended Harlow's calculated provocations. He looked at the man across from him, really looked at him for the first time since he'd sat down, and what he saw shifted something in his understanding.

Harlow's eyes, for all their calculating observation, held a particular hollowness that Jack recognized – the empty space where connection should be. His casual cruelty wasn't random; it was targeted at what he himself lacked. The realization didn't diminish Jack's anger, but it transformed it, contextualizing it within a broader understanding of the man attempting to provoke him.

"When did you lose someone?" Jack asked quietly, the question emerging not as a counterattack but as a genuine inquiry.

Harlow blinked, the calculated smile faltering briefly. "What?"

"The person who mattered to you," Jack continued, his voice steady, his eyes holding Harlow's with calm intensity. "When did you lose them? Before you came in, or after?"

The mess hall seemed to still around them, the ambient noise receding as attention focused on this unexpected turn in the conversation. Cam's posture shifted slightly, a subtle readjustment that communicated his surprise at Jack's approach.

Harlow's face underwent a remarkable transformation – the practiced smile slipping, confusion replacing calculation, followed by a flash of something raw and unguarded before his features rearranged themselves into forced nonchalance.

"Don't know what you're talking about," he said, but the edge had left his voice, replaced by a defensive flatness that betrayed his discomfort.

"I think you do," Jack replied, not pressing the advantage but simply acknowledging what he'd seen. "It's why you focus on other people's connections. On what they might lose." He paused, allowing the observation to settle between them. "It's easier than dealing with what you've already lost."

Harlow's eyes narrowed, but the calculated provocation had disappeared, replaced by genuine wariness. The dynamic between them had shifted, the power balance altered by Jack's unexpected insight. What had begun as an attempt to expose Jack's vulnerability had instead revealed something of Harlow's.

"You don't know anything about me," Harlow said, but the statement lacked conviction, the words emerging with defensive brittleness rather than his earlier smooth confidence.

Jack shrugged. "Maybe not specifics. But I recognize the pattern." He held Harlow's gaze for a moment longer before returning his attention to his meal, the deliberate shift communicating that the exchange was concluded on his terms.

Harlow remained seated for several seconds, the calculated performance abandoned as he recalibrated. Around them, conversations gradually resumed, though with an altered quality – assessment continuing beneath the surface as inmates processed what they'd witnessed. Without another word, Harlow finally gathered his tray and stood, moving away from their table with less assurance than he'd approached it with.

Cam waited until Harlow was well out of earshot before speaking. "Interesting approach," he observed. "Not where I thought that was going."

Jack continued eating, his movements deliberate and controlled. "It was never about Tabby," he said quietly. "It was about finding a way past my guard."

Cam nodded, understanding without need for elaboration. "Most guys would have taken the bait. Thrown hands, landed in solitary."

"That's what he wanted," Jack acknowledged. "Reaction proves vulnerability."

They finished their meal in companionable silence; the incident already being absorbed into the prison's constant assessment and reassessment of its inhabitants. Jack's wedding band caught the light as he gathered his tray – a reminder of what was real beyond Harlow's provocations, beyond these walls, beyond the years stretching between now and home.

He rolled his shoulders slightly, releasing the tension that had built during the exchange. The flash of insight that had allowed him to turn Harlow's provocation back on itself hadn't been calculated strategy but genuine recognition – one man seeing through another's defenses to the loss beneath. In a place designed to strip away humanity, that moment of connection, however uncomfortable, had paradoxically reinforced Jack's own.

17

Meeting Simon

The visitation room at South Woods held the particular quiet of spaces designed for momentary connection – a hush broken only by murmured conversations, the occasional laugh quickly stifled, and the ever-present hum of the intercom system that reminded everyone of the institutional machinery governing even these most human of interactions. Today wasn't an ordinary visit. Today, his son would enter this room.

His prison-issued clothing was as neat as he could manage – shirt tucked in precisely, collar straightened, the creases maintained through careful folding rather than the luxury of an iron. Jack's hands remained steady on the table, but beneath them, his legs tensed and released in a controlled rhythm, the only outward sign of the anticipation that coursed through him like an electrical current.

June had come and gone and somewhere beyond these walls, his son had entered the world. Jack had received the call – Tabby's voice tired but joyful, the sound of a newborn's cry in the background. "Seven pounds, four ounces," she had told him. "Ten fingers, ten toes. Dark hair, like yours." The details had sustained him through the subsequent weeks of waiting for today's visit, for the moment when prison bureaucracy would finally allow him to see his child.

The door opened, and Jack's head lifted, his body responding to the sound before his mind had fully processed it. Tabby entered first, her steps slower than her usual determined stride, her face bearing the particular exhaustion of new motherhood – skin paler than before, dark circles beneath her eyes, but a glow emanating from within that transcended physical fatigue. Ruby followed close behind, one hand supporting Tabby's elbow with subtle steadiness, the other helping to balance the small bundle wrapped in a pale blue blanket.

Jack rose to his feet in a single fluid motion, his hands remaining on the table as if to anchor himself. His eyes locked with Tabby's across the room, a moment of connection that bridged the physical space between them. Her smile – tired but genuine – reached him before she did, carrying recognition of the magnitude of this moment for both of them.

"Sit, sit," Ruby urged Tabby gently as they reached the table. "You're still recovering."

Tabby complied, lowering herself carefully into the chair across from Jack, the bundle cradled protectively against her chest. Ruby remained standing, her hand resting lightly on her sister-in-law's shoulder, her eyes briefly meeting Jack's with a silent communication of support and shared responsibility.

"Hi," Tabby said, the single syllable carrying the weight of everything that had happened since their last visit – the birth, the sleepless nights, the absence of the person who should have been beside her through it all.

"Hi," Jack replied, his voice steady despite the pressure building in his chest. His eyes dropped to the blanket, to the small movements visible beneath the soft fabric.

Tabby adjusted her position slightly, wincing as she found a more comfortable angle. "He's been fed and changed," she said, practicality asserting itself even in this emotional moment. "Should be calm for a little while."

Jack nodded, unable to form words as Tabby began to unwrap the blanket with careful movements, revealing what it contained inch by precious inch. First a tiny hand, fingers curled into a miniature fist. Then the curve of a cheek, impossibly soft and round. Finally, the entire face – eyes closed in sleep, dark lashes against skin that still carried the newborn flush, a small mouth that worked briefly in dreams before settling.

"This is Simon," Tabby said softly, her eyes moving between her son and her husband. "Simon West."

Jack's hands trembled slightly as they hovered over the table, an involuntary response that he couldn't quite control. The sight of his son – this perfect, complete person who existed because of him yet entirely separate from him – created a pressure in his chest that threatened to crack his careful composure.

Jack leaned forward, eyes cataloging every detail of the small face before him – the shape of the nose, the subtle arch of eyebrows that would likely darken with time, the particular curve of the upper lip. He committed each feature to memory with methodical thoroughness, storing images against the long absence to come.

"He's so calm, observant when he's awake. Watches everything," Tabby declared.

Jack nodded, his throat too tight for speech. The reality of what he was missing – what he would continue to miss – settled over him with crushing weight. First smiles, first steps, first words – all would happen in a world he couldn't access, all would be conveyed to him through secondhand accounts during brief visits or truncated phone calls.

"Do you want to hold him?" Tabby asked, the question gentle but direct.

"Inmates are permitted limited physical contact with visitors, including infants," the guard near the door stated, his voice carrying the practiced neutrality of someone reciting regulations. "You can hold the child while seated at the table. No standing or moving around the room with the infant."

Jack nodded acknowledgment without looking away from Simon. His hands, which had handled chainsaws with confidence eighty feet above the ground, now felt clumsy and oversized as he prepared to receive his son.

"Like this," Ruby said, stepping forward to demonstrate the proper support for the baby's head and neck. "Cradle your arm... yes, that's it."

Jack positioned his arms as instructed, his movements deliberate and careful. Tabby leaned forward, transferring their son with the practiced motion she'd recently developed. The bundle settled into Jack's arms – impossibly light yet somehow containing the entire weight of the future.

As Simon's warmth registered against his chest, Jack's carefully maintained control slipped, just for a moment. His breath caught, his eyes burned, and something profound shifted beneath the surface of his composed exterior. He looked down at his son's face, at the life he had helped create but would largely miss unfolding and felt an emotion too complex to name wash through him – love and loss and determination so tightly interwoven they formed a single, overwhelming response.

Simon stirred slightly, tiny eyelids fluttering but not opening, one small hand working free of the blanket to wave briefly before settling again. Jack held perfectly still, afraid to disturb this moment of peace, aware of how quickly it would pass, how long it would need to sustain him.

Simon weighed almost nothing in Jack's arms yet somehow contained the gravity of planets. Jack adjusted his hold carefully, cradling the small head in his palm, feeling the soft pulse of the fontanel beneath wisps of dark hair. The baby's scent reached him – a complex blend of powder, laundered cotton, and something else, something intrinsic and new that bypassed Jack's conscious mind and registered directly in some ancient, parental part of his brain. This is my son, that part recognized with absolute certainty. This is my blood.

The visitation room continued its hushed activity around them – guards shifting positions with practiced boredom, other families engaged in their own reconnections – but Jack's awareness had contracted to the small bundle in his arms. Simon's face held the particular newborn quality of being simultaneously unique and universal – features that hinted at future definition but remained soft with the malleability of new life. His eyes, when they briefly fluttered open, revealed irises of indeterminate color that would settle into their permanent shade in the coming months. His miniature fingers, perfect down to the translucent half-moons of tiny nails, curled reflexively around Jack's thumb when it brushed against his palm.

"His grip is strong," Jack observed, his voice low and slightly rough, as if emerging from somewhere deeper than usual.

Tabby nodded. "Yeah, especially when he gets a good fistful of hair," Tabby said with a smile.

Jack bent his head, pressing his lips gently to Simon's forehead. The skin there was impossibly soft, warmer than he'd expected. He breathed in deeply, consciously committing the scent to memory, storing it away against the months and years ahead when this direct connection would be replaced by photographs and secondhand reports. His lips lingered against his son's skin, the closest thing to a blessing he could offer.

"Tell me about the birth," he said finally, raising his eyes to meet Tabby's. The question was both request and permission – an invitation for her to share what he couldn't witness himself.

Tabby tucked a strand of hair behind her ear, her wedding ring catching the fluorescent light as it matched the movement of Jack's earlier. "It was fast," she said, her voice taking on the storytelling quality of someone who had already related these details multiple times. "Faster than they expected for a first baby. My water broke around two in the morning, and he was born by noon."

"She called me at three, saying contractions were already five minutes apart," Ruby added, her hand resting lightly on Tabby's shoulder.

Jack nodded, picturing the scene – Tabby alone when labor began, reaching for the phone instead of waking him. The image created a brief tightness in his chest that he carefully controlled, focusing instead on the practical details they were sharing.

"Ruby was amazing," Tabby continued, reaching up to briefly cover her sister-in-law's hand with her own. "Did everything the books said you would do." Her eyes met Jack's, acknowledging the substitution without resentment. "Counted through contractions, got ice chips, didn't complain when I crushed her hand."

"My bones have almost recovered," Ruby interjected, her dry humor a familiar counterpoint to the emotion of the moment.

Simon stirred in Jack's arms, his small face contorting briefly before settling again. Jack adjusted his hold slightly, supporting the baby's head with careful attention. His calloused fingers, marked by years of rope work and chainsaw operation, looked almost absurdly large against Simon's delicate skull.

"He's perfect," Jack said, the simple statement containing layers of meaning.

Tabby's eyes filled briefly before she blinked the moisture away. "The pediatrician says he's textbook healthy. Birth weight right on target, all reflexes normal." She paused, then added with quiet pride, "He's already lifting his head a little during tummy time. The doctor says that's advanced."

Jack stored these details away, filing them alongside the physical impressions he was gathering – the weight of Simon in his arms, the particular rhythm of his breathing, the way his eyebrows drew together momentarily when the overhead intercom crackled with an announcement in another part of the facility.

"He's a good sleeper," Tabby continued, her eyes never leaving the bundle in Jack's arms. "Usually gives me a four-hour stretch at night already. And he seems to know my voice – calms down when I talk to him, even when he's fussy."

"What about when he cries?" Jack asked, his question revealing one of the many practical concerns that had occupied his thoughts during the waiting period between Simon's birth and this first meeting. "Is he colicky?"

Tabby shook her head. "Not so far. He gets hungry, he lets us know. Needs changing, same thing. But once those needs are met, he settles." A small smile touched her lips.

Ruby's hand squeezed Tabby's shoulder lightly. "Except at bath time," she added. "He's decided that's worth protesting."

The image of Simon being bathed – tiny limbs flailing in displeasure, face red with indignation – created a sharp pang in Jack's chest. Another moment he would miss, one of thousands to come. First smile, first tooth, first steps, first words – all would happen beyond these walls.

"Jason built the changing table," Ruby said, filling the silence that had settled between them. "Put it together last weekend. It matches the crib."

Jack continued his careful observation of Simon, but his jaw tightened slightly at the mention. The changing table had been on his list – one of the many nursery preparations interrupted by his sentencing. He had researched models, compared safety features, settled on the one that best combined stability and functionality. Now another man had assembled it, had taken over this task as he had taken over so many others that should have been Jack's.

The thought carried no anger toward Jason, whose support for Tabby and Simon reflected nothing but loyalty and generosity. The ache was directed inward, at the circumstances Jack had created through his own actions, at the absence that would define his son's earliest years. Simon would learn to crawl, to walk, to speak in a home where his father existed primarily in photographs and weekly visits. He would form his understanding of the world without Jack's direct guidance, would navigate childhood with a father present only in carefully structured intervals.

"I've been keeping a journal," Tabby said softly, as if reading the direction of his thoughts. "Writing down everything – when he first focused his eyes on me, the sounds he makes, how his hair sticks up in the morning." Her voice grew firmer, more determined. "So you won't miss it. Not really. It will all be waiting for you when you come home."

Jack looked up from Simon's face to meet his wife's eyes, finding in them the same steady resolve that had characterized her throughout the pregnancy, throughout his case, throughout the separation forced upon them. In her gaze, he saw not just the acknowledgment of what they had lost but the determination to preserve what remained – to build a bridge across the years that would allow him to reclaim his place in their family when his sentence ended.

"Thank you," he said simply, the words inadequate to express what her efforts meant to him.

Simon's tiny fingers flexed against Jack's hand, curling reflexively around his thumb in a grip disproportionate to his size. The sensation – this small, instinctive connection between father and son – created a pressure behind Jack's eyes that he controlled through practiced discipline, allowing himself to feel it fully while preventing its outward expression.

"Ten-minute warning, folks." The announcement crackled through the intercom system, the guard's voice flat and impersonal. Jack felt the words like a physical pressure against his skin, each syllable peeling away seconds from the already insufficient time with his son. He had known this moment was coming – had prepared for it during the sleepless night before – yet the reality of it struck with unexpected force. Ten minutes. Six hundred seconds to store away enough of Simon to sustain him through the time until their next visit.

Simon stirred in his arms, tiny eyelids fluttering open to reveal unfocused eyes that would eventually sharpen into awareness of the world around him. Jack studied them intently, searching for hints of color that might eventually emerge – would they be brown like his own, or hazel like Tabby's? Another detail he would learn secondhand, another development he would miss witnessing directly.

"I should take him back," Tabby said gently, her hands already extending across the table. "He'll need feeding soon."

Jack nodded, acknowledging the practical truth of her statement while his arms tightened fractionally around the bundle, an involuntary resistance to the impending separation. The contradiction – knowing he must relinquish his son while his body refused to comply – created a peculiar paralysis that lasted precisely three seconds before his training in self-control reasserted itself.

"Of course," he said, his voice steady despite the pressure building behind his sternum.

Ruby stepped forward, her movements efficient but gentle as she helped with the transfer. Her hands adjusted the blanket that had loosened during Simon's time in Jack's arms, tucking it securely around the small body with practiced ease.

"Support his head," she reminded Tabby unnecessarily, the instruction serving more as acknowledgment of the moment's weight than practical guidance. "There you go."

The warmth of Simon's small body left Jack's arms, the absence immediately registering as a physical sensation – a ghost impression of weight and heat that lingered after the actual contact had ended. He watched as Tabby settled their son against her chest, his dark hair barely visible above the blue blanket. The sight created a tableau that Jack knew would revisit him during the long nights ahead – his family, complete and separate from him, continuing their life beyond these walls.

"How's your recovery?" he asked, the question emerging from the practical part of his mind that had been cataloging concerns during the weeks since Simon's birth. "Any complications?"

Tabby adjusted her hold on Simon before answering. "Standard postpartum stuff. Better each day. Dr. Winters says everything is healing normally." Her response matched his in tone – factual, composed, prioritizing information over emotion. It was their established pattern, this exchange of practicalities that allowed them to navigate impossible circumstances without breaking.

"And financially?" Jack continued, his hands now flat on the table before him, wedding band catching the light. "The medical bills? Has the insurance covered everything we expected?"

Ruby's hand settled on Tabby's shoulder, a quiet gesture of support that Jack noted with the same attentiveness he applied to all details of his family's circumstances. The unspoken communication between the two women – developed and strengthened during his absence – was both reassuring and painful to witness.

"All covered," Tabby confirmed. "And Jason's firm sent a ridiculously expensive baby gift basket that included enough diapers to last through the first month." She attempted a fragile smile. "We're managing, Jack. One day at a time."

He nodded, absorbing this information along with the subtext beneath it – that they were finding ways to continue without him, that systems of support had formed in his absence, that life outside these walls refused to pause despite his removal from it. The knowledge was both comfort and knife-edge, cutting in multiple directions simultaneously.

"Simon's healthy," Tabby added, correctly interpreting his next unasked question. "Perfect APGAR scores, gaining weight right on schedule. The pediatrician says he's textbook."

Jack's jaw tightened slightly, then relaxed with deliberate control. These medical details – numbers and assessments that reduced his son to data points – were simultaneously too much and not enough. They told him nothing about the particular way Simon's face scrunched when displeased, the specific rhythm of his breathing during sleep, the unique scent that would change as he grew. Yet they were all he would have for weeks at a time – facts without texture, information without experience.

"I wish you could stay," Tabby said suddenly, the words emerging with an uncharacteristic lack of filtering. Her composed façade cracked momentarily, revealing the raw emotion beneath – exhaustion and longing and the particular loneliness of single parenthood forced by circumstance rather than choice.

Jack didn't answer directly. Words were inadequate to the moment, would only emphasize the impossibility contained in her wish. Instead, he nodded once, the gesture containing acknowledgment of everything that remained unspoken between them – regret, determination, the shared understanding that wishing changed nothing about their reality.

"Five minutes remaining," the guard announced, his voice carrying the particular detachment of someone who delivered the same message multiple times daily, who had witnessed countless separations without being touched by any of them.

Tabby glanced at Ruby, who nodded and began gathering their belongings – the extra blanket in case the air turned cool, the folder of photographs they'd brought to leave with Jack. These preparations for departure had a terrible efficiency to them, movements practiced and perfected through repetition.

"The next visiting day is the twenty-eighth," Jack said, maintaining his focus on practical details as a defense against the emotion threatening to breach his careful control. "Will Ruby be able to drive you again?"

"Of course," Ruby answered immediately, her tone suggesting the question was unnecessary. "We've worked out a system for the car seat. Getting better at it each time."

Jack nodded, filing away this additional evidence of their adaptation to his absence. His hands remained flat on the table, but his knuckles had whitened slightly, pressure building beneath the skin as his fingers pressed against the metal surface.

"Visiting hours have concluded," came the final announcement. "All visitors please proceed to the exit."

Tabby stood carefully, cradling Simon against her chest as she adjusted to the shift in balance. The movement was still tentative; her body not fully recovered from birth despite her assurances. Jack rose as well, the motion automatic despite knowing it would only emphasize the impending separation.

"I'll see you on the twenty-eighth," Tabby said, her voice steady once more, control reasserted. "Both of us will be here."

Jack nodded, his eyes moving from her face to the small bundle against her chest. Simon had settled into sleep again, oblivious to the institutional machinery that governed his contact with his father, unaware of the years that would pass before they could exist in the same space without supervision and time limits.

"May I?" Jack asked, gesturing toward Simon.

The guard nearby gave a curt nod, permission granted for this final contact. Jack reached out, his calloused finger gently touching his son's cheek – a brief connection, skin against skin, before pulling back. The touch lasted less than three seconds yet contained everything he couldn't say aloud.

Ruby guided Tabby toward the exit, one hand supporting her elbow with the same steady presence she'd maintained throughout the visit. Jack remained standing, watching their progress across the room, memorizing the image of his family in motion – Tabby's careful steps, Ruby's protective stance beside her, Simon's dark hair just visible above the blue blanket.

At the door, Tabby paused and turned back. Their eyes met across the room – a moment of connection that transcended the institutional setting, that reached across the space between them to acknowledge everything they were fighting to preserve despite the years of separation ahead. Then she was gone, the door closing behind her with the particular finality of prison architecture.

Jack remained standing until the guard's voice broke the spell.

"Back to your block, West."

He sat down slowly, hands gripping the edge of the table with white-knuckled intensity. Around him, other inmates were being escorted out, their own visits concluded, their own momentary connections severed. Jack didn't move immediately; his eyes fixed on the door through which his family had disappeared.

His face revealed nothing of the storm beneath its surface – not to the guards who waited with professional impatience, not to the other inmates who passed by on their way out. Only his hands, curled around the table's edge with a force that threatened to bend metal, betrayed the cost of maintaining that control.

Soon he would stand and walk calmly back to his cell block. Soon he would resume the careful navigation of prison life that had become his means of survival. But for these few remaining seconds, he allowed himself to feel the full weight of separation – from his son, from his wife, from the life that continued without him beyond these walls.

18
Jason's Visit

Jack sat with his back straight, hands resting flat on the table's cool surface in the visitation room at South Woods State Prison, wedding band catching the harsh light as he rotated it with his thumb – a gesture that had become as unconscious as breathing during his months of incarceration. His eyes tracked the movement around the room without appearing to focus on any particular point, counting the minutes until Tabby would walk through those doors with Simon in her arms.

Three months since Simon's birth. Each visit revealing new developments – the strengthening of neck muscles, the more focused gaze, the increasing awareness in those dark eyes that studied Jack's face with an intensity that seemed impossible in one so young. Jack had memorized every detail: the particular whorl of hair at the crown of Simon's head, the tiny fingernails perfect as shells, the specific weight and warmth of his small body when temporarily transferred to Jack's arms under the watchful eyes of the guards.

The door at the far end of the room opened, and Jack's attention sharpened, muscles tensing slightly in anticipation. His composed expression revealed nothing of the hunger he felt for the sight of his family, for those precious minutes of connection that sustained him through the days between visits. But instead of Tabby's familiar figure with Simon bundled against her chest, Jason entered alone, his civilian clothes – jeans and a button-down shirt – marking him as distinctly separate from the institutional environment.

Jack's fingers stilled on his wedding band, the momentary break in his habitual movement the only outward sign of his disappointment. His eyes met Jason's across the room, and he knew immediately that something had changed in their planned visit. Jason's posture – shoulders slightly hunched, steps more hurried than his usual measured pace – communicated concern before he even reached the table.

"Hey," Jason said, settling into the chair opposite Jack. His hand rested briefly on the folder he'd brought – the usual collection of photos and updates that supplemented their visits. "Tabby sends her apologies. She couldn't make it today."

Jack's face remained composed, but beneath the table, his hand curled into a tight fist, knuckles whitening with pressure before he deliberately relaxed them. "Simon?" he asked, the single word containing all necessary questions.

"He's got a fever," Jason confirmed, his expression softening with understanding of what this news would mean to Jack. "Started last night – nothing serious, the doctor says. Just over a hundred and one. Probably a minor virus, but Tabby didn't want to bring him out, risk exposing him to more germs or stressing his system."

Jack nodded once, processing this information with the same outward calm he applied to all challenges. Inside, concern for Simon battled with the selfish disappointment of missing one of his preciously few chances to see his son. He recognized both emotions without judgment, acknowledged them, then set them aside to focus on what mattered – Simon's wellbeing.

The fluorescent lights buzzed overhead, one fixture at the far end of the room flickering in an erratic rhythm that matched the disjointed thoughts racing behind Jack's careful mask. Simon, sick for the first time. Tabby handling it alone. The fever that was "nothing serious" but serious enough to keep them home. All normal parental concerns made extraordinary by the concrete and steel that prevented him from being where he should be – at his son's side, at his wife's side, carrying his share of the worry.

"The doctor saw him?" Jack asked, voice level despite the pressure building in his chest.

Jason nodded. "Tabby took him in first thing this morning. Pediatrician on call said it's a standard virus. Gave the usual advice – fluids, rest, Tylenol for the fever. Said to bring him back if it goes over a hundred and three or lasts more than three days." He hesitated, then added, "Ruby's with them now. She stayed over last night when the fever started."

Jack absorbed this information, cataloging it alongside his growing mental file of Simon's development and care. The silence stretched between them, heavy with all the things Jack couldn't do, couldn't say, couldn't change. In another life – the one that should have been – he would be the one staying up through the night, monitoring his son's temperature, calling the doctor, supporting Tabby through their first experience with a sick child. Instead, he sat in this room with its institutional furniture and regulated interactions, receiving information about his family secondhand.

"Is he eating?" Jack asked after a moment, focusing on practical concerns rather than the emotions threatening to breach his control.

"Tabby says his appetite is down but he's still nursing," Jason replied, clearly relieved to be discussing concrete details. "Not as long as usual, but regularly. The doctor said that's a good sign." He shifted in his seat, the plastic chair creaking slightly under his weight. "He's not fussy, either. Just a little more tired than normal. Sleeps, wakes up, looks around with those serious eyes of his, then goes back to sleep."

Jack's hand returned to his wedding band, rotating it once, twice, three times – a physical manifestation of thoughts turning over problems he couldn't solve from here. "And Tabby?" he asked. "She's handling it okay?"

Jason's expression softened slightly. "She's tired. You know how she gets – researching everything, making charts of temperature readings and feeding times. But she's steady." He paused, choosing his next words carefully. "Ruby's making sure she rests when Simon does. They've got a system going."

Another silence settled between them, filled with the ambient sounds of the visitation room – murmured conversations at other tables, a child's laugh quickly hushed, the squeak of the guard's shoes as he patrolled the perimeter. Jack's eyes moved past Jason to the door through which Tabby and Simon should have entered, his mind filling in the details of what he was missing – Simon's warm weight against his chest, the subtle changes that time would have brought to his developing features, the quiet updates from Tabby about milestones reached and challenges overcome.

"She wanted me to show you these," Jason said finally, opening the folder he'd brought. He slid several photographs across the table – Simon sleeping in his crib, Simon awake on a play mat, his dark eyes focused on something beyond the camera's frame, Simon held carefully in Ruby's arms, his tiny hand wrapped around her finger. "These were taken a few days ago, before the fever."

Jack's fingers hovered over the images, not quite touching them, as if the glossy surfaces might somehow connect him physically to the moments they captured. His son's face looked back at him from each photo – healthy, alert, changing already in the brief time since Jack had last held him. In one image, Simon's expression held a particular seriousness that Jack recognized from his own reflection, a focused intensity that seemed impossibly mature in such a young face.

"Tabby said the fever started to come down with the Tylenol," Jason added, watching Jack study the photographs. "She's monitoring it every four hours. Ruby's staying again tonight to help with the night shifts."

Jack looked up from the photos, his eyes meeting Jason's directly. "Thank you," he said simply. "For coming. For letting me know."

The words were plain but carried the weight of everything unspoken between them – gratitude for Jason's support of Tabby and Simon, acknowledgment of the uncomfortable position he occupied, recognition of the boundaries being navigated by everyone involved in this complex arrangement forced upon them by circumstance.

Jason nodded once, accepting both the spoken thanks and the unspoken complexity behind it. "I brought the visitor log for you to sign," he said, sliding another paper across the table. "Tabby thought you'd want to add Simon officially, even though he couldn't come today."

Jack took the pen Jason offered, adding his son's name to the list of approved visitors with careful, measured strokes. The simple act – acknowledging Simon's existence in the official record of his incarceration – carried a weight that momentarily threatened his composure. His son was real, was ill, was being cared for by others while Jack sat in this room, helpless to do anything but write his name on a form.

"Tell Tabby—" he began, then paused, recalibrating. "Tell her I'm thinking of them both. That I trust her judgment about Simon's care." He met Jason's eyes again. "And tell her I'll be waiting to see them next time."

Jason nodded, understanding all that remained unspoken in Jack's measured words.

Jason rubbed the back of his neck, a tell Jack recognized – the unconscious movement that preceded difficult conversations. The air in the visitation room seemed to thicken, conversations at nearby tables fading to background noise as Jack recognized the shift in Jason's posture, the gathering of resolve visible in the set of his shoulders.

"Look, there's something I need to say," Jason began, his voice pitched low enough that neighboring tables couldn't overhear. "About me, Tabby, and Simon."

Jack's face remained composed, but his wedding band pressed harder against his finger as his hand tensed slightly. He waited, neither encouraging nor discouraging the conversation, his eyes steady on Jason's face.

"I know Harlow tried to get under your skin about me being around so much," Jason continued, nodding toward the separate waiting area, where familiar visitors exchanged polite chitchat—a routine that helped fill the silence before visitation began—"And I know you shut him down. But I still feel like we should talk about it directly."

Jason's words confirmed what Jack had long suspected. Prison gossip moved both ways, traveling beyond these walls through visitors and phone calls, carrying details of his confrontations to the outside world. Jack nodded once, a minimal acknowledgment that allowed Jason to continue without revealing his own thoughts on the matter.

"I'm there when they need me," Jason said, leaning forward with the earnest intensity that characterized his approach to all moral questions. His forearms rested on the table; hands open as if physically offering his honesty for inspection. "But I know my place, Jack. I'm not – I would never – I mean, Tabby is..." He stumbled over the words, eloquence failing him in the face of this delicate territory.

"I know," Jack said quietly, offering rescue from the verbal tangle.

But Jason shook his head, determined to finish what he'd started. "No, let me say this properly. I care about Tabby and Simon. They're family to me. But I'm careful about boundaries – both for them and for myself." His eyes, direct and unflinching, met Jack's. "I help with practical things

– driving to appointments, carrying in groceries, assembling furniture. I come when Ruby can't be there or when Tabby needs an extra set of hands. But I'm always clear about my role. I'm the friend, the brother-in-law by extension. Not anything else."

Jack watched Jason's face as he spoke, noting the mix of discomfort and determination in his expression. Jason had always worn his emotions like badges – displayed openly, almost proudly, as if transparency itself were a moral virtue. Now that openness revealed his genuine struggle with the complex position he occupied – wanting to help without overstepping, to support without replacing.

"I know you're respecting boundaries," Jack said, each word measured and precise. "I've never doubted that."

A slight relaxation showed in Jason's shoulders, tension releasing at this direct acknowledgment. "Good. That's good." He ran a hand through his hair, disheveling it. "Because sometimes I worry that I'm doing too much or not enough, you know? That I'm either overstepping or not being there when I should be."

Jack's fingers found his wedding band again, rotating it once before stilling. "It's not easy for me either," he admitted, the words emerging with careful control. "Depending on others to care for my family. Knowing someone else is there when Simon has a fever, when Tabby needs support." He paused, selecting his next words with precision. "But if it has to be someone, I'm glad it's you. Someone who understands what matters."

The admission cost him something – a small surrender of the self-sufficiency he valued, an acknowledgment of his current limitations. But it offered something in return – a bridge across the unspoken tension that had existed between them since his incarceration, since Jason had stepped into the support role that should have been Jack's.

"I struggle with it sometimes," Jack continued, his voice dropping lower, the admission meant for Jason alone. "Seeing the photos, hearing the updates. Knowing I'm missing everything." His hands remained flat on the table, controlled despite the emotion behind his words. "Knowing others are there when I can't be."

Jason nodded, understanding without need for elaboration. "I can't imagine how hard that is," he said simply. "And I know nothing I do changes that. I just—I want you to know that I'm trying to help without replacing.

The PA system crackled to life above them, a disembodied voice announcing: "Attention all visitors. Visiting hours will end in fifteen minutes. Please begin concluding your visits."

The announcement created a subtle shift in the room's energy – conversations intensifying as time grew shorter, promises to return next week offered with varying degrees of conviction. Jack felt the familiar pressure of the countdown, the mechanical diminishment of connection that characterized every visit.

"I appreciate what you're doing," Jack said, the words emerging with unusual directness. His typical economy of expression gave way to something more explicit, more vulnerable than his standard careful measurements. "Thank you for being there when I can't be."

The simple statement hung between them – neither dismissal nor absolution but acknowledgment of the reality they were both navigating. Jason's expression shifted, relief mixing with a complicated emotion that might have been pride or determination or something uniquely his own.

"I'll keep looking out for them," Jason promised. "While respecting that they're your family. That I'm just helping temporarily." He gathered the photos, straightening them with precise movements before returning them to the folder. "And I'll keep bringing you every detail, every update. So you don't miss more than you have to."

Jack nodded, the gesture containing both acceptance and gratitude. Around them, other visits were concluding – inmates saying goodbye to wives, children, parents, the particular pain of separation playing out in dozens of individualized performances across the room. Guards moved with practiced efficiency; their attention heightened during this transition period when emotions ran highest.

"Five minutes remaining," came the announcement, more urgent than the last.

Jason extended his hand across the table – an offer of connection beyond words. Jack took it without hesitation, their grip firm and brief, communicating in that simple contact what remained difficult to articulate aloud. They were something more complex than just friends– two men bound together by their connections to the same woman, the same child, navigating the uncharted territory created by Jack's absence.

"Tell Tabby I hope Simon feels better," Jack said as they released the handshake. "And that I'll call her soon."

Jason nodded, gathering his jacket from the back of the chair. "Will do. And I'll make sure she knows you're thinking about them."

A guard approached their table, his presence signaling the imminent conclusion of visiting hours. Jason stood, offering a final nod before turning toward the exit. Jack watched him go – this man who represented both support and reminder of all he couldn't provide himself, both ally and unintentional rival.

As the door closed behind Jason, Jack remained seated, his expression revealing nothing of the turbulence beneath its composed surface. His thumb found his wedding band again, the metal warm against his skin. The visitation room emptied gradually around him, families separating with varying degrees of emotion, inmates returning to the reality of confinement after brief tastes of connection.

When the guard finally approached to escort him back to his cell block, Jack rose with the same controlled movements that characterized all his actions inside these walls. His face betrayed nothing of his disappointment at missing Simon, his concern about the fever, his complex feelings about Jason's role in his family's life. Those emotions existed beneath the surface, acknowledged and contained, fuel for the discipline that would carry him through the years still stretching between this moment and his return home.

19

Renee's Letter

The letter arrived on a Tuesday, slipped under his cell door with the casual indifference of routine mail delivery. Jack West stared at the cream-colored envelope, its edges crisp and unmarked by the usual institutional handling. The return address hit him like a physical blow—Renee Torres, a name he'd never seen written down but recognized instantly. His victim's sister had found him; had chosen to reach across the void he'd created between their lives with something as mundane as a letter.

Jack sat on the edge of his narrow bunk, the mattress dipping beneath his weight in the familiar hollow worn by three years of identical mornings. The envelope lay on his thigh, lighter than it had any right to be, considering the weight of what it represented. The prison hummed around him—metal doors clanging in distant corridors, the murmur of conversations muffled by concrete, the perpetual background noise of confinement that he'd learned to filter out.

His thumb traced the edge of the envelope, feeling for weakness. There were a thousand reasons not to open it. The letter could contain anything—rage, accusations, detailed descriptions of a family's suffering that he already understood too well. Jack had made his peace with what he'd done, had accepted the justice of his sentence. He protected Ruby. That was the beginning and end of it.

But the letter remained, insistent in its ordinariness.

"You gonna stare at that all day?" Cam's voice came from the sink where he was brushing his teeth, the words garbled around his toothbrush.

Jack didn't answer. Instead, he slid his thumb under the flap and tore a clean line across the top. Inside was a single sheet of paper, folded in thirds. The handwriting was neat and controlled, not the angry scrawl he'd half-expected. Each letter was formed with deliberate care, as if the writer had taken her time, considering each word before committing it to paper. It struck him as the handwriting of someone who had drafted and redrafted, who wasn't writing in the heat of emotion but after long consideration.

Jack unfolded the letter completely, aware of his heartbeat quickening against his ribs.

Dear Mr. West, it began. Not Jack. Not murderer. Just the formal address of one stranger to another.

I've written this letter many times in my head over the past three years. I'm a high school counselor, so I spend my days helping teenagers articulate difficult feelings, yet I've struggled to find the right words to say to you. Perhaps there aren't any perfect words for this situation, so I'll simply tell you about my brother.

Jack's throat tightened. He had never thought of Brad Torres as someone's brother. In his mind, Brad had been stripped down to a core identity—Ruby's rapist.

Brad loved spicy food so much that he carried hot sauce in his backpack through all of high school. He had a ridiculous collection of movie tickets saved in a shoebox under his bed—every film he'd ever seen in theaters. He taught himself to play guitar from YouTube videos and was terrible at it, but so earnest that we never had the heart to ask him to stop practicing at family gatherings.

The words blurred slightly as Jack blinked. His hands were steady—they were always steady—but something inside him trembled. These details were dangerous, more threatening than any accusation could have been. They formed a person where Jack had allowed only an act to exist.

When our mother was diagnosed with breast cancer, Brad drove her to every appointment and took meticulous notes that he organized in color-coded folders. He made inappropriate jokes that somehow made her laugh when nothing else could. He was twenty-one then, and postponed his plans for a year to be there for her.

Jack shifted on the bunk, uncomfortable with the growing shape of Brad Torres in his mind. The prison air felt suddenly thinner, insufficient. He wanted to stop reading, to fold the letter back into its envelope and push it deep under his mattress, but his eyes kept moving down the page as if compelled.

I'm not writing to tell you that Brad was perfect. He wasn't. He had a temper that got worse when he drank. He could be selfish, stubborn, and sometimes cruel when he felt cornered. He made choices I couldn't understand or defend. But before he was any of those things—before he was the man who hurt your sister, before he was the reason you're in prison—he was my big brother who checked my closet for monsters and taught me to ride a bike.

This was what he had feared—the erosion of his clean narrative. He had reduced Brad Torres to a single dimension because necessity had demanded it. Killing a person required it.

I'm not writing to ask for your remorse or to demand an apology. I understand that you did what you did to protect someone you love, just as I loved my brother despite his flaws. I'm writing because Brad existed beyond his worst action, just as I imagine you do. He was a son, a brother, a friend—a person composed of ordinary moments, small kindnesses, and terrible mistakes.

The final paragraph hit Jack with a physical force so strong it stole his breath.

I don't expect a response. I only wanted you to know that while the legal system processed this as a case and the prison system processes you as an inmate, I process this as the irreversible absence of my brother. Brad is gone, and he won't ever get to be more than the sum of what he was in his twenty-seven years. Whatever he might have become—better or worse—that possibility died with him. I'm still learning how to live with that finality.

It was signed simply: *Renee Torres.*

He slipped the letter back into its envelope and held it between his palms like something volatile, something that could detonate if handled carelessly.

The morning bell rang, signaling movement to breakfast. Jack tucked the letter into his shirt pocket, its edge pressing against his chest.

Jack stood before his open locker, the metal door hanging ajar like a mouth waiting to swallow secrets. The narrow cabinet contained what passed for his life now—three paperbacks with creased spines, a stack of letters from Ruby tied with a shoelace, photos of Tabby and Simon, and the miscellaneous debris of incarceration. He pulled the Torres letter from his pocket, its edges softened from a day of unconscious handling, and slid it beneath the bundle of Ruby's correspondence, as if his sister's words could neutralize Renee's.

The prison day had dragged with the peculiar elasticity of institutional time—stretching endlessly through work detail, then suddenly contracting during the brief outdoor hour when the sky opened above the yard. As the evening approached, its tempo shifting once again, Jack arranged his possessions with the precision that had become his hallmark in South Woods. Everything in its place, a small rebellion against a system designed to strip away control. His toothbrush aligned perfectly with his state-issued soap. His extra uniform folded in identical thirds. The photograph of Tabby positioned so her face caught what little light filtered through the high window. Order created the illusion of autonomy.

But the letter wouldn't stay buried. Each time he closed the locker door, Jack pictured it beneath the stack, Renee's careful handwriting facing upward in the darkness. He found himself opening the metal cabinet again, ostensibly to retrieve a book, but his eyes strayed to the corner where the cream envelope peeked from beneath Ruby's letters. He shoved it deeper, tucking it under his spare t-shirts, then slammed the door with more force than necessary.

"Thing bite you?" Cam asked from his position on his bunk, not looking up from his magazine—an issue of National Geographic with a well-thumbed cover showing the Serengeti at sunset.

"Just stuck," Jack muttered, testing the latch with unnecessary thoroughness.

Evening bled into night. Lights dimmed to the perpetual half-dark of prison nights, where true darkness was deemed a security risk. Jack lay on his bunk, arms crossed behind his head, staring at the ceiling. Jack studied this familiar landscape rather than close his eyes, where Renee's words waited.

Sleep came in fractured increments, shattered by the usual nocturnal soundscape of the prison—snoring, distant arguments, the regular footfalls of night guards. Jack woke feeling as though he hadn't slept at all, his mind still circling the letter like water around a drain.

In the morning, Jack moved through the breakfast routine on autopilot. The cafeteria buzzed with the controlled chaos of two hundred men eating on a schedule. Plastic trays slid along metal counters. The institutional oatmeal sat in his bowl, congealing as he stirred it absently, his spoon creating spiral patterns in the pale mush.

Across the table, Cam watched him with the practiced patience of a man who had learned that observation was its own form of currency. Cam's forearms rested on the table, sleeve tattoos telling stories in faded blue ink—an anchor, a cross, a woman's name partially obscured by a newer design.

"You planning to hypnotize that oatmeal?" Cam asked, his voice pitched low enough to remain private despite the crowded table.

Jack looked up, momentarily disoriented, as if he'd forgotten where he was. "What?"

"You've been stirring that same bowl for ten minutes. Either eat it or don't, but watching you play with it is killing my appetite." Cam's words carried the gruff concern of a man unaccustomed to expressing worry directly.

"Not hungry," Jack said, pushing the tray away a few inches.

Cam leaned forward slightly, his broad shoulders creating a barrier between their conversation and the rest of the table. "You've been somewhere else since yesterday. Walking around like your body's here but the rest of you is on vacation."

Jack met his cellmate's gaze with a studied neutrality that had served him well inside. "Just thinking through some things."

"Bullshit." Cam's response was immediate but without heat. "This started when that letter came. The one you've been opening and closing your locker to check on like it might sprout legs and walk off."

The accuracy of the observation caught Jack off guard. He'd thought his movements casual, unremarkable. But of course Cam would notice—noticing things was how he'd survived twelve years inside.

"It's nothing," Jack said, the denial automatic.

Cam snorted. "Sure. That's why you can't finish a sentence in conversation. That's why you missed the count bell last night until the CO was practically standing in our cell."

Jack's hand tightened around his plastic spoon, an instinctive response to feeling cornered. He forced his fingers to relax, placed the utensil deliberately on his tray. "It's from Brad Torres' sister."

The name hung between them. Cam knew why Jack was inside—they all did. Prison offered little privacy, and stories traveled with the efficiency of a nervous system.

"And?" Cam prompted, after the silence stretched too long.

"And nothing. She wrote a letter. I read it. End of story." Jack's tone suggested a finality he didn't feel.

"Right." Cam's expression remained skeptical. "That's why you're hiding it under your shirts and staring at your oatmeal like it contains the secrets of the universe."

Jack felt a flicker of irritation, quickly suppressed. Cam wasn't probing out of idle curiosity. In their environment, unusual behavior drew attention—from other inmates, from guards. Attention was dangerous.

"She wrote about him," Jack finally said, his voice low enough that Cam had to lean closer to hear. "Not about what happened. About who he was. Brother. Son. Friend. The whole human package."

Cam nodded slowly, understanding passing across his weathered features. "And you'd rather he stayed a one-dimensional asshole who deserved what he got."

The bluntness was typical of Cam, who had long ago abandoned social niceties in favor of brutal clarity. Jack didn't answer immediately, considering the accusation.

"I thought I could just shove the letter away," he admitted finally. "File it under 'not my problem' and move on. But—"

"But it doesn't work like that," Cam finished for him. "Never does."

Around them, inmates began standing, trays in hand, as breakfast period wound down. The noise level rose with sounds of footsteps and renewed conversations.

"I can't make it unhappen," Jack said, the words emerging more vulnerable than he'd intended. "I can't unfeel what reading it did."

Cam gathered his empty tray, movements efficient and economical. "So, stop trying," he said simply, as if the solution were obvious. "You can hide the letter under every piece of clothing you own, but you already read the damn thing. It's in your head now. Pretending otherwise is just wasting energy you don't have to spare in here."

The bell rang, signaling the end of the meal period. Jack stood, his untouched breakfast a pale island on his tray.

The counseling office existed in strange opposition to the rest of South Woods—a space deliberately designed to feel unlike prison. No metal furnishings bolted to the floor, no institutional paint in soul-deadening beige. Instead, a desk of actual wood faced a chair upholstered in fabric rather than vinyl, and the fluorescent lights were supplemented by a lamp that cast a warmer glow against one wall. The illusion of normalcy was both comforting and disorienting, like stepping into a memory of the world outside.

Jack sat with his back straight, hands resting on his thighs, his posture revealing nothing of the reluctance that had nearly caused him to cancel this appointment. Three years inside had taught him to wear neutrality like armor, to reveal nothing in his expression or body language that could be exploited. The counseling office, with its invitation to vulnerability, represented its own kind of danger.

Dr. Abrams sat across from him, her notepad balanced on crossed knees. She was neither young nor old, her age disguised by a certain timelessness in her appearance—sensible shoes, hair cut to fall just below her ears in a style that required minimal maintenance, reading glasses hanging from a beaded chain around her neck. Her face bore the subtle lines of someone who listened more than she spoke.

"You requested this session, Jack," she said after the silence had stretched long enough to become its own statement. "What's on your mind today?"

Jack's hand moved to his breast pocket, where Renee's letter had taken up residence again after his failed attempt to banish it to the locker. The paper had softened with handling, its creases worn into fabric-like flexibility. He removed it carefully, as if it might disintegrate.

"I received this," he said, the words inadequate to explain why he was here, why this particular piece of mail had disrupted the careful equilibrium of his sentenced life.

Dr. Abrams accepted the letter. "Who is it from?"

"Brad Torres' sister." Jack's voice didn't waver—he refused to let it. "The man I killed."

She nodded, unsurprised. Such communications weren't uncommon, though they took many forms—rage, questions, sometimes even forgiveness.

"What would you like to discuss about it?"

The question seemed simple but wasn't. Jack stared past Dr. Abrams's shoulder, where a framed print of a mountain landscape hung on the wall—the kind of generic art found in waiting rooms, notable only for being neither institutional nor challenging.

"I'm not sure," he said finally. The truth, but not all of it.

Dr. Abrams studied him for a moment, her expression thoughtful rather than judging. "You've been sentenced for what you did. You're serving your time. Has this letter changed any of that?"

"No."

"Has it changed what happened to your sister?"

"No," Jack said again, more firmly.

"Then perhaps what it's changing is your ability to compartmentalize—to keep Brad Torres in a box labeled 'deserved it' and yourself in a box labeled 'did what was necessary.'"

The observation struck with uncomfortable precision. Jack had survived these three years by maintaining those exact distinctions—clean lines between cause and effect, action and consequence, justice and punishment.

Jack leaned forward slightly, elbows on knees, hands loosely clasped. The position felt more natural than his previous rigid posture. "So, what am I supposed to do with this? She didn't ask for a response. She didn't demand anything."

"That's true. She hasn't placed any obligation on you." Dr. Abrams returned the letter, watching as Jack carefully refolded it along its worn creases. "Which means you have a choice."

"A choice," Jack repeated, testing the concept.

"You can acknowledge receipt of her letter or not. You can respond or not. You can engage with what she's shared or not." Dr. Abrams's voice remained measured, presenting options rather than directives. "The question is, what do you want to do?"

Jack hadn't considered that his own desires might be relevant in this situation. He'd been reacting to the letter's arrival, to its content, to the disruption it created in his carefully ordered existence. The idea that he might choose a direction rather than simply defend against an intrusion shifted his perspective subtly but significantly.

"I don't know yet," he said, which was more honest than he'd intended to be.

"That's a perfectly reasonable position," Dr. Abrams assured him. "But I'd suggest considering what staying silent means versus what responding might offer—to Ms. Torres, yes, but also to yourself."

Jack tucked the letter back into his pocket, its presence now familiar against his chest. "And if I respond, what do I even say? 'Sorry I killed your brother, but he had it coming'?"

Dr. Abrams's expression didn't change at his bitter tone. "I think you're capable of more nuance than that, Jack. The fact that you're sitting here, troubled by her words rather than dismissing them, suggests you're already engaging with the complexity of this situation."

"I'll think about it," he said as he stood, signaling the end of the session.

Jack paused with his hand on the doorknob, but as he stepped back into the institutional reality of the corridor, with its echoing surfaces and watchful eyes, he knew he had already crossed some internal boundary. The question was no longer whether to acknowledge what Renee Torres had shared, but how to live with the understanding it had forced upon him.

The torn notebook pages formed a scattered archipelago across the concrete floor of the cell, each island a failed attempt at response. Jack sat cross-legged on his bunk, a fresh sheet balanced on the hardcover of a borrowed library book, his hand hovering above the blank page. The prison-issued pen felt inadequate for the task, its cheap plastic casing and inconsistent ink an absurd contrast to the weight of what he needed to convey. How did you acknowledge the humanity of someone you'd deliberately removed from the world?

The cell offered what passed for privacy in South Woods—a temporary solitude dependent on Cam's absence during his laundry work shift. Even this limited space for vulnerability felt like a luxury. Jack had spent the past week drafting and discarding versions of this letter, each attempt falling short of what he sensed was necessary. Not just what Renee Torres might need to hear, but what he needed to articulate, even if only to himself.

Writing had never been Jack's natural medium. Before prison, his communication had been direct and action-oriented—problems identified and solved through work, through physical intervention, through the applied knowledge of his hands. Words were functional tools, not vessels for complex emotion. Yet here he was, struggling to shape language precise enough to cross the divide he had created with his actions.

The discarded attempts told their own story. Some began with formal apology, a reflexive "I'm sorry for your loss" that rang hollow even as he wrote it. Others attempted explanation, laying out the sequence of events as if clarifying the timeline might somehow justify the outcome. One draft veered into his own suffering, the consequences he'd faced, before he recognized the self-serving nature of that approach and crumpled the page mid-sentence.

Jack studied the blank page before him, conscious of time passing. The institutional clock on the wall outside his cell ticked away the minutes of Cam's shift. Soon the relative quiet would be broken by the return of his cellmate and the evening lockdown procedures. Whatever he wrote needed to be completed in this window of solitude.

He placed the pen against the paper and began writing, the letters forming with careful deliberation. His handwriting was precise and measured, each word considered before it was committed to the page.

Ms. Torres,

He paused, considering the formality. It felt right—neither presumptuous nor coldly distant.

I've read your letter many times since receiving it. Initially, I tried to put it away and not think about what you'd written. That didn't work. Your words about your brother have stayed with me, impossible to ignore or forget.

Jack stopped, reviewing what he'd written. The admission felt exposing, an acknowledgment that her letter had penetrated defenses he'd carefully maintained. But it was true, and anything less would be dishonest.

There's nothing I can say that will change what I did or bring your brother back to you. I won't offer excuses or explanations that might ease my conscience at the expense of your grief. Brad belongs to those who loved him—to you, to your family, to his friends. You have the right to remember him fully, as the complex person you knew him to be.

Jack paused again, struck by the truth of what he'd just written. Until Renee's letter, he hadn't considered that his action had claimed more than Brad's life—it had also attempted to define Brad's identity, reducing him to a single act and a deserved punishment. There was a kind of arrogance in that, a presumption that Jack was now seeing clearly for the first time.

I honor the truth of your grief without asking for your forgiveness. What I did took your brother from you permanently, and no words can adequately address that loss. I recognize that writing to me required courage and a generosity of spirit that's remarkable under the circumstances.

Jack hesitated over how to close the letter. Traditional endings seemed inappropriate—neither "sincerely" nor "regards" could possibly convey the complex relationship between them. After consideration, he opted for simplicity.

Thank you for telling me about Brad.

Jack West

He read the completed letter twice, searching for unintended implications or hollow sentiments. The words weren't perfect—how could they be?—but they were honest. They acknowledged Renee's loss without diminishing it. They respected Brad's humanity without excusing Jack's action. And perhaps most importantly, they didn't ask for anything from Renee—not understanding, not absolution, not continued correspondence.

Jack folded the letter carefully along precise thirds, creasing each fold with the edge of his thumb. The physical act felt like a ritual, a deliberate handling of something valuable and fragile. He'd need an envelope from the commissary, and he'd have to wait until mail call to send it. These practical considerations grounded him after the emotional effort of composition.

The letter wouldn't change what had happened. It wouldn't shorten his sentence or ease Renee's grief. But it represented a kind of truth that Jack hadn't previously acknowledged—that Brad Torres had been more than a target, more than a justification. He had been someone's brother. Someone's son. A person composed of ordinary moments, small kindnesses, and terrible mistakes.

Just like Jack himself.

The letter arrived three weeks after Jack had sent his response, the envelope identical to the first—same cream color, same neat handwriting. When it arrived, Jack felt a strange lightness in his stomach, as if he'd missed a step on a staircase. He hadn't expected Renee to write again. Hadn't asked for it. Had been careful, in fact, not to invite further correspondence. Yet here was her name in the upper left corner, waiting like an unspoken question.

Jack held the envelope without opening it through the remainder of the day's routine—through dinner in the crowded cafeteria, through the structured tedium of evening recreation period with its worn checkerboards and monitored conversations. He carried it like something volatile, a small weight in his pocket that seemed to grow heavier with each passing hour.

When lockdown finally came Jack sat on the edge of his bunk, beneath the cone of light from the single fixture overhead. Cam, sensing the significance of the moment, turned his attention ostentatiously to his magazine, creating what passed for privacy in their shared eight-by-ten space.

Jack ran his thumb beneath the sealed flap, the tearing sound unnaturally loud in the evening quiet. Inside was a single sheet, folded with the same careful precision as before. Renee's handwriting remained neat and controlled, but Jack noticed subtle differences from her first letter—the pressure slightly heavier, the letters more firmly drawn, as if she'd written with greater certainty this time.

Mr. West,

Thank you for your response. I wasn't sure you would write back, and I appreciate that you took the time to do so.

I've considered carefully what I want to say to you, and I've decided that the most respectful approach is simple honesty: I don't forgive you for killing my brother, and I don't hate you for it either. Both reactions would require more emotional energy than I'm willing to give this situation. What happened can't be undone. Brad remains gone, and your acknowledgment of his humanity, while meaningful to me, doesn't change that fundamental reality.

Jack's breath caught slightly, the directness of her words landing with unexpected force. There was no artifice in her statement, no performative emotion or hidden agenda. Just the unvarnished truth—she neither absolved nor condemned him. The simplicity of this position hit harder than either extreme would have.

You wrote that Brad belongs to those who loved him, and I've thought about that phrase many times since reading it. There's a generosity in that perspective that I wasn't expecting. Most people in your position might have continued to define him only by his worst action, as justification for what followed. Your willingness to see him as more than that single moment suggests a capacity for reflection that serves you well.

His hands tightened slightly on the paper's edges. Renee's assessment felt dangerously close to praise, something Jack neither wanted nor believed he deserved. Yet her observation was accurate—his response had acknowledged Brad's complexity rather than reducing him to a convenient villain in Jack's narrative.

I don't know what you hope to gain from this correspondence, and I don't know what I hoped to gain by initiating it. Perhaps there was nothing to "gain" at all—just a human impulse to connect across the divide created by violence. To remind us both that behind these terrible events are people trying to make sense of what can never truly make sense.

This will be my final letter. Not because I'm angry or dissatisfied with our exchange, but because I believe we've said what needed to be said. I will continue my life, carrying Brad's memory and absence. You will continue yours, carrying whatever weight your actions have placed upon you. Neither of us can change what happened, but perhaps this exchange has changed, in some small way, how we carry it.

Renee Torres

Jack read the letter twice more, each time struck by its calm clarity. There was neither the false comfort of forgiveness nor the familiar territory of condemnation. Instead, Renee had offered something he hadn't realized was possible—an acknowledgment of what had happened without allowing it to define either of them completely.

He sat with the letter in his hands, the paper light yet somehow substantial. Outside the cell, the prison continued its nighttime routine—distant voices, the occasional metallic sound of a door or gate, the soft-soled steps of guards making their rounds. Inside, a different kind of space had opened—not freedom, not escape, but a subtle shift in perspective.

The subtle shift inside him wasn't dramatic—no sudden lightening of his burden, no theatrical moment of catharsis. Rather, it was a quiet realignment, like a bone that had been set improperly beginning to find its natural position. The guilt remained, as did the responsibility. But something else had entered the equation—a recognition that he could not control how others bore their loss or defined Brad's memory.

From the lower bunk, Cam's voice broke the silence. "Bad news?"

Jack looked down, momentarily disoriented, as if he'd forgotten he wasn't alone with Renee's words. "No," he said after a pause. "Not bad."

"Not good either, from the look on your face."

Jack considered this assessment. "True," he acknowledged. "But mayb e... honest."

Cam nodded, understanding without requiring elaboration. In their world, honesty was currency more valuable than comfort. Jack folded Renee's letter along its original creases, the action now familiar from the handling of her first communication. This letter, like its predecessor, would not be hidden away or denied. It had earned its place in his consciousness, a marker of something significant even if he couldn't yet fully articulate what that significance might be.

Jack stood before his open locker; Renee's folded letter balanced on his palm like a small white bird. The narrow metal cabinet gaped before him; its contents arranged with the careful precision that had become his signature in South Woods. Unlike his previous impulse to bury her first letter deep beneath his other possessions, he now considered the spaces thoughtfully, weighing options as deliberately as a chess player contemplating the board.

Three weeks ago, Jack had shoved Renee's first letter beneath his extra T-shirts, a physical manifestation of his desire to bury its implications. He'd tried to treat her words as an intrusion, something to be hidden away and forgotten. That attempt had failed spectacularly, with the letter's contents expanding in his mind until they occupied more space than the physical paper could possibly contain. Hiding it had only emphasized its power.

Now, Jack placed Renee's final letter deliberately at the front of the locker, propped against the metal side where its cream-colored edge would be visible each time he opened the door. The action wasn't impulsive but considered—a choice made after hours of reflection. He positioned it carefully, adjusting its angle so that Renee's name was partially visible on the folded exterior.

Three years into his sentence, Jack had perfected emotional efficiency—channeling his thoughts toward survival, not regret. It kept him functional, safe, sane. But Renee's letters had forced a shift, exposing the limits of that approach. This placement marked a step away from denial, from the reflexive self-protection that had shaped his early response.

The block settled into its nighttime rhythm—coughs, murmurs, the scuff of guards' shoes. Jack lay still, hands folded over his stomach, Cam already asleep. In this liminal space between institutional day and true night, a reckoning took shape. It wasn't insomnia that kept him awake—he'd mastered the prison skill of sleeping through almost anything——but a deliberate choice to sit with the truths that had crystallized from Renee's letters, counseling, and his own stubborn wrestling.

This wasn't about forgiveness or absolution. It was about recognizing that human complexity extended to them all—Brad, Renee, Ruby, and himself. They were more than the worst thing that had happened to them or the worst thing they had done.

20
Ruby's Visit

The guard at the entrance checked his clipboard, nodded, and opened the door. Ruby stepped through, her blonde hair pulled back in its customary practical style, her movements precise and deliberate. She wore khaki pants and a green polo shirt with the Garden Center logo embroidered on the breast pocket. She must have come directly from the nursery where she cultivated plants and flowers, organizing the natural world into orderly rows. The irony wasn't lost on him - his sister who tended growing things, and him, locked away in a place where nothing grew.

"Hey," she said, sliding into the seat across from him. The single syllable carried the weight of everything unsaid between them.

"Hey yourself," Jack replied, his voice dropping into the comfortable cadence they'd established over three years of these visits. Ruby took her seat, her posture mirroring his—straight-backed, composed, revealing little. The resemblance between them had always been more in mannerism than appearance, in the particular way they carried themselves.

"How's the greenhouse?" Jack asked, beginning with safe territory as they typically did, establishing connection before moving to anything more substantial.

"Busy. Spring rush is starting early this year. We can barely keep up with demand for vegetable seedlings. Mr. Peterson put me in charge of the entire perennial section. Said my organizational skills were 'transformative.'"

Jack nodded, noting the hint of pride she allowed herself. "He's right. You've always had a talent for creating systems that work."

"It's just plants," Ruby said, her typical deflection of praise, but a small smile touched the corner of her mouth. "The inventory software helps. I'm learning the backend management now too."

Jack leaned forward slightly, genuinely interested. "Management track?"

"Maybe." Ruby's fingers smoothed an invisible wrinkle from her pants. "Peterson mentioned something about assistant manager training next fall." She shrugged, the gesture deliberately casual. "We'll see."

"That's good," Jack said. "You deserve it."

A brief silence settled between them, not uncomfortable but charged with something unspoken. Jack watched as Ruby's eyes tracked around the room, noting the other visiting families, the guards positioned at intervals along the walls, the institutional clock marking time in measured increments. Her gaze returned to him, more focused than before, her expression shifting subtly.

"I got a letter yesterday," she said, her voice dropping slightly though her composure remained intact. "From Renee Torres."

Jack felt the air leave his lungs in a slow, controlled exhale. He should have anticipated this, should have known that once Renee had reached out to him, she might extend that reach to Ruby as well. "What did she say?"

"She told me you two had been corresponding. That she wrote to you about Brad, and you wrote back." Ruby's voice remained even, but her knuckles whitened as she clasped her hands together on the table. "Why didn't you tell me?"

Jack couldn't meet her gaze. "I didn't want to burden you with it."

Ruby sighed. "That's the problem, Jack. Everything you do to protect me becomes my burden anyway."

Jack felt a familiar defensiveness rise in his chest, the reflexive justification that had sustained him through years of imprisonment. "Ruby—"

"No. Let me say this." She took a deep breath before continuing, "You killed a man for me, and every single day I live with that weight. I never asked you to kill for me, Jack. I never wanted that sacrifice."

"I couldn't let him hurt you again," Jack said, his voice dropping to nearly a whisper. "I couldn't stand by and do nothing."

Ruby held Jack's gaze. "Tell me the truth. Not the version you've been telling yourself for three years. Not the story you crafted to make this bearable. What really happened that day? Why did you go to his apartment?"

Something cracked inside Jack—a hairline fracture in the narrative he'd carefully built. He looked at his sister—really looked at her—not as the traumatized victim he'd cast her as in his mind, but as a strong, determined woman demanding honesty. She deserved that much. Perhaps she always had.

Jack exhaled, a shaky breath bracing himself. "Do you remember that night at the tavern? Three years ago? With that guy... Dylan?"

Ruby looked up slowly. The memory had never really left. "The one who wouldn't leave me alone." She paused, her voice tightening. "You nearly choked him to death."

Jack gave a shallow nod, absorbing the words like punishment. He stared at the table before speaking again. "I didn't sleep that night."

Silence filled the space.

"I stayed up, replaying every moment of your assault. From five years earlier." His voice strained against the memory. "That's when I knew—what Brad did... what I couldn't stop... it would haunt everything. Forever."

Ruby said nothing.

Jack continued, each word a deliberate act. "Early the next morning, I drove to his apartment. He'd just gotten out of prison. I thought if I could face him—say what I needed to—I might be able to let it go. Start fresh. Be the father Simon needed. Be whole for Tabby."

Around them, the murmur of voices in the visitation room drifted in and out, distant and irrelevant. The space between them had collapsed into something raw and confessional.

Jack fell silent. Ruby waited, then prompted gently, "And then?"

He swallowed. His voice dropped. "I lost it. Again. Like I did with Dylan." The words stripped away any illusion that his actions had been measured—that they had served some righteous purpose.

Jack's admission hovered between them, fragile and damning.

"I couldn't convince him to leave you alone. To leave all of us alone. And then—it all came rushing back. How you asked me to protect you five years earlier. How I failed. Finding you after the assault."

He hesitated, then—

"How I almost lost you."

Ruby inhaled, her chest rising slowly. "From my suicide attempt, " she said quietly, naming what neither had said yet. The trauma of Brad's assault had led Ruby to that moment.

Jack didn't look up. But something in him flinched.

"You were the one who found me," she said softly. "You got me help."

Jack's voice was even, but his eyes betrayed something raw, something fractured. "After I killed him, I told myself I eliminated a threat—that it was the only way to keep my family safe."

His hand curled into a fist.

"But that wasn't it. I lost control. I was so afraid of failing again… of something happening to you. To Tabby."

Ruby saw it clearly now. He hadn't lashed out in anger. He had unraveled.

The brother who had carried her burdens, who had made her pain his own, had finally broken under the weight of everything she'd once asked of him. They had both been drowning—reacting instead of thinking, hurting instead of healing.

After a long silence, Ruby spoke, her voice trembling. "I blamed myself, Jack. All these years. I thought… if I had never gotten involved with Brad in the first place, if I hadn't leaned on you—maybe you'd still have your life. You'd be home. With Tabby. With Simon."

Jack shook his head slowly. "Ruby… none of this is your fault."

She looked at him, her expression hard to read. "It's not all yours, either."

His brow furrowed.

"You don't get to carry this like a martyr," she said. "We all made choices. Me, you…even Brad. And we each have to own what came of them."

Jack absorbed that, the words her words settling in.

She leaned forward, barely above a whisper. "But Jack… Tabby and I aren't just people you protect. We love you. We need you here, with us—not sacrificing yourself on our behalf."

A guard strode by, voice clipped and indifferent. "Ten minutes."

The hum of the room sharpened around them—voices growing urgent, gestures quickening.

Jack stared at his hands. "I don't know how to make this right."

The words sounded different now. Stripped of defense. Hollowed by truth.

Ruby's voice softened. "Maybe you don't. Maybe there's no 'right.' Just the truth. And where you go from here."

That landed hard.

Jack looked up. Slowly, he nodded.

Ruby reached across the table, her fingers stopping just short of his in deference to the prison's no-contact rules.

"Time's up," called a guard from near the entrance. Around them, families engaged in hurried goodbyes, final embraces where allowed, promises to write or call.

"Think about what I said. Really think about it." Ruby said.

Jack remained seated. "I will," he promised, meeting her eyes with sincerity.

He watched as Ruby walked toward the exit, her back straight, her stride purposeful. She didn't look back—she never did during these departures, a personal rule she'd established during her first visit. Jack had always assumed it was to hide her tears, to maintain her composure. Now he wondered if it was something else entirely—an assertion of forward movement, of continuing her life despite the pause his imprisonment created.

Later, back in his cell, Jack lay on his bunk staring at the ceiling that had become a familiar canvas for his thoughts.

He thought about Renee's final letter, still in his locker, still in plain sight, a daily reminder that he can't erase the past. Two women, connected by violence he had perpetrated, both refusing to let him simplify their experiences into something tolerable. Jack closed his eyes, not to escape their truths, but to fully absorb them—to begin the difficult work of seeing beyond his own perspective to the broader consequences of his actions.

21
Freedom

Jack resumed his walk across the plaza, each step carrying him further from the past eight years and closer to the life that had continued without him. The duffel bag containing his meager possessions weighed against his shoulder, a physical reminder of how little he had accumulated during his incarceration and how much he had lost. His eyes remained fixed ahead, searching for the parking lot where Tabby had promised to wait, where his son—no longer the infant he had held during those first prison visits but now an eight-year-old boy he knew primarily through supervised conversations—would see his father as a free man for the first time in his life.

The concrete beneath his feet gave way to asphalt as Jack reached the visitor parking area. He paused at this new boundary, another invisible line crossed. Inside, surfaces were institutional—polished concrete, painted cinder block, stainless steel worn dull by thousands of hands. Here, the world presented itself in textures he'd almost forgotten—rough asphalt with its pebbled surface, the soft movement of new spring leaves on trees planted along the perimeter, the unpredictable patterns of clouds drifting across the horizon. His senses, calibrated for years to the limited stimuli of confinement, struggled to process this sudden abundance.

Freedom, Jack realized, would require its own kind of adjustment. His body still moved according to prison rhythms—the measured steps, the contained gestures, the careful positioning that avoided accidental contact with others. He consciously lengthened his stride, letting his arms swing more naturally at his sides, small rebellions against ingrained habits. The clothes Tabby had sent for his release—jeans, a button-down shirt, a light jacket—felt strange against his skin after years of identical prison-issued garments. The fabric moved differently, the fit more precise, another reminder that he was reclaiming his identity one sensation at a time.

Jack scanned the parking lot methodically, the habit of surveillance not yet broken. A dozen or so vehicles occupied spaces near the entrance—family members waiting for releases, staff finishing their shifts, the occasional official visitor. His eyes moved across each one with the automatic assessment he'd developed inside, calculating potential threats, identifying surveillance points. He caught himself mid-thought and deliberately relaxed his shoulders, forcing his mind away from prison calculations and toward the simple task of finding his family.

And then he saw them, standing beside the familiar shape of his old Lexus. The car itself startled him first—a tangible piece of his previous life preserved but visibly aged, the once-glossy black finish now dulled by years of sun exposure, a small dent visible on the passenger door that hadn't been there when he last drove it. The sight of this mechanical witness to his absence hit him with unexpected force, this object that had continued to exist and serve its purpose while he remained static within South Woods' walls.

But the car was merely background to what truly mattered. Tabby stood by the driver's side, one hand resting on the roof, the other holding Simon's shoulder. She wore a white dress flecked with faded cherries that caught the spring breeze, the fabric rippling slightly around her calves.

And Simon—Jack's breath caught in his chest. His son stood straight-backed beside his mother, dark hair falling across his forehead in a way that echoed Jack's own. Not the infant Jack had first held in the visitation room, not the toddler who had walked tentative circles around the metal tables under guards' watchful eyes, not even the schoolboy who had brought report cards and careful drawings to share during their weekly hours. Here stood a child on the cusp of adolescence, with a serious set to his jaw that Jack recognized from his own reflection.

Jack's feet moved before his mind fully registered the command, carrying him toward them with increasing urgency. The distance between them—no longer measured in institutional rules and visitation schedules but in simple yards of asphalt—diminished with each step. He watched as Tabby spotted him, her hand tightening briefly on Simon's shoulder, her face transforming with a smile that began in her eyes before reaching her lips. Simon straightened, his expression intensely focused, as if memorizing every detail of his father's approach.

They had seen each other just four days ago, during Jack's final prison visit. They had spoken the usual words, made the usual plans, exchanged the usual carefully moderated touches allowed under supervision. But this—this was different. This was the beginning of the life they had discussed in hypotheticals, the reality they had constructed in letters and phone calls and one-hour visits suddenly manifesting before them.

When only ten feet separated them, Simon moved first, slipping from beneath his mother's hand and closing the final distance at a run. Jack dropped his duffel bag without thought, kneeling to meet his son at eye level. Simon crashed into him with the uninhibited momentum of childhood, arms wrapping around Jack's neck with a fierce grip that spoke volumes about the years of carefully constrained hugs they had endured.

"Dad," Simon whispered, the single syllable containing everything that couldn't be said aloud.

Jack's arms encircled his son, feeling the solid reality of him—the warmth, the rapid heartbeat, the slight tremor in the small shoulders. Simon smelled of shampoo and the faint trace of peanut butter from lunch and something indefinably young and alive. Jack buried his face briefly in his son's hair, allowing himself this moment of pure sensation. Eight years of fatherhood compressed into weekly visits had created a strange familiarity between them, but this—this unguarded physical connection—was new territory for both.

His hands registered the details his eyes had missed during prison visits—the exact breadth of Simon's shoulders, the texture of his hair. For years, he had been allowed only brief hugs at the beginning and end of each visit, always aware of guards' observant eyes and ticking clocks. Now, he could simply hold him, without countdown or constraint.

Simon pulled back slightly, his dark eyes—so like Jack's own—studying his father's face with that serious, analytical gaze that had always seemed beyond his years. "You're really here," he said, not a question but a confirmation, as if he needed to state the obvious to fully believe it.

"I'm really here," Jack confirmed, one hand moving to cup the side of Simon's face. His expression carried the particular watchfulness Jack had noted in their visits—the careful observation of a child who had learned to analyze adult behaviors for hidden meanings.

Movement caught his eye, and Jack looked up to see Tabby approaching, her steps measured as if giving father and son this moment before inserting herself. The sight of her—not seated across an institutional table but standing in the open air, moving toward him without restriction—created a constriction in Jack's chest that was both painful and exquisite. He rose to his feet, one hand remaining on Simon's shoulder, unwilling to break contact even momentarily.

"Jack," Tabby said, her voice carrying the slight tremor he recognized from moments of intense emotion. She stopped just short of him, a hand's breadth of space between them that seemed to contain all the years of their separation.

And then the space vanished as Jack stepped forward, pulling her into an embrace that erased all the years of carefully monitored contact. His arms wrapped around her waist, lifting her feet clear of the ground as he drew her against his chest. The familiar scent of her jasmine shampoo enveloped him, unchanged after all these years, a constant in a world that had continued without him. He felt her arms circle his neck, her face press into the curve of his shoulder, her body relax into his with the trust that had sustained them through the years of separation.

Jack tightened his embrace. In the prison visitation room, their physical contact had been limited to carefully choreographed interactions under constant surveillance. Now, with her body pressed fully against his, with no guards monitoring their every move, with no clock counting down the minutes until separation, something long-frozen within him began to thaw.

He spun her in a small circle, her feet still off the ground, her dress flaring slightly with the movement. The simple joy of this action—this unplanned, uncalculated expression of emotion—felt foreign after years of measuring every gesture, containing every impulse. He heard her laugh, a sound so rarely experienced in the visitation room where conversations remained measured and subdued by institutional necessity. The sound traveled through him like electricity, awakening nerve endings deadened by years of forced restraint.

When he set her down, his lips found hers with an urgency that surprised them both. In prison, kisses had been quick, perfunctory things—the brief contact allowed at the beginning and end of visits, performative affection under watchful eyes. This kiss contained eight years of absence, of longing, of connection maintained across impossible distance. Her hands moved to frame his face, fingers tracing the contours that had aged in subtle ways during their separation, relearning him through touch as he was relearning her.

They broke apart only when Simon cleared his throat, the sound carrying the particular mix of embarrassment and amusement unique to children witnessing parental affection. Jack laughed—a rusty sound, unfamiliar after so long—and extended his arm, drawing Simon back into their circle. His other arm remained firmly around Tabby's waist, unwilling to relinquish the connection so recently reestablished.

Standing there in the prison parking lot, one arm around his wife and the other around his son, Jack experienced a completeness he had preserved in memory but almost forgotten in physical reality. The sensation was overwhelming—not just happiness but a more complex emotion that encompassed relief, gratitude, disbelief, and an undertow of grief for the years lost.

"Let's go home," he said, the word 'home' catching slightly in his throat. For so long, 'home' had been an abstract concept, a place that existed in letters and photographs and stories shared across visitation tables. Now it was a real destination, a physical space where he would sleep tonight without locks and guards, where he would wake tomorrow without count bells and institutional routines.

Simon pressed against his side, still maintaining contact as if afraid his father might disappear if he let go. "We fixed up your workshop," he said, the words tumbling out with suppressed excitement. "Mom let me help organize all your tools. Everything's ready for when you want to start working again."

Jack looked down at his son, struck by this evidence of careful preparation, of life arranged to welcome him back. "Thank you," he said, the simple words inadequate for the emotion behind them. “I can’t wait to see it.”

Tabby’s hand found his, fingers interlacing with familiar precision. “Ruby and Jason wanted to be here too,” she said, “but we thought it might be better—just us, at first.”

Jack nodded, grateful for this understanding. As much as he loved his sister and valued Jason’s steadfast support of his family during his incarceration, this first moment of freedom belonged to the three of them alone. There would be time for wider reunions, for navigating the complex relationships that had evolved during his absence. For now, this was enough—more than enough. It was everything.

“We should get going,” Tabby said softly. “Traffic will be picking up soon.”

The practical consideration—so characteristic of her approach to challenges—brought Jack back to the immediate present. He reluctantly loosened his hold on them both, bending to retrieve his fallen duffel bag. As he straightened, his eyes caught sight of the prison in the distance, its concrete walls and guard towers still visible across the plaza he had traversed. For a moment, he felt the phantom weight of those walls pressing against him, the ingrained caution of years under constant surveillance.

Then Simon’s hand slipped into his, small fingers gripping with surprising strength. “Dad?” his son asked, sensing his momentary distraction. “Are you okay?”

Jack turned away from the prison, deliberately focusing on the faces before him—his wife, his son, the family that had waited for him, that had maintained connection across impossible barriers. “I’m better than okay,” he said, and meant it. Whatever challenges lay ahead—reintegration, rebuilding, relearning the rhythms of family life—they would face them together, without bulletproof glass or time limits.

He followed them to the Lexus, watching as Tabby unlocked the doors with the familiar electronic chirp. Simon immediately claimed the back seat, buckling himself in with practiced efficiency. Jack paused before the passenger door, his hand hovering over the handle. Such a simple action—opening a car door—yet it represented a freedom of movement he hadn’t experienced in eight years.

"Jack?" Tabby's voice came from across the roof of the car, her eyes meeting his with understanding. "Take your time."

He nodded, grateful for her perception, for her patience with the small adjustments that would mark his return to everyday life. Drawing a deep breath, he opened the door and slid into the passenger seat, the leather cool against his back. The interior smelled of Tabby's jasmine and Simon's candy and the particular scent of the car itself—familiar yet strange, like so much else in this moment of transition.

As Tabby started the engine and guided the car toward the exit, Jack watched the prison recede in the side mirror. As they merged onto the main road, Jack felt the past press against his chest like a phantom weight. He had traveled this stretch once before—shackled in the back of a transport van, his old life shrinking into the distance. That day, his name had become a number, his choices reduced to sentences in a case file.

Now, he was returning by the same route but in reverse. No chains. No van. Just the quiet presence of his family beside him, their steady breathing tethering him to the present. He wasn't just going home—he was reclaiming himself, piece by piece.

The years in prison had carved hard truths into him: that accountability couldn't erase the past regardless of the sentence imposed, that healing wasn't found in avoidance, and that neither his pain nor Ruby's could be buried and forgotten. The only way forward was through—and for the first time, he felt ready to face it.

22
Home

The Lexus rolled to a stop in the driveway, tires crunching softly on the familiar gravel. Jack stared through the windshield at the house—his house—that had existed for so long as nothing more than stories told across visitation tables and images captured in photographs mailed to South Woods. The reality of it struck him with unexpected force: the soft yellow paint he'd never seen before, the new mailbox with "WEST" stenciled in Tabby's careful script, the flower beds edged with stones that Simon had described collecting from the creek during a summer project two years ago. It was both exactly as he'd pictured from their descriptions and entirely different, like a familiar face altered subtly by time.

"We're home," Tabby said softly from the driver's seat, her hand finding his across the console. She squeezed gently, her wedding band pressing against his skin—a physical anchor pulling him back from the disorientation of seeing his life's setting transformed.

In the backseat, Simon unbuckled with practiced efficiency. "Can I show Dad the workshop?" he asked, already reaching for the door handle, vibrating with the particular energy of childhood that couldn't be contained by momentous occasions.

"Let's get inside first," Tabby replied, her voice carrying gentle authority.

They walked toward the house together, Simon darting ahead while Jack measured his steps carefully, still adjusting to movement without institutional constraints. The front walkway had been replaced—concrete now instead of the cracked flagstones he remembered. Three ceramic pots flanked the steps, filled with plants he couldn't name, their purple flowers nodding in the spring breeze.

At the front door, Jack paused. Years of missing this threshold—of imagining crossing it—had built the moment into something momentous in his mind. Now faced with the actual door (new, he noticed, with a different knocker than he remembered), he found himself suddenly paralyzed by the simple act of stepping inside.

"Dad, come on!" Simon called from where he'd already bounded up the steps, hand on the doorknob. "Aunt Ruby said she's making your favorite for dinner."

Jack nodded, one foot on the bottom step, eyes taking in details that letters and photographs couldn't convey—the precise shade of the new door, the slight tilt to the porch railing that had always needed fixing, the wind chime hanging from the eave that hadn't been there before. Time had continued here without him, marking its passage in these small alterations to the landscape of his memory.

The door swung open before Simon could turn the knob. Ruby stood in the entryway, her blonde hair caught up in a loose knot, her eyes already bright with unshed tears. Behind her, Jason lingered a few steps back, hands in his pockets, his expression a careful mix of welcome and restraint.

"You're here," Ruby said, the simple statement laden with everything unsaid between them—years of visits where she'd been the one leaving at the end of the hour, returning to this place that Jack could only imagine.

Simon pushed past her legs with the casual entitlement of a child in his own home, dropping his backpack beside the living room couch with practiced familiarity. "We played the alphabet game on the way back from prison," he announced to no one in particular, disappearing into the kitchen.

Jack remained on the threshold, taking in the entryway with its new coat of sage green paint. The sideboard had been moved from the right wall to the left, topped now with a collection of framed photographs charting Simon's growth from infant to boy. And there, taped to the wall at child height, a series of crayon drawings—wobbly houses, stick figures with disproportionate limbs, a tree with a square nestled in its branches. Simon's artwork, displayed with the casual pride of everyday family life.

Tabby's hand settled on his lower back, a gentle pressure guiding him forward. "Come in," she said quietly, the words an invitation to more than just physical entry. Jack stepped across the threshold, the familiar creak of the third floorboard sending a jolt of recognition through him—a sound his body remembered even as his eyes adjusted to the changes around him.

Ruby moved then, closing the distance between them. Her arms wrapped around him with surprising strength, her face pressed against his shoulder. Jack felt the slight tremor in her frame, heard the shaky breath she drew before pulling back to look at him properly.

"Welcome home," she said, her voice steady despite the tears that had spilled onto her cheeks. Her fingers gripped his forearms briefly before releasing him, a tactile reassurance that he was real, that he was here.

Jason stepped forward, extending his hand. "Good to have you back, Jack," he said, the simple greeting carrying the weight of their complex history. His handshake was firm, direct—an acknowledgment between men who had navigated an impossible situation with as much grace as they could manage.

"Thanks," Jack replied, the word encompassing far more than this moment. "For everything." His eyes held Jason's briefly, communicating what couldn't be said aloud—gratitude for the support Jason had provided to Tabby and Simon during his absence, acknowledgment of the boundaries he had respected.

"Something smells good," Tabby said, breaking the moment with deliberate lightness. Her hand remained on Jack's back, guiding him gently toward the kitchen.

They moved as a group through the living room, where Jack noted more changes—a new sofa replacing their old one, different curtains framing the windows, Simon's toys occupying spaces once reserved for Jack's woodworking magazines. The physical evidence of life's continuation surrounded him, years of small decisions and acquisitions that had happened without his input.

In the kitchen, dinner simmered in the oven, filling the air with the savory scent of garlic and rosemary. Ruby moved immediately to the counter, where a half-assembled salad waited. Her hands resumed their work with the easy rhythm of someone comfortable in this space, tossing greens with practiced motions.

"The bus schedule changed again last month," Jason said, settling into a chair at the kitchen table. "They moved the stop from Maple to Elm, which adds about ten minutes to the morning commute."

Jack recognized the offering for what it was—normal conversation, everyday concerns, a deliberate step away from the extraordinary circumstances of his return. "Is it still the 22 route?" he asked, accepting the unspoken agreement to focus on the mundane.

"No, they renamed it the Blue Line now," Tabby replied, moving to the cabinet for glasses. Her actions in the kitchen were fluid, automatic, the product of years navigating this space. "Part of the city transit rebranding."

"The lawnmower broke last week," Ruby added, her voice steadier now as she tipped cherry tomatoes into the salad bowl. "Jason tried to fix it, but I think we need a professional."

"The motor's shot," Jason confirmed. "I looked up a replacement part, but it's an older model."

Simon reappeared, clutching a folder he'd retrieved from his backpack. "Dad, I need to finish my science fair project this weekend. It's about tree rings and how they tell time. Can you help me? Mom says you know all about trees."

Jack felt something loosen in his chest at the casual way Simon incorporated him into future plans, as if his presence was already an accepted fact rather than a fragile new reality. "I'd like that," he said, his voice rougher than he intended.

"Simon's been reading everything he can find about dendrochronology," Tabby said, the scientific term rolling off her tongue with the ease of someone who had heard it repeated countless times by an enthusiastic child. "He checked out seven books from the library last week."

They continued like this—passing ordinary information back and forth, rebuilding the framework of family life around Jack's presence. No one mentioned prison directly. No one referenced the eight-year gap. Instead, they focused on the broken lawnmower, the bus schedule, Simon's science project—the texture of everyday life that Jack had been denied for so long.

As they talked, Jack watched them all—Tabby reaching into the refrigerator with the same unconscious grace she'd always possessed, Ruby's hands moving confidently among ingredients she'd assembled for this homecoming, Jason leaning casually against the counter in a space that had become familiar to him over years of supporting this family, Simon moving between adults with the assurance of a child securely attached to all of them.

They were a complete family again, yet irrevocably changed by the years of separation. Jack felt both absolutely essential to this tableau and strangely superfluous—a missing piece returned to a puzzle that had reshaped itself in his absence. The contradiction created an ache behind his sternum, not quite pain but something deeper—the simultaneous joy of return and grief for what could never be recovered.

Yet beneath that ache lay something else—the quiet certainty that they would find their way forward together, building something new from the foundations that had endured despite everything.

Ruby set the ceramic dish on the table with the ceremonial care of someone placing an offering on an altar. Steam rose from the golden-brown crust of meatloaf—Jack's favorite, prepared exactly as he remembered it, with the precise ratio of breadcrumbs to meat that had made it a weekend staple in their life before. The scent hit him with the force of memory: Sunday dinners around this table, Tabby laughing at something he'd said, Ruby arguing good-naturedly about politics. The normality of it—the sheer ordinary wonder of family dinner—made his throat tighten unexpectedly.

"Garlic mashed potatoes," Ruby announced, setting down another dish before returning to the counter for the green bean casserole topped with crispy fried onions. "And homemade rolls." The spread before them represented hours of preparation, a welcome home constructed from butter, flour, and deliberate care.

"This looks amazing," Jack said, his voice steadier than he felt. Eight years of institutional food—of meals designed for efficiency rather than pleasure—had recalibrated his expectations. The table before him now, with its mismatched serving dishes and carefully prepared comfort food, seemed almost surreal in its ordinariness.

"We eat family-style now," Simon informed him with the serious authority of a child explaining important household protocols. "You take what you want and pass it to the left. Mom says it's more civil than everyone reaching."

Jack nodded gravely, accepting this information with the weight Simon clearly felt it deserved. Another small evolution in family life he'd missed—the establishment of dinner table protocols as Simon grew from toddler to boy.

Tabby began passing dishes, and soon their plates were filled with slices of meatloaf, mounds of garlic mashed potatoes, and generous portions of green bean casserole. The first bite hit Jack with unexpected intensity—flavors sharp and distinct after years of institutional blandness. He closed his eyes briefly, savoring the simple perfection of Ruby's cooking, of food prepared with attention and care.

"Dad, did Mom tell you about my rocket?" Simon asked around a mouthful of potatoes, his enthusiasm overriding table manners. "I built it from a kit, but I modified the fins to make it more aerodynamic. It went so high we almost lost it in the Petersons' yard."

Jack smiled, cutting another piece of meatloaf. "She mentioned it during visits, but I'd like to hear all about it."

This was all the invitation Simon needed. He launched into a detailed account of his model rocket construction, hands gesturing animatedly to illustrate the dimensions of fins and the trajectory of flight. His vocabulary was precise, technical terms dropping into conversation with the casual confidence of a child who had internalized scientific language through passionate interest.

"Ms. Abernathy—she's my science teacher—she says I have a natural aptitude for engineering principles," Simon continued, the adult phrase sounding endearingly formal in his young voice. "I told her that's because I'm going to build houses someday. Or maybe be an arborist like you were." He paused only long enough to take another bite before transitioning seamlessly to stories about his classmates.

"Tyler's the fastest runner in our grade, but he's terrible at math. And Emma knows everything about sharks—she has seventeen books just about different shark species. Her dad took her to the aquarium in Cincinnati where they have a touch tank, and she got to feel a bamboo shark."

Jack watched his son as he spoke, cataloging the small details that prison visits couldn't fully convey—the particular way Simon's eyebrows pulled together when he was making an important point, the unconscious gesture of pushing hair from his forehead that mirrored Jack's own habit, the rapid shift of topics that revealed a mind constantly moving, connecting, exploring. This animated, unrestricted Simon was different from the more measured child who had visited South Woods, where conversations happened under observation and time constraints shaped every interaction.

The entirety fatherhood compressed into weekly visits had created a peculiar dynamic—Jack knew his son in carefully structured increments, but this unrehearsed, natural flow of Simon's thoughts and interests revealed dimensions he was only now discovering. Pride mixed with grief as Jack recognized the years of everyday moments he'd missed—the gradual emergence of Simon's personality, interests, and habits that couldn't be fully captured in photos or brief visits.

"I have eleven library books right now," Simon continued, unaware of Jack's internal reflection. "Mom says that's too many to keep track of, but I have a system. The space books stay by my bed, the animal books go on my desk, and the mystery books are for reading during silent time at school."

Under the table, Tabby's hand found Jack's thigh, her fingers squeezing gently. When he glanced at her, she was already looking at him, her eyes communicating understanding of his complex emotions. The silent message was clear: She saw his struggle, his wonder, his grief—and she was beside him through it all. Her thumb traced a small circle against his leg, a private gesture of connection that grounded him in the present moment.

"Simon's reading at a sixth-grade level," she said, her voice carrying a mother's pride. "We can't keep enough books on hand for him at the library."

"I like knowing things," Simon stated matter-of-factly, scraping the last of his mashed potatoes from his plate. "Books know everything."

Jason laughed, the sound genuine and warm. "Can't argue with that logic."

As dinner wound down, they began clearing plates to the counter. Jack moved to help, the institutional habit of immediate cleanup deeply ingrained, but Ruby waved him back to his seat. "You're the guest of honor tonight," she insisted, stacking dishes with practiced efficiency. "We've got this."

Jack settled back into his chair, feeling strangely out of place in this familiar routine. For almost a decade, his movements had been dictated by prison schedules and protocols. Now, the simple freedom to remain seated while others cleared the table felt foreign, almost uncomfortable.

Ruby glanced at Jason as she set the last plate on the counter, a look passing between them that Jack recognized as the silent communication of a long-established couple. Jason nodded slightly, understanding without words what she was suggesting.

"Oh!" Ruby exclaimed, her tone of sudden realization so perfectly calibrated that Jack might have believed it genuine if not for the preceding look. "We forgot dessert. I meant to make your favorite apple pie, Jack, but with everything else..." She let the sentence trail off with a convincing display of remorse.

"We could go get a cake," Jason suggested, the casual proposal clearly part of this choreographed moment. "That bakery on Elm is still open for another hour."

Simon perked up immediately. "Can I come? They have those chocolate things with the sprinkles."

"Perfect idea," Ruby agreed, her eyes briefly meeting Jack's with a flicker of mischief that reminded him of their shared childhood, of her orchestrating situations with the same deliberate care. "Simon, want to help us pick out a cake?"

Simon was already on his feet, dinner forgotten in the prospect of dessert. "Can I get the one with the chocolate shavings on top? Or maybe the one with the filling? Or both?"

Jason stood, fishing car keys from his pocket with a jingle that seemed to accelerate Simon's excitement. "We'll see what they have," he said diplomatically, exchanging a brief look with Tabby that confirmed the adults were all aligned in this manufactured errand.

Ruby ushered Simon toward the front door with gentle efficiency, her hand on his shoulder guiding him forward. "We'll be back in about forty-five minutes," she said, the specific timeframe making the intention of their absence even clearer. "Maybe an hour, depending on how busy the bakery is."

Jack caught Tabby's eyes across the table as Ruby and Jason maneuvered Simon toward the door. The look that passed between them carried all the years of separation, of desire held in check by institutional rules, of physical connection reduced to brief hugs under watchful eyes. In that single glance was everything they couldn't say aloud—recognition of what Ruby had just engineered, anticipation of what would follow, gratitude for this gift of privacy in a day otherwise filled with careful navigation of family dynamics.

"Thanks, Ruby," Tabby called after them, her voice remarkably steady despite the color rising in her cheeks. "Take your time."

As the front door closed behind them, the house fell into a sudden, expectant silence. Jack reached across the table, taking Tabby's hand in his. Her fingers interlaced with his, warm and familiar yet thrillingly new in this context of genuine privacy.

"So," he said, his voice low and intimate in the quiet kitchen, "I think my sister just gave us some time alone."

Tabby's slow smile contained everything he'd dreamed of during long prison nights. "I think you're right," she agreed, rising from her chair without releasing his hand. "What should we do with it?"

Jack pulled Tabby against him, years of carefully restrained desire breaking through institutional discipline. The kiss was nothing like the measured, watchful embraces of prison visits—this was hunger and homecoming wrapped into a single desperate connection. Her body melted against his, familiar curves pressing through the fabric of her dress, her hands sliding beneath his shirt to touch skin that had been forbidden to her for eight years.

"Bedroom," she whispered against his mouth, the single word carrying all the yearning of their separation.

Jack didn't hesitate. He swept her into his arms with a strength born of prison routines—push-ups in a cell, pull-ups in the yard, every repetition imagined as preparation for this moment of return. Tabby's surprised laughter bubbled up, her arms circling his neck as he carried her down the hallway toward their bedroom—their bedroom, not just hers alone as it had been for too long.

The room had changed—new curtains, different bedside lamps, a quilt he didn't recognize covering the mattress they'd chosen together in what felt like another lifetime. But none of that mattered as he set her gently on the edge of the bed, her hands already working at the buttons of his shirt with an urgency that matched his own.

"I've thought about this every day," she said, her fingers trailing across his chest as she slid his shirt off his shoulders. Her touch explored the changes prison had wrought in his body—harder muscles, new definition carved by years of systematic exercise that had been both physical outlet and mental discipline.

Jack's hands found the buttons of her dress, fingers remembering their dance despite the years between. Each newly revealed inch of skin was both achingly familiar and thrillingly new—the freckle below her collarbone, the soft curve where neck met shoulder, the delicate hollow at the base of her throat where he pressed his lips, breathing in the jasmine scent of her.

"You're beautiful," he murmured, sliding the fabric down her arms to reveal the simple cotton bra beneath. No lace, no special occasion lingerie—just the everyday intimate garment of a woman who hadn't expected this moment until later, if at all. The ordinariness of it struck him as unbearably precious.

Tabby's hands moved to his belt, fingers working the buckle with determined focus. Her palm pressed against him through the denim, a bold touch that sent heat surging through his body.

Jack leaned forward, capturing her mouth again as his hands unfastened her last of her buttons with reverent care. He was already shrugging out of his jeans, his body responding to her touch with an urgency that threatened to overwhelm his self-control, when a voice called from the kitchen.

"Mom? Dad? I forgot my Gameboy!"

They froze, foreheads touching, breath mingling in the sudden silence. Simon's voice echoed again, closer now, footsteps moving through the house. "Mom, where's my Gameboy? I need it for the car ride!"

"One second, Simon," Tabby called, her voice remarkably steady despite the flush spreading across her chest. "We're just... talking."

Jack pressed his forehead against hers, suppressing a laugh that was equal parts tension and genuine humor. "Talking," he repeated in a whisper. "Is that what the kids call it these days?"

"Shh," she admonished, though her eyes sparkled with shared mischief. "He's eight. He still believes in Santa Claus."

Ruby's voice drifted down the hallway, closer than expected. "Simon, I'll help you find it. Your parents are... busy."

Jack and Tabby remained perfectly still, listening to the sound of Ruby's footsteps guiding Simon back toward the front of the house. "I think it might be in your backpack, by the couch," Ruby suggested, her voice growing fainter as she steered Simon away from the bedroom.

"But I already looked there," Simon protested, his voice trailing off as Ruby successfully redirected him.

"Let's check again," Ruby insisted, her tone leaving no room for argument. "And then we need to get going if we want to pick out a good cake."

A moment later, they heard Ruby's reassuring call from the front door. "Found it!" The front door clicked shut for the second time, followed by the distant sound of car doors and an engine starting.

Tabby's laugh broke the silence, tension releasing in a sound of pure joy that Jack hadn't heard in years. "God, I love your sister," she said, falling back onto the bed and pulling him down with her. "Even if her timing could use some work."

"She's always had my back," Jack agreed, his hands returning to their exploration of Tabby's body with renewed purpose. "Now, where were we?"

Her answer came in the form of a kiss that ignited everything they'd momentarily set aside. Clothes fell away with increasing urgency, revealing bodies both familiar and changed by time—the slight roundness to Tabby's belly from carrying Simon, the new definition in Jack's shoulders and arms, the small scar on her knee from a gardening accident three summers ago, the prison tattoo on his upper arm he'd never fully explained in letters.

They came together with none of the tentativeness Jack had feared during lonely nights in his cell. There was no awkwardness, no hesitation—just the perfect recognition of bodies that remembered each other despite the years apart. Tabby arched beneath him, her breath catching as he entered her, the sensation overwhelming in its immediacy after so long with only memory and imagination.

"Jack," she breathed, his name both prayer and affirmation on her lips. Her hands traced the muscles of his back, feeling them flex with each movement, relearning the rhythm of their shared pleasure. Her legs wrapped around him, drawing him deeper, erasing the years of separation with each pulse of connection.

The intensity built too quickly—years of abstinence and anticipation making control impossible. Jack buried his face against her neck, breathing in her scent as his body surrendered to the overwhelming wave of release. Tabby followed moments later, her soft cry muffled against his shoulder, her body tightening around him in the familiar pattern he'd carried in memory through countless prison nights.

They lay tangled together afterward, sweat cooling on their skin, the rumpled sheets a testament to their passionate reunion. Jack traced lazy patterns on her bare shoulder, marveling at the simple freedom to touch her without guards watching, without time limits, without institutional constraints.

"In my fantasies, I lasted longer," he said finally, a self-deprecating smile touching his lips. "Eight years of build-up, and I barely made it five minutes."

Tabby laughed, the sound vibrating against his chest where her head rested. "We have time," she reminded him, fingers tracing the line of his jaw. "All the time in the world now."

The distant hum of a car engine broke into their private bubble, reality intruding once again. Jack glanced at the bedside clock, surprised to find that nearly forty minutes had passed. "They're back," he said, reluctantly disentangling himself from Tabby's embrace.

They scrambled into clothes with the frantic energy of teenagers caught by parents rather than adults interrupted by children. Jack had just fastened his jeans when they heard the front door open, followed by Simon's animated voice describing the cake selection process in detail to no one in particular.

"Mom! Dad! They had chocolate AND vanilla, and Aunt Ruby said we could get both because it's a special occasion."

Tabby smoothed her dress, fingers combing quickly through tousled hair as she shot Jack a look of mingled amusement and frustration. "Perfect timing," she whispered, pressing a quick kiss to his lips before calling out, "We'll be right there, honey!"

They emerged from the bedroom with what Jack hoped was casual nonchalance, though he suspected their flushed faces and Tabby's hastily rebuttoned dress told their own story. Ruby's knowing smile as they entered the kitchen confirmed his suspicion, but her discretion held as she busied herself setting out plates for the cake.

"Look what we got, Dad." Simon said, pointing proudly to an elaborate confection on the counter—a two-layer cake, one chocolate and one vanilla, decorated with swirls of frosting and a simple "Welcome Home" written in blue icing. "Jason let me pick the colors, and Aunt Ruby asked them to write the special message."

"It's perfect," Jack said, his voice rough with emotion that had nothing to do with their interrupted lovemaking and everything to do with the simple acceptance in Simon's excited face. His son held none of the hesitation or wariness Jack had feared—only genuine joy at having his father home, at being a complete family again.

Jason handed out forks while Ruby cut generous slices of cake, the domesticity of the moment wrapping around them all like a comfortable blanket. As they gathered once more around the table, Jack felt Tabby's hand find his under the surface, their fingers interlacing in silent communication.

They had reclaimed the physical connection that prison had denied them, but the true homecoming wasn't just in their passionate reunion. It was here, in this kitchen, with Simon's animated chatter about cake flavors, Ruby's knowing smile, Jason's quiet support, and Tabby's hand warm in his—the complete circle of family, once broken and incomplete, but now, finally, whole again.

23
The Oak Tree

The oak tree cast dappled shadows across the backyard as Jack measured the plank of wood with practiced precision. Six weeks after his release, the simple act of handling wood without supervision still carried a weight of freedom that occasionally caught in his throat when he least expected it.

"Is that one going to be the floor?" Simon asked from his perch on a nearby stump, legs swinging in small, controlled arcs. His dark eyes tracked every movement of his father's hands with the particular intensity Jack had come to recognize as uniquely his son's—analytical, absorbing, cataloging.

"This piece will be part of the railing," Jack replied, marking the cut line with a carpenter's pencil. The mark was straight and unwavering, much like the boundaries he'd maintained in prison. Some habits would take longer to fade than others. "Safety first. Don't want anyone falling off the platform."

Simon nodded with a seriousness that seemed impossibly adult in his eight-year-old face. "Mom says you always think about safety. Even before."

Before. The word hung between them, their shared shorthand for the years of Jack's incarceration. Neither of them ever said "prison" directly, as if naming it might somehow summon it back.

"Your mom's right about that," Jack said, setting the wood against the sawhorses. He positioned the saw, its teeth gleaming in the spring sunlight. "Want to see how to make a straight cut?"

Simon slid off the stump, approaching with the careful deliberation that characterized all his movements. He stood beside Jack, his shoulder barely reaching his father's elbow, his posture a miniature mirror of Jack's straight-backed stance.

"Hold the saw like this," Jack demonstrated, his hands dwarfing the tool in a way that Simon's couldn't yet. "Fingers wrapped but not too tight. Let the saw do the work." He began cutting, the rhythmic rasp of metal against wood filling the space between heartbeats. Sawdust collected on his boots in small golden piles.

Simon watched, his forehead creased with concentration. "The angle matters," he observed, not asking but stating, having absorbed this fact from previous demonstrations.

Jack nodded, pride warming his chest. "Exactly right. Too steep and the cut's sloppy. Too shallow and you'll be here all day." He completed the cut with a final, deliberate stroke, then handed Simon a piece of sandpaper. "Want to smooth the edges?"

Simon accepted the paper with careful hands, approaching the freshly cut wood as if it were a living thing requiring respect. His small fingers worked the sandpaper along the edge, his technique imperfect but earnest.

"Is it sixty grit or eighty?" Simon asked, his vocabulary reflecting hours spent organizing Jack's workshop during the years of waiting, learning names and purposes for tools he couldn't yet use.

"Eighty," Jack confirmed, watching his son's methodical movements. "Good for finishing without removing too much material."

Simon nodded, filing away this information alongside all the other details he collected and categorized. "Is this how you did it when you worked on trees?"

"Similar principles," Jack said, selecting another board for cutting. "Though trees are less forgiving than lumber. They're alive, with their own ideas about which way they want to grow."

"Like people," Simon said, the observation dropping from him with the casual profundity of childhood.

Jack paused, the saw halfway through a new cut. His son's perception occasionally ambushed him like this—moments of insight that seemed beyond his years. "Yeah," he agreed softly. "A lot like people."

They worked in companionable silence for several minutes, the only sounds the rasp of the saw and the gentle susurration of sandpaper against wood. Jack occasionally glanced at Simon, still surprised by the simple fact of his presence, by the freedom to watch his son without counting down minutes until a guard called time.

"Ready to try hammering?" Jack asked as they finished preparing the railing pieces. He held out a hammer sized for smaller hands—purchased during his second week home, part of the careful accumulation of objects that would allow Simon to work alongside him.

Simon's eyes widened slightly, his composure slipping to reveal the excitement beneath. "You think I'm ready?"

"I do," Jack confirmed, selecting a nail from the coffee can he'd repurposed as hardware storage. "Start with the frame piece here. I'll hold it steady."

Simon accepted the hammer with a reverence that made Jack's throat tighten. He positioned the nail with careful deliberation; his tongue caught between his teeth in concentration.

"Don't worry about getting it perfect," Jack said, sensing his son's anxiety. "First time's about learning the feel of it."

Simon nodded but remained focused, his entire body tensed with effort. His first swing missed the nail entirely, connecting with wood instead. He looked up quickly, apology forming on his lips.

"That's normal," Jack assured him before the words could emerge. "Try again, but looser in the wrist."

Simon adjusted his grip, determination hardening his features. His second attempt connected with a satisfying ping. The nail sank a quarter-inch into the wood.

"There you go," Jack encouraged, holding the board steady as Simon continued. "Nice and easy."

The nail progressed in fits and starts, Simon's technique improving with each swing. When the head finally sat flush against the wood, a smile broke across his face—not the careful, measured expression he usually wore, but something wider, more spontaneous.

"I did it," he said, a hint of wonder in his voice.

"You sure did," Jack agreed, allowing his own smile to match his son's. "Want to do the next one?"

Simon nodded eagerly, already reaching for another nail.

They progressed to the platform assembly, Jack guiding Simon through the process of connecting the frame pieces. When it came time to attach the floorboards, Jack handled the heavier work while Simon secured each plank with screws, his small fingers growing more confident with the screwdriver as they progressed.

"This one's wobbling," Simon noted as they tested the last board, his tone concerned.

Jack knelt beside him, examining the unstable plank. His first instinct was to take over, to fix the problem with the efficiency that had defined his pre-prison life. The urge to protect, to perfect, to control outcomes remained strong within him. But as he watched Simon's careful assessment of the problem, something shifted in his approach.

"What do you think is causing it?" he asked instead.

Simon ran his hand along the board, testing pressure points with methodical thoroughness. "This end isn't attached properly," he concluded. "And maybe the board isn't straight."

Jack nodded, pleased with the analysis. "What would you suggest?"

Simon considered the question with the seriousness he brought to all challenges. "We could unscrew it and try again? Maybe check if the board is warped first?"

"Good thinking," Jack confirmed. "Let's try that approach."

Together they removed the screws, examined the board for warping, and repositioned it with greater care. Jack guided Simon's hands as they replaced the screws, but allowed his son to do the actual work, resisting the temptation to ensure perfection at the cost of Simon's learning.

When they finished, Simon tested the board again, pressing his full weight against it. "It's solid now," he announced, satisfaction evident in his voice.

"Good job troubleshooting," Jack said, the praise simple but sincere.

They stepped back to assess their progress; the platform now complete with its railing securely attached. It wasn't perfect—the corners didn't meet with the precision Jack would have achieved working alone, and one section of the railing sat slightly higher than the rest. But it was solid, safe, and most importantly, it was theirs—something built by four hands working in tandem, learning each other's rhythms.

Jack ruffled Simon's hair, the gesture still new enough to feel like a discovery. Simon leaned into the touch, his body relaxing in a way Jack had rarely seen during prison visits, where his son had always maintained the careful alertness of a child in an unpredictable environment.

"We make a good team," Jack said softly.

Simon looked up at him, his expression serious once more, but with warmth behind it. "Yeah," he agreed. "We do."

The simple truth of it settled between them, more solid than any structure they could build.

Jack unscrewed the thermos cap, the smell of fresh lemonade rising between them like a memory of summers he'd missed. He poured the pale yellow liquid into the cap-cup and handed it to Simon, who accepted it with the careful precision that characterized all his movements, as if each ordinary gesture deserved full attention. They sat in the dappled shade of the oak tree; wood shavings scattered around them like confetti from a celebration of their shared work.

Simon took a small, deliberate sip before setting the cup on a level patch of grass beside him. His fingers reached out to sift through the wood shavings, collecting a few in his palm and bringing them closer to his face for inspection. Jack watched the familiar tilt of his son's head, the slight narrowing of his eyes that indicated deep concentration—expressions he'd cataloged during visits but now could observe freely, without the artificial constraints of prison visitation rooms.

"The shavings from the cedar are different than the pine," Simon observed, separating them in his palm with the tip of his index finger. "They curl differently. And they smell better."

Jack nodded, pouring lemonade for himself after Simon handed back the cap. "Cedar contains natural oils that pine doesn't. Those oils protect the tree from insects and rot. They're also what gives it that distinctive smell."

Simon inhaled deeply over his palm. "Like pencil shavings, but stronger."

"Exactly," Jack confirmed, pleased with the comparison. "Those same properties make cedar ideal for outdoor projects. Resists decay better than most woods."

Simon carefully returned the shavings to the ground, arranging them in a small pile rather than scattering them. His movements were economical, nothing wasted, nothing overlooked—a trait Jack recognized from his own methodical approach to tasks.

"What other kinds of wood could we use?" Simon asked, turning toward Jack with that serious expression that made him seem older than his years. "For future projects, I mean."

The phrase 'future projects' settled in Jack's chest with unexpected weight. A lifetime of absence compressed into those two words—the simple assumption of continuity, of shared tomorrows stretching ahead uninterrupted. He took a sip of lemonade to cover the sudden tightness in his throat.

"Depends on what we want to build," Jack answered, setting his drink aside. "Oak is strong but heavy. Maple takes detail work well—good for smaller projects with intricate parts. Cherry develops a beautiful patina over time."

Simon nodded, absorbing this information with his characteristic intensity. "Did you work with all those types when you were saving trees?"

"Most of them, yes," Jack said, leaning back on his palms, feeling the cool grass beneath his fingers. "Every tree species has its own personality, its own challenges."

"Like the oak you saved?" Simon prompted, his expression suggesting he'd heard fragments of this story before, perhaps from Tabby or Ruby during Jack's absence, and wanted the full version directly from its source.

Jack glanced up at the massive oak that dominated their backyard, its sprawling branches now supporting the beginnings of their treehouse. "That one was actually a different oak, across town. Massive thing—must have been over a hundred years old. The owners wanted to remove it because it had developed a disease in one section."

Simon's eyes widened slightly. "And you climbed it?"

"All the way to the top," Jack confirmed, the memory of that ascent still vivid despite the years between. "Eighty feet up, secured with climbing ropes and a harness. The owner watched from below; certain the tree was beyond saving."

"Were you scared?" Simon asked, leaning forward slightly.

Jack considered the question with the honesty he'd always tried to offer his son, even during the constrained conversations of prison visits. "Not of the height. I was more afraid of making the wrong cut, of causing more harm than good."

"But you saved it," Simon said, not a question but a statement of faith in his father's abilities.

"I did," Jack nodded. "Identified the diseased sections, pruned them away, treated what remained. Last I heard, the tree was still standing, still healthy." He didn't add that he'd often thought of that tree during his incarceration—how sometimes removal was necessary for survival, how healing required precision and care, how some things could be saved if approached with the right knowledge and tools.

Simon reached for the thermos, pouring himself another small cup of lemonade with careful concentration. "I think our treehouse needs a rope ladder," he said, the transition typical of his conversational style—observing, processing, then moving to the next logical point without unnecessary elaboration.

"Smart thinking," Jack agreed. "More flexible than a fixed ladder, and we can pull it up if we want privacy."

Simon's eyes brightened at this. "And a pulley system? For sending things up and down without climbing?"

"Definitely doable," Jack said, watching as Simon's usual reserve gave way to growing excitement. "Maybe even a small platform with a rope attached, like an elevator for supplies."

"Or secret messages," Simon added, his imagination expanding beyond the purely practical for the first time since they'd begun work. He reached for a fallen twig, using it to sketch in the soft dirt beside him. "We could put the pulley here," he traced a circle near the edge of his crude drawing of the treehouse. "And maybe a trapdoor for entering?"

Jack watched his son's fingers move through the dirt, creating a vision of their shared project. Simon drew with the same precision he brought to all tasks, but there was a freedom in his movements now, a loosening of the careful self-control that had been his hallmark during Jack's incarceration.

The sight created a complex emotion in Jack's chest—pride in his son's creativity mingled with a sharp awareness of all he had missed, all the moments when Simon's imagination might have flowered if Jack had been present to nurture it. He had protected his son in the only way available to him while incarcerated—by being predictable, by never missing a visit, by maintaining connection through consistent presence despite institutional barriers. But that protection had come with its own constraints, had perhaps encouraged Simon's serious, watchful nature.

"This is getting pretty elaborate," Jack said with a smile, nodding toward Simon's increasingly detailed dirt sketch. "Think we should get back to work so we can make some of these ideas happen?"

Simon nodded eagerly, abandoning his drawing and rising to his feet in a single fluid motion. "Can we start on the rope ladder now?"

"Let's do it," Jack agreed, collecting the thermos and cups as he stood. "I bought some special rope last week that should work perfectly."

They returned to their workstation beneath the oak, where coils of rope and additional lumber awaited their attention. Jack demonstrated how to measure and cut the rope to appropriate lengths, how to secure it properly to the wooden rungs they would create. Simon absorbed each instruction with his characteristic focus, asking clarifying questions when necessary but mostly learning through careful observation.

As the afternoon progressed, they assembled the ladder together, Jack handling the more complex knots while teaching Simon the simpler ones. When the finished ladder lay before them, Simon ran his hand along the rough fiber of the rope, testing its strength with a slight tug.

"Ready to try it out?" Jack asked, gathering the completed ladder.

Simon nodded, his expression serious once more but with an undercurrent of anticipation visible in the slight tension of his shoulders, the way his weight shifted forward onto the balls of his feet.

Jack secured the ladder to the platform railing using the cleats they'd installed earlier, testing each connection before standing back. The ladder hung against the trunk of the oak, its rungs spaced at intervals suitable for Simon's shorter legs.

"I'll be right here," Jack said, positioning himself at the base of the ladder. His instinct was to offer more—to hold the ladder steady, to place a protective hand on Simon's back as he climbed, to remove all possibility of failure or fall. But he restrained these impulses, recognizing them as remnants of his own fear rather than necessities for Simon's safety.

Simon approached the ladder with deliberate steps, grasping the sides with both hands. He tested the first rung with his foot, pressing down to ensure its stability before transferring his weight. Jack remained below, close enough to intervene if necessary but allowing his son the space to navigate the ascent independently.

With methodical care, Simon climbed the ladder, each movement precise and considered. Halfway up, he paused, glancing down at Jack with a flicker of uncertainty crossing his features.

"You're doing great," Jack encouraged, his voice steady. "Take your time."

Simon nodded and continued upward, his confidence visibly growing with each successful step. When he reached the platform, he pulled himself up with surprising strength, turning to sit with his legs dangling over the edge. His face transformed with a smile of genuine accomplishment—not the careful, measured expressions Jack had grown accustomed to during visits, but something wider, freer.

"I can see the whole yard from here!" Simon called down, his voice carrying a note of wonder that made him sound, for the first time all day, exactly like the eight-year-old he was.

Jack looked up at his son, silhouetted against the dappled light filtering through oak leaves, and felt something shift in his chest—an easing of a tension he'd carried.

"What do you see?" he called up, stepping back to gain a better view of Simon's perch.

"Everything," Simon answered, the simple word containing multitudes.

www.ingramcontent.com/pod-product-compliance
Lightning Source LLC
Chambersburg PA
CBHW021624030826
48979CB00036B/2037/J

9798991852548